A Scandalous Husband

Bev Pettersen

DEDICATION

To Barb and Ulf Snarby
Thanks for your love, compassion and support.

CHAPTER ONE

"No worries," Dani Tattrie muttered. "Who needs a husband when they have a dog and a handyman?"

She stooped to pat Red, dismissing the splintered fencepost. She'd been pretending everything was fine for so long, it had become a habit. But her dog was tougher to fool. He stared at the sagging post. One of his eyes was brown, the other blue—both were full of concern.

"Don't worry," she repeated, giving his head another reassuring pat. "We'll manage." Red was great company but like her, he'd aged much over the last few years. He still slept by the front door, waiting and hoping. The dog was definitely loyal. Far more loyal than her husband.

A familiar lump settled in her throat. She impatiently tugged on her battered work gloves and struggled to straighten the post. Six of the paddocks, as well as the huge pasture, required new fencing. With two people it was an arduous job. Alone, it was dauntingly difficult.

She placed several rocks around the base of the damaged post, a temporary fix until she had more time. And maybe Jeffrey could help. He was always happy to act as her handyman or at least try. However, although his intentions were good, his carpentry skills were rather suspect. Besides, she didn't like to take advantage of a family friend, no matter how many times he offered.

She swiped her brow, determined not to agonize over the state of the ranch. Too many things screamed for repair and the list was multiplying. Even if she had the expertise, horses needed riding and after grueling hours in the saddle, she was always exhausted.

A chestnut gelding wandered over to the fence and sniffed curiously at the rocks. But unless he kicked the post again it should hold, at least until she could rent some equipment. If Dex were here, he'd pound in a new post in minutes, but she didn't have half his strength or know-how. She needed to fix the fencing soon though. Clients wouldn't be very impressed if they spotted their horses wandering loose along the road.

She slipped through the rails of the paddock and scratched the horse's neck. Spunky was a five-year-old Quarter Horse labeled as incorrigible. But after three months of training, he'd finally settled.

Admittedly, the first month had been rough. He'd dumped her four times. Not only that, he'd charged through two fences, stomping Red and leaving the dog limping. Spunky had been just as difficult to handle from the ground, fully justifying his outlaw label.

She'd actually considered sending him back. Broken bones meant she couldn't do her job, and any lay-up would be disastrous. But the owner had offered an enticing bonus if the Double D would retrain his horse. And she'd always been drawn to the bad boys. Besides, someone had to help these horses and she was no quitter.

"You've come a long way, Spunky," she said, running a hand down his front leg. The horse stood rock-still, obediently lifting his hoof even though he was unrestrained. He didn't even pin his ears at Red, his former arch enemy.

The owner would definitely be happy. Previous trainers had thrown up their hands in disgust, and Dani knew she had been a last resort. Spunky's owner had hauled the horse all the way from northern California to their Double D Ranch.

Double. She winced, accepting the ranch's name needed to be changed. Unfortunately the Single D didn't have quite the same ring. Of course, if she didn't make her mortgage payment, the name would be moot.

Damn him.

She dropped the horse's hoof to the ground and clasped her stomach. Her gut always churned when she thought of her husband. Dex wasn't an easy man to forget...or forgive. But she'd get through it. Spunky was the toughest horse she'd trained without his help. It proved she could succeed on her own. And the bonus money would certainly appease her nervous creditors.

"Let's go inside and make some calls, Red." She turned and strode toward the house, the attentive dog trotting at her heels.

Once inside, she gathered the phone and her achingly short client list, then settled in a chair by the kitchen table. The file on Spunky was thin, containing his medical history, feeding instructions and contact information. Most of her customers were personal referrals, but this man had discovered her training services on the Internet.

At least she had the owner's name and number—Richard Higgins, Santa Clara— along with a short description of Spunky: six-year-old chestnut QH gelding. Previously successful in the show ring but now bucks under saddle. Requires experienced rider and handler. Hates dogs.

Not anymore.

Smiling, she pressed Mr. Higgins's number and settled back in the chair. Hopefully he'd tell his friends. She'd never had any clients from northern California before and had only met the man once, when he'd hauled into her driveway and despairingly tossed her Spunky's lead line. However, word-of-mouth referrals were always the best. She couldn't remember Mr. Higgins's face, only that he was fifty pounds overweight and at his wits' end as to how to handle his horse.

Fortunately Spunky was a gorgeous animal. If he'd been ugly, it was doubtful the man would have risked any more money on training fees. No matter what anyone said, looks did matter.

An impatient voice answered, pulling back her attention.

"Spunky is ready for pickup, Mr. Higgins," she said into the phone.

"Really?" The man turned quiet for a moment. "You mean he's rideable? Even at a lope?"

"He's behaving perfectly," Dani said. "Both in the ring and out. And he's no longer bothered by dogs."

"But what about his lead changes?" Mr. Higgins sounded more incredulous than happy. "He always bucks with leg pressure. I don't want to be the laughing stock at another show."

"His changes are excellent," Dani said. "And he moves quietly off the leg. He's really a responsive fellow. When you come, I'll give a lesson and demonstrate the most effective cues."

"I don't need a riding lesson," the man said. "I've been around horses way longer than you. Let me speak to your husband."

Dani's fingers tightened around the phone. "He isn't here right now. And I've done all the training. So it's best I give the lesson."

"You've done the work? But I was paying top dollar for a professional cowboy. That's why I offered a bonus."

"My riding background was more appropriate for this type of training," she said, trying to keep her voice level. "And of course the lesson is included in the fee, the price we agreed upon."

"Yeah, but groundwork was a condition for the bonus. The website claimed your husband had a rodeo background. And I want him to fix Spunky's ground manners. The damn horse is no good to me if he won't load."

"But he does load," Dani said. "I've had him on our stock trailer dozens of times. You just have to point and he'll walk on. I guarantee you'll be satisfied."

"You're lying." The man's voice rose. "You want me to believe a little thing like you could fix my horse? That I can load him without a tranquilizer?"

Dani opened her mouth to snap but swallowed her retort. Spunky's problems had been the result of poor riding and even poorer handling. But owners tended to blame the horse. When Dex was here, aggressive clients had never been a problem. No one turned belligerent around Dex. No one had dared.

"I'm not in the habit of lying," she said, her words clipped now. "And Spunky is ready to haul to a show. To be fair to the horse, you should have a lesson first. But whether you accept my advice or not, your total fee is thirty-five hundred dollars."

"I just can't believe he'll load easily," Mr. Higgins said. "If we need help, is there a competent man around? Your husband perhaps?"

"He's away. But I assure you Spunky would load in the dark. He had some fear issues but they've settled now and with consistent handling, you can ensure they don't return. You can also call me anytime, should you want some training tips."

"Yeah, all right," Mr. Higgins muttered. "I'll come down on Saturday. But I really didn't think a woman like you could change a horse like that."

"I liked him," Dani said. "He was fun." She closed the file, remembering the times Spunky had slammed her face into the dirt. Not much fun then. But the risk had proven worthwhile. The horse's fees would cover some overdue bills and give a welcome reprieve from the collection calls. "See you on the weekend," she said.

She cut the connection, grabbed a calculator and tallied her net profit. She'd have her regular expenses, of course.

Spunky was an enthusiastic eater, and hay and grain weren't cheap. She'd also have to pay for his vet and farrier visits along with all the fence repairs. But adding in her bonus, she'd pocket almost eighteen hundred dollars, enough to cover the overdue mortgage. Her time didn't bring in much, only about four dollars an hour, but she enjoyed her job and it was impossible to put a price tag on something she loved.

Best of all, she'd finally be able to afford an evaluation of Dex's Thoroughbred. Tizzy was a four-year-old who had yet to set foot on a racetrack. There had been no time or money. However, the colt's younger brother had just run second in the Santa Anita Derby, proving once again that Dex had an excellent eye for a horse. Dani didn't know much about racehorses; her background was in western riding. But she had a friend who was a jockey.

She speed-dialed Eve.

"I just finished a training job," Dani said, "and finally have a little cash. So could you come by and gallop Tizzy? Let me know if he has any potential?"

"Sure," Eve said. "It'll be great to get together. I'll arrange a sitter for tomorrow night. And you definitely don't have to pay me."

"But I want to pay for your time," Dani said. "I know what it's like trying to make money riding horses."

Eve laughed. "And I know what it's like to be broke. See you tomorrow. I'll bring the wine."

She ended the call before Dani could argue.

Dani sighed and patted Red, her fingers absently working through the long hair around his neck. Eve was a professional jockey and a single mom. Her time was scarce and it wasn't fair to ask her to drive all the way out to the Double D for free. But like Jeffrey, Eve would never accept Dani's money.

Of course, it was difficult to charge friends. Dani knew that firsthand. Three of the horses in her paddocks belonged to neighbors who'd dropped them off for a little tune-up. She never wanted to see anyone hurt, horse or rider, so she always helped, generally on a gratuitous basis.

Owners had been much quicker to pull out their wallets when Dex was around. Not that he'd ever said anything; the man wasn't a big talker. Dex just glanced at the sign with the Double D training rates and crossed his arms. People always paid.

'This is our business and we have to charge,' he'd said. And then he gave her that gentle smile, the one he didn't show to many people. 'You look after the riding,' he said. 'I'll take care of the collections.'

And though they hadn't been rich, clients never expected services for free. It might have been because Dex was a Tattrie. Nobody crossed that family, reputedly not without a visit from someone swinging a tire iron. Of course, Dex wasn't involved in that side of the Tattrie business... Or she'd thought he wasn't.

Her father warned bad blood always showed. She'd refused to listen. Sure, Dex was related to some shady characters but underneath his tough exterior, he was really a softie. He was always so patient with the animals, with people, with her. In fact, she'd been deliriously happy for their three short years of marriage. Had been head-over-heels in love. She thought he'd been happy too.

She gave Red one last pat and scraped back her chair. She couldn't stop Dex from hounding her dreams but she refused to brood about him during the day. Their life together was over. He'd accepted that.

She only wished she could.

CHAPTER TWO

"You're all I want." Dex cupped her face, his dark eyes solemn. "Marry me, sweetheart."

Dani's chest tightened with both joy and shock. For a moment she couldn't speak. They'd only been dating for three months and while she knew she was falling too hard, too fast, she'd never dreamed he felt the same way. "I'm not sure a minister's daughter would make the best biker's wife." She hid her wistfulness behind a flippant smile. "My family would disown me."

"I'll sell my bike."

"Then your family would disown you."

"Doubtful," he said. "But if they did, it wouldn't matter. I was always on the fringe anyway."

"But what would we do?" Her heart pounded with a wild hope. It was hard to tell with Dex. He teased with a straight face. But right now he seemed totally serious. "Would you keep working at the garage?"

"No," he said. "I have a little money. Enough for a down payment on an acreage."

Her fingers tightened around his shoulders. This was more than she'd ever dared hope. He'd leave the Tattrie business, the Tattrie way of life? She didn't believe every rumor but it was common knowledge Dex's family never worried unduly about the law.

People said the Tattrie biker club kept folks safe from the really violent gangs. On the other hand, while her dad grudgingly accepted that his daughter was friends with a Tattrie, he never expected she'd date one. And now marriage? The poor man would have a heart attack. At the very least he'd create problems. And she feared the Tattrie garage might not hold up to much scrutiny.

Dex's voice softened, as if reading her mind. "Don't worry. This is clean money. It won't buy a huge spread but a little ranch is all we need. You can ride as many horses as you want. I'll make you happy, Dani."

"But would *you* be happy?" She tilted her head, studying the rakish curve of his jaw. She'd been training horses for two years, ever since graduating from high school. And she loved her job. But it wasn't nearly as exciting as the Tattrie business which, depending on the whispers one believed, involved everything from stolen cars to prostitution, and even drug running.

"You make me happy," Dex said, tucking her against his hard chest. "You always have."

"You'd really sell your bike? To climb out of bed and clean stalls?"

His chuckle was quick and amused and slightly rueful. "At least I won't have to drive to every weekend rodeo to see you." His voice turned gruff. "I like horses too, Dani. And I do love you. Say yes, sweetheart."

Despite the worry about facing her father, a smile split Dani's face. "Yes," she said quickly, pure joy leaking from the sides of her mouth. She'd been enthralled with Dex Tattrie ever since she was eighteen. Since he'd roared onto the fairgrounds with his big black bike, swung his leg over the seat and watched her barrel race. She'd never been close to a Tattrie before, had never seen any man so sinfully attractive. Maybe that's why her concentration had been shot, and she and her horse had wiped out rounding the third barrel.

She couldn't remember hitting the dirt, only that he'd been the first to reach her side. And she was too shaken and disoriented, unable to suck enough air in her lungs, to ask about her loose horse. She couldn't see Peppy but she could hear his frantic hoofbeats as he tore around the arena. Dex was the only one who understood.

"Don't try to talk," he whispered. "I'll look after your horse." And he did, catching and walking Peppy for almost an hour while the paramedics checked her out. When he'd sauntered over leading her horse, her riding friends had instantly shifted to the periphery.

"Your horse is fine," he said, in a voice so surprisingly rich and velvet it sent shivers of pleasure down her neck. "The ground around that last barrel was too slick." And then he nodded, returned to his bike and roared away.

She never knew when he'd re-appear, but that summer she'd entered every barrel race at any rodeo within a five-hundred-mile radius. Sometimes he showed up to compete. More often he didn't. But she gathered a lot of ribbons in the process and learned much about his event—bareback riding.

Dex was considered an aberration, a biker from the wrong side of the tracks who was freakishly good at riding a horse. The buckle bunnies whispered he was good at other kinds of riding too, and while the circuit cowboys might resent his presence—Dex collected more than his share of prize money and women—they weren't stupid. They treated him with cautious respect although they never let him join their fraternal ranks. And Dex, for his part, seemed content to remain aloof. Which suited Dani just fine.

They struck up an odd relationship, the loner biker cowboy and the horse-crazy teenager. Dex generally waited by the in-gate to watch her barrel race, and she always stayed to whoop him on during his bareback event. They shared corn dogs and conversations. However, their friendship was cemented the day a thin scruffy dog wandered onto the rodeo grounds, barking and nipping at horses and making the riders curse.

"That dog is going to get hurt," Dani said, wincing as a black Chevy almost squashed the animal.

Dex nodded, shook off the brunette plastered to his side, strode over and scooped the dog out of harm's way.

"He's still a pup," he said, walking back to Dani with the wiggling dog safe in his arms. "Some sort of shepherd-Aussie mix. Be a good dog for a horse person like you."

Dani gave a wistful sigh. "I can't get a dog yet. Not until I move out and have my own place. Dad wouldn't like it."

"Then I'll keep him for you," Dex said. "Until you're ready."

"Really?" She patted the dog's head, studying his mismatched eyes and laughing when he licked her nose and then Dex's dark stubbled jaw. "I have a job working at Equine Excellence this fall," she said. "But it might be a while before I can afford my own apartment."

"It doesn't matter," Dex said, his face inscrutable. "I'll keep him for you… As long as it takes."

She'd named the stray Red, but the dog had always been Dex's. She'd visited Red at the Tattrie garage, every Monday and Thursday evening, faithfully bringing toys and food and trying to teach him tricks. Later, she'd sit by Dex as he worked beneath a car, handing him a wrench or a beer, and telling him stories about the horses she'd trained. A few times she'd shown up unannounced, but her heart had been crushed when she saw the gorgeous women snuggled up to him on the seat of his powerful bike. After that, she never arrived without calling first.

Her father had been horrified at her association with a Tattrie. "What happens if you see them stripping a stolen car?" Even her younger brother, Matt, had looked aghast. But when the engine fell out of Matt's treasured Camaro, her brother had been more than happy to have Dex find replacement parts—unbeknownst to their disapproving father.

Low growls yanked at Dani's consciousness, prodding her awake. She groaned and curled closer to Dex's side of the bed, her arms squeezing his pillow. These moments, halfway between waking and sleeping, were the best part of her life now. No one could steal her memories. Her world may have imploded, but at night dreams could be indulged. Dex was here. Red was here. And that's all she'd ever wanted.

If only Red would shush. It was impossible to stay immersed in her shadow world when the dog made such a racket. She clamped the pillow over her head, desperate to remain in the Tattrie garage, to replay Dex's expression when she'd told him she had a boyfriend… And that they were considering sharing an apartment.

Dex had been tinkering with a car, but he dropped his wrench on the concrete that day. She remembered the discordant clang, how he'd looked at her with such an odd expression. "What's the guy's name?" he finally asked, pulling a rag from his back pocket and deliberately wiping his hands.

"Why?" she asked. "Because my dad and Matt are bad enough. I don't want you scaring him away. I just want to get out on my own."

Dex tossed the rag aside and gestured at the seat of his bike. "Hop on."

"But you said I'm too young to ride with you."

"Not anymore," he said.

She gripped the pillow tighter, pretending it was Dex's lean hips she was clutching. After he sold his bike, they'd replaced it with horses, often riding double around the ranch. Dex had grinned and said it was an important part of any horse's education to carry two people…and to stand patiently as required. Even Red had learned to flop on the grass and wait out their impromptu kissing.

But the dog wasn't being patient tonight. At some point, his growls had changed to a deep-throated bark. The last time he'd been so aggressive was the night a coyote had wandered onto the porch.

Dani reluctantly opened her eyes. Red was like Dex; he didn't make unnecessary noise. If the dog was upset, there had to be good reason. She tossed aside the sheets and checked the illuminated clock. Four-ten. Coyotes didn't generally bother full-grown horses, but it was dangerous to let them grow too bold.

She yawned, pulled on her jeans and shirt, then shuffled to the front door, unable to hear anything over Red's frantic barking. She grabbed Dex's wooden baseball bat in one hand and Red's collar in the other. The dog was too fearless. She didn't want him bolting into the night to be chewed up by a pack of coyotes.

She clicked the lock and swung the door open. Cool air pricked her awake, but it still took a moment to process the dark box rolling down the driveway.

A trailer with no lights?

She blinked in disbelief then charged forward. "Come back, you sonofabitch!" she hollered. Red jerked from her hand and bolted over the gravel, past Spunky's open paddock gate, intent on catching the truck and trailer.

"Here, Red," she called, her voice choking with frustration. Any scumball who would sneak onto her property to remove a horse, simply to avoid paying, might not hesitate to run over a dog.

Red turned back, still growling, his hackles ridged.

"It's okay, fellow," she said. "I should have listened to you earlier." *Instead of wallowing in old memories.*

"Everything's okay," she repeated. But her hands fisted in despair as the trailer disappeared into the night, carrying Spunky along with all hope of making her mortgage payment.

CHAPTER THREE

"Thanks for coming so quickly," Dani said, filling Jeffrey's cup with coffee and joining him at the kitchen table.

"No problem. I was working night shift when your call came in." Jeffrey rose and pulled a carton of milk from her fridge, sniffing it suspiciously before adding it to his mug. "And of course I want to help. I'm not sure what the police can do though. Even if we find this guy, it's his horse. And there was no signed agreement."

Dani lowered her head in her hands. "I was thinking of typing up an agreement," she said. "But most of our clients are local. And Dex and I always operated on a handshake."

"Dex was more intimidating than you. This really isn't a sensible business for a woman." Jeffrey's voice softened. "I understand it's hard to make changes. But I don't like watching you struggle."

His empathy moved her, much more than her father's cutting disapproval, and her lower lip gave an uncharacteristic tremble. She fumbled for her mug. But Jeffrey was quicker. He covered her hand, his voice pleading. "You have to give this up. You're wearing yourself out. This place needs a man. The house, your equipment, the old fencing. Everything is crumbling."

"I never realized how much Dex did," she said, her shoulders slumping. "How good he was…at everything."

"But it couldn't last," Jeffrey said. "Men like Dex crave excitement. I remember him in school. You and the ranch were never going to be enough." He squeezed her hand. "You can move on though. Stop clinging to something that's gone and find another life."

Dani forced a trembling smile. "You sound like my dad."

"That's because I care for you too," Jeffrey said. "Very much."

"I'm not even sure how to go about selling," she said, pulling her hand away and rubbing her forehead. "If I should fix it up or walk away. But no bank would finance any repairs. The mortgage is always in arrears."

She didn't hear Jeffrey's chair slide back, but suddenly he was there, surprising her by pulling her close. "I can help," he whispered. "We'll splash some paint on. I know a good real estate agent. The main thing to remember is that you're not in this alone."

His hand rubbed her shoulders, his voice low and soothing, and her breath escaped in a ragged sigh. It had been a long time since she'd spilled her fears, a long time since she'd felt safe. And it was rather nice. She'd never considered Jeffrey as anything but a friend. He'd been several years ahead of her in school, but she'd always thought he looked very handsome in his deputy sheriff uniform. He'd occasionally stopped her on the highway, asking where the rodeo was, and warning that her truck wasn't in any condition to haul a horse trailer.

But he'd been wrong about that. Because Dex had fixed up her old truck just fine. Everything worked perfectly when Dex was around. Of course, he wasn't around now.

"You need to push for a divorce," Jeffrey said. "End this farce of a marriage."

Dani lifted her head, slightly bemused. Being with Dex had never felt like a farce. Never.

Jeffrey's mouth lowered, covering hers in a sudden kiss.

She stilled but it wasn't too bad. And she was rather curious. His mouth was a little too soft though, a little too wet. He'd obviously eaten a mint recently so that earned some points. Still, this kiss was nothing like Dex's. Nothing like that first day when he'd driven his bike into a stand of oak trees and purposefully cut the engine. He'd turned, pulled her into his arms and she couldn't remember much after that, just that the buckle bunnies had been absolutely correct.

"You better find that old boyfriend," Dex had said afterwards, as he helped her adjust her clothes, "and let him know you won't be sharing an apartment."

"And you better let your old girlfriends know there won't be any more bike rides."

"All right," he'd said.

It had been so easy, and so right. She stiffened, annoyed at how her mind seemed to have left her body at a very crucial time. One minute of inattention, but already Jeffrey's hand covered her breast, his gun poked her hip, and his breathing had turned thick and aroused.

"I'm glad you didn't wear a bra," he said. "Let's move to the bedroom."

He seemed to believe she'd dressed to simplify his night visit, and the inference was rather annoying. "I threw these clothes on when that man took Spunky," she said. "And I'm still married."

"Dex has been in prison for over two years." Jeffrey's thumb caressed her nipple. "And everyone knows you weren't the last woman *he* had sex with."

She winced. Jeffrey was right. The night Dex was arrested, he had been holed up with a prostitute named Tawny.

Jeffrey's mouth dipped lower, exploring her neck, and a shiver of awareness swept her. He may not be a world-class kisser but he had her T-shirt lifted and he was definitely handling her breasts competently. Not like Dex, of course, but it wasn't fair to compare. And why should her estranged husband have all the fun? She liked Jeffrey. He liked her.

Something hard and hairy pressed against her thigh.

"Dammit," Jeffrey muttered, lifting his head. "What's that dog doing?"

Dani looked down and couldn't stop her laugh. Red had poked his head between her and Jeffrey, his lip curled in disapproval. "Guess he thinks I should return to the bedroom alone," she said, still smiling, "and that you should go back to your patrol car. And I do believe he's right. Come on, I'll walk you to the door."

"Dex probably trained the dog to do that," Jeffrey grumbled. "But I guess this is progress. How about dinner tomorrow?"

"I can't. A friend is coming to gallop Tizzy. She's going to let me know if he has any race potential."

"Hopefully he does." Jeffrey pressed a lingering kiss on her mouth. "But if you sell, you won't have to worry about horses any longer. Guess I'll see you at church?"

"Yes," Dani said. "And thanks for coming so quickly. I'm glad it was you who took the call."

"You know I'll always look after you," Jeffrey said, his gaze drifting over her white T-shirt. "But you need to let me."

"You stacked hay last week and now you're going to track down Mr. Higgins. You already do too much," she said, deliberately misunderstanding him. There'd be time to think about this development later, after she grabbed more sleep. She'd never thought of Jeffrey like this. It had been years since she'd thought about anyone but Dex. "I'll see you Sunday," she added. "Maybe we could go for lunch after church."

"It's a date," Jeffrey said. He nodded, adjusted his gun belt and walked out with a hint of a swagger.

Red watched him go, then tilted his head and looked at Dani, his eyes reproachful.

"Oh, stop that," she said. "We can't wait forever. Especially since Dex told us not to bother. Come and sleep in my room tonight. I'll get you a treat."

But Red ignored her bribe. He circled twice, let out a heavy sigh, then flopped down in his usual spot—waiting for Dex by the front door.

CHAPTER FOUR

Dani climbed onto the tractor seat and turned the key, listening with bated breath. The engine gave a feeble kick then died. It was a little stronger on the second try. But on the third attempt, it roared to life. She gave the steering wheel an approving pat. It was difficult to imagine life without the big green tractor, but she didn't have to worry about that today.

She gestured at the passenger's seat and Red scrambled up beside her. He liked to follow whenever she dragged the ring. However, his last dustup with Spunky had left him chronically stiff, and if he had too much exercise he limped for days. Besides, it was safer to let him ride on the seat, high above those big black wheels.

She gave his head a pat and turned the tractor toward the hayfield. Red shot her a puzzled look, as though questioning where they were going. His confusion was understandable. It had been months since she'd dragged the large makeshift track that skirted the hayfield. Most of the horses sent to the Double D were pleasure horses. Occasionally though, they received a Thoroughbred destined to race or merely chilling from hectic track life, and it was handy to have a half-mile track for galloping. Both she and Dex enjoyed taking a horse out for a run, savoring the pure exhilaration of raw speed.

It had been a long time though since she'd ridden for fun. Daylight hours were too precious, and the chore list on her fridge kept growing. But Eve was coming tonight to check out Tizzy, and it was important that the track have safe ground.

She chugged four complete circles around the oval, stopping the tractor several times to toss aside an occasional rock, but after an hour and a half, the smooth dark dirt was groomed to perfection. It looked safe. However, the best way to check the footing would be to ride a horse over it. She'd have to hurry though. Eve was arriving at five.

She returned the tractor to the drive-in shed, parking it behind Matt's Camaro, and rushed to the fourth paddock, selecting a stocky bay Quarter Horse named Gunner. This horse was a reiner, excelling at slides and spins, but the owner felt he was a little sour in the show pen and wanted him freshened.

"Nothing better than a little ride around the track," she said, dragging a brush over Gunner's back and belly. She picked out his feet, then tossed on her worn saddle. The reining-trained horses were generally a pleasure to work with, standing still but eager to work. This one was no exception.

Gunner obligingly lowered his head, lifting the bit from her hand and practically putting on the bridle himself. "You're a good fellow," she said.

She led him from the paddock, mounted then turned him away from the ring and toward the track.

He stepped out with a relaxed and confident walk, ears pricked, eager to see something other than a riding ring. Red followed at his heels, nose close to the horse's tail. Dex had always felt a horse should learn to accept distractions and after Dani's firm correction, Gunner ignored the dog. It had taken Spunky much longer to accept Red's presence, but Spunky had a totally different personality.

Her hand tightened around the reins at the thought of Spunky. Hopefully Jeffrey would be able to track down Mr. Higgins and persuade him to pay. Unfortunately Jeffrey hadn't been too optimistic. And without a lesson, the poor horse would no doubt revert to bucking again. Which was a shame—Spunky deserved better.

Gunner tossed his head, sensing her agitation, and she straightened her thoughts. It wasn't cool to be thinking of another horse. Almost like cheating. And horses didn't like cheaters.

Neither did she.

She moved him into a trot, half hoping he'd shy and keep her mind occupied. But the horse behaved perfectly, enjoying the expanse of track and relaxed now with Red's presence. Her thoughts veered back to last night.

Selling the ranch was probably inevitable. But the admission hurt. There had been so many tears, so many wrecked dreams. The conversation with Jeffrey still felt surreal, as did his embrace. It shouldn't be totally surprising though. He'd been her rock over the last two years. It would only be natural if they ended up together.

And it most certainly wasn't cheating. She gave an emphatic headshake.

Dex wanted a divorce. He'd prepared the papers two years ago. She simply hadn't had the time or energy to deal with that...or admittedly, the desire to make big changes. Daily survival had been enough of a challenge. But Jeffrey was right. She was delusional thinking she could make a go of the ranch. Even Dex had known.

A red-tailed hawk swooped from a fencepost, but Gunner's steady stride didn't falter. He had a lovely bold trot but wasn't allowed to use it much. Reiners didn't trot in their show patterns, and some riders avoided it like the plague, afraid they'd break stride and be penalized. However, this horse was a seasoned pro and knew when he was in the ring. He was pleasantly normal. Just like Jeffrey.

Her father would be pleased with their liaison. "You should be with a decent man," he'd said. "Jeffrey's a churchgoer and a policeman. He contributes to society."

Gunner's stride shortened, almost imperceptibly, and she tugged her mind back to her job. The track was a little deeper on the north side, and she noted the change in footing about ten feet beyond the oak tree. It would be best if Eve galloped to the inside of the section here. But it was excellent stopping ground.

She raised her hand slightly. "Whoa," she said, relaxing her seat. Gunner tucked his hind end and slid to a long smooth stop. Even on a strange track, he listened beautifully, with no thought but to please his rider.

She loosened the reins and sat for a moment, letting the horse stand on a long rein. Red flopped to the ground beside them, tongue hanging out and panting. Birds chirped and a truck roared from the distant highway but Gunner stood like a rock, not fidgeting, simply awaiting her next signal.

She picked up the reins and deepened her seat. He backed up, tucking his butt and moving backwards twelve precise steps.

She blew out an admiring breath. If all horses sent for training were as obedient as this fellow, she'd feel guilty about ever accepting money. And clearly his owner remembered her Double D lessons. Dani had started Gunner as a two-year-old, then gave him another four months' training as a three-year-old. Four years later, the animal was as sharp as ever. And horses didn't stay tuned without consistent riding.

"You won the lottery with owners," she said, patting his neck. Poor old Spunky wasn't nearly as lucky. Mr. Higgins would have the horse totally confused within a week. Naturally Spunky would rebel. It could have been a win for all, but now it was a complete and utter failure. Like the Double D ranch. And if she couldn't help horses and make a livable wage, what was the sense?

"Let's go back," she said, abruptly turning Gunner. They'd circled the track twice and other than one soft spot, it seemed safe. Hopefully, Tizzy would gallop well for Eve. If he sold before the end of the month, the mortgage could be brought up to date, and there'd be money left for ranch repairs. Perhaps she should talk to Jeffrey's agent and listen to the lady's suggestions.

Red was tired now, his limp noticeable, so she stopped and patted the front of the saddle. He leaped up, gave her cheek a grateful lick, then balanced over the saddle horn. The reliable horse flicked an ear but if Gunner thought it strange to carry a dog, he didn't show it.

If the owner wasn't vacationing, Dani would have suggested she pick up her horse early. Gunner was as dependable as her old barrel horse. Like Peppy, he didn't need schooling, just a little trail riding to relax his brain, and she had never felt comfortable taking people's money unnecessarily. Besides, she'd have to empty the barn soon.

It was gut wrenching to abandon her dream but just like Red, she was worn-out. She blew out a despairing sigh. Despite her best efforts, the ranch was doomed. Jeffrey and her father had been correct all along. She'd simply been too foolish and too stubborn to accept the truth.

CHAPTER FIVE

"He definitely has potential!" Eve called. She slowed Tizzy to a trot and circled in front of Dani. "I knew you'd have him well trained, but he feels like a racehorse. His stride is huge and when I stretched him out on the far side, he wanted to run. I'll talk to my boss. Jack always has owners looking to buy. It would be a waste if this horse wasn't given a chance to race."

"Dex thought he'd be a good one," Dani said, reaching up and looping the lead line through Tizzy's bridle.

"Whose name is on the registration papers?" Eve asked, vaulting to the ground.

"I'm not sure," Dani said. "Probably Dex. He looked after all that stuff. But everything should be filed in the house."

"He'll have to sign the papers. Do you see him regularly?"

"Not since he was sentenced," Dani said. "I'm not approved for his visitors' list."

"Oh, you bad girl," Eve teased. "I guessed you were an adrenaline junkie, by the way you ride. But the authorities can be so picky. They think anyone who ever had a scrape with the law is probably plotting a prison break."

"It wasn't the authorities," Dani admitted, fighting the suffocating twist in her chest. "It was Dex who didn't approve."

"Oh." Eve pulled off her helmet and fluffed her short hair. "My cousin said regular visitors were what kept him going." She gave a dismissive shrug. "But everyone has a different experience in prison."

Dani nodded, her breath coming a little easier. Eve's easy acceptance was one of the reasons they'd developed a friendship. Dani's old school friends were aghast that her husband was serving time. Yet Eve tossed it off with a casualness that showed she'd seen much in her life and wasn't inclined to judge.

"How's your cousin doing now?" Dani asked.

"He never made it out." Eve turned and removed her saddle. "He joined a gang. Bad move. But when you're stuck between a rock and a hard spot, what do you do?"

It wasn't really a question so Dani kept her mouth shut. Her father said that Dex probably knew half the people in prison and besides, guards kept the inmates safe. But when she'd questioned Jeffrey about actual prison life, his eyes had flickered and he avoided her gaze. It made her stomach churn with nausea. Even if she didn't love Dex anymore, he wouldn't do well locked in a cell. There was nothing he'd enjoyed more than the freedom and exhilaration of riding his bike. Or a horse.

"I've decided to sell this place," she said abruptly. She wasn't sure when she'd accepted the inevitable. Possibly it was Spunky's disappearance or Jeffrey's prodding. More likely the decision had been percolating in the back of her mind for months and she'd simply refused to let it surface.

"It must be a lot of work," Eve said, glancing at the paddocks and outbuildings. "It's amazing you even have time to ride. What about your husband? Will you get a divorce?"

Dani nodded, the tightness in her throat making her words unusually husky. "He had his lawyer draw up divorce papers before he went to prison. I just have to sign off on the division of assets."

Eve's eyes widened. "But you can't agree to anything without seeing your own lawyer first. You need advice too."

"But Dex made the down payment," Dani said. "The only thing I contributed was my truck and trailer. And my truck isn't worth much... Not unless the gas tank is full. Besides, I can't afford a lawyer."

"What about the horse that left today? Use that money."

"Actually, Spunky left last night." Dani's fingers tightened around Tizzy's lead line. "Rather unexpectedly," she added. "The police are trying to track down the owner. But even if they do, they don't hold out hope that I can collect on the training fee."

"Asshole," Eve muttered. "Scott told us to make sure we hold the horse's papers when they come in for training. People won't risk losing those. It keeps everyone honest."

"Who's Scott?"

"Private investigator, married to my son's aunt. He's the one who recovered Joey's body in Mexico, back when everyone thought Joey was dealing heroin. Scott and Megan are little Joey's godparents."

Dani's stomach gave a painful lurch. Heroin had killed the hooker Dex was with. She wanted to ask if Joey had ever encountered laced heroin, but she didn't like people asking painful questions. No doubt, Eve felt the same way.

"Scott keeps a lawyer on retainer," Eve went on. "He could review your divorce papers."

Dani glanced hopefully at Eve. "Would he do that? I could pay a little. I don't want to take advantage."

"He won't mind," Eve said. "He's a good guy. He and Megan are driving out from LA tomorrow. And Scott's fair. He'll see both sides."

A weight lifted from Dani's shoulders. The most valuable horse they owned was Tizzy, who clearly belonged to Dex. And Dex also deserved the bulk of the ranch. But if she could get a few dollars from the sale maybe she could find an apartment in town, something to tide her over until she found another job.

"Who picked out this Thoroughbred?" Eve asked, as if reading Dani's mind.

"Dex. He bought him at a yearling sale. Tizzy was the first foal out of that Tiz The Time dam who's a hot commodity after the Santa Anita Derby."

"She sure is hot," Eve said. "And if Tizzy is anything like his younger brother, he'll burn up the track. You'd probably get a better price after a race or two though. I'll talk to my boss. See if Jack will put some training on him."

Eve's helpfulness was rather overwhelming, and Dani tightened her grip on Tizzy's lead line. She wasn't accustomed to accepting help or even talking about her situation. Jeffrey had tried to do more, but he already resented the ranch and how it gobbled up her time. And her dad still bristled about Dex, seeming to take his conviction as a personal offence.

"You're solving all my problems today," she said, her voice thick with emotion.

Eve squeezed Dani's shoulder. "I know how tough it is being alone. My life would have been hell without Megan and Scott. After Joey died, it felt like my insides had been ripped out. It was scary being a single parent, knowing no one else would ever love my son as much as me."

"I can't imagine having a child in the mix," Dani said. "It hurts just to get rid of the animals."

"What will you do?" Eve asked.

"Move to town," Dani said. "Find a job."

"But will you work with horses?"

"Not fulltime." Dani shook her head. "That's over. Too much sweat and tears. Too many broken dreams."

"But you can't cut out everything you love."

"I'll find new things," Dani said, squaring her shoulders. "Jeffrey can help fix the fences, then the sign goes up."

"Jeffrey is your handyman?"

"Yes, but also a close friend. Someone who's always been around."

"Oh, I understand. One of those." Eve gave a knowing smile, her eyes bright and curious. "Let's cool out this horse and open the wine. Sounds like we both have some interesting stories to tell."

CHAPTER SIX

"So then Dex walked into the bar," Dani leaned further over the kitchen table, laughing as she told the story, "and the bouncer returned my ID and hid in the bathroom."

"Wow, is this Dex?" Eve tugged at the photo album, nearly tipping her drink. "He looks dangerous. Dangerous but delicious."

"He was all right." Dani didn't look at the picture. She picked up the second bottle of wine and instead concentrated on topping up their glasses.

"He's much more than all right." Eve's voice rose. "He's a stud. Men would hate him. Women must love him."

"Yes, well, I guess one woman did," Dani said. "Unfortunately Dex gave her some bad heroin. He called an ambulance but she died on the way to the hospital."

"At least he called for help. Drug addicts sometimes bolt."

"Dex wasn't an addict," Dani said quickly. "He didn't do drugs. Never even smoked." She flushed, hating how she still rushed to defend him. According to Jeffrey, wives were always the last to know.

But Eve only shrugged and continued flipping through the album. "Strange he'd pay a prostitute. Guys like him would have no problem getting it for free."

"I thought he was getting enough at home," Dani said, rather surprised at her candidness. But Eve had agreed to stay overnight and abundant wine had a way of loosening conversation. More than that, Eve's own experiences made

her an ideal confidante. The drug cartel that had murdered
Joey made the Tattrie clan seem like choirboys.

"Maybe there was more to it," Eve said. "Who was
running the prostitute? Was she working for the Tattries?"

"I'm not sure. They were in a motel outside town. Dex
didn't have much to do with the family business. He sold his
bike, which displeased them. Sometimes he'd go to their
garage and help fix cars. He was an excellent mechanic." And
carpenter, plumber, friend and lover.

"There wasn't much he couldn't fix," Dani added, fiddling
with the stem of her glass. "That's why I missed him, you
know…because he was so good around the ranch."

Eve hooted and flipped the album shut. "Fess up. A
woman would miss this guy if he couldn't tell a hammer from
a shovel. How much time did he get?"

"Five years."

"That means he'll be up for parole soon."

Dani's glass tilted. Wine splashed the table, then dripped
onto her lap. "Parole? You think he'll get out early?" She
ignored the wine, her voice high and squeaky. "Jeffrey said it
was unlikely."

"He probably didn't want to get your hopes up," Eve said,
grabbing a napkin and wiping ineffectually at the red blotch.
"But yes, if Dex manages to behave himself, he might make
early parole. Depends how many enemies the Tattries have
and if he had to join a gang for protection. Sometimes it's
impossible to stay out of trouble."

"That's what Jeffrey said."

"For a handyman," Eve said dryly, "Jeffrey has plenty of
opinions."

"He's also a cop."

"Figures." Eve wrinkled her nose in distaste. "Scott says
there are plenty of good cops. But I haven't met one yet."

Dani ignored Eve's dig, unable to suppress a spurt of hope. *Parole*. It didn't change her situation, of course, but it would be wonderful for Dex.

Her cell phone chirped. She checked the display then dismissed it with a grimace. "It's just the bank. The collections department now calls on weekends."

"Persistent bloodsuckers," Eve said. "But it'll be awhile before they can kick you out. Unless it's with that new credit company on Main Street. I hear they're total dicks."

"Our mortgage isn't with them. Dex felt the same way."

"Sounds like he's a smart man," Eve said, "other than his taste for heroin and hookers."

"I didn't see it coming," Dani admitted, enjoying Eve's bluntness. "But Dad said it was inevitable—Dex being a Tattrie. Unfortunately Dad was right."

"Are you going back to your maiden name?"

"I don't know. That seems cowardly. Like I'm trying to cover up past mistakes." She couldn't stop her mischievous grin. "And sometimes it's nice to see Dad's grimace when I say my last name. He's very proud of my brother. Not so much of me."

"Is your brother into horses too?"

"Heck, no. Matt only cared about his Camaro and pleasing Dad. I think that's why he volunteered for the mission in Africa. Now he's building orphanages and Dad is bursting with pride. I miss my brother but I'm glad he finally got away. Our house was rather straitlaced."

"It must have been tough looking like you," Eve said, "and growing up in a minister's house."

Dani self-consciously tucked a tendril of blond hair back into her ponytail. She'd never cared much for jewelry or makeup, but it still stung to have her shortcomings pointed out, especially since Dex's attraction for flashy hookers was public knowledge. "I like my boots and jeans just fine," she said stiffly.

"And you look stunning in them," Eve said. "What I meant is that your father must have gone crazy dealing with all the boys knocking on the door."

"The only guys who came around were the ones interested in horses, so it was okay. I made a lot of money giving them lessons, enough to buy an old truck and trailer."

Eve rolled her eyes. "Not many high school guys like horses. They were just smart enough to wheedle their way onto your property and not spook your dad."

Dani shrugged. It was irrelevant why so many guys had hung around her back yard. The money they handed over had enabled her to compete at horse shows...and meet Dex. "I like your necklace," she said, angling for a more comfortable subject.

Eve fingered her silver necklace. "Scott's wife makes jewelry. She donates a lot of the proceeds. Your father would approve."

"I didn't mean to complain," Dani said, "but he's always been judgmental. My brother was terrified to bring a girl home. Matt never had much of a life."

"He didn't have a tough guy like Dex to help him escape," Eve said. "Probably easier to volunteer abroad."

Dani blinked. Eve was painfully honest as well as insightful. Matt had waited six months to be accepted as a Christian missionary. And when the call had come, he'd been thrilled to go. He'd been very sheltered and there was no one besides family who cared if he stayed or went. He only asked that Dani park his car out of the sun before he hugged her good-bye and hopped a plane. Probably her father *had* driven him away.

"You don't pull your punches," Dani said.

"Sorry." Eve had the grace to blush. "Being a mother softened me, but I still tend to speak without thinking."

"I like it," Dani said, raising her glass. "Here's a toast to honesty."

"And here's to women like you." Eve grabbed her glass. "Beautiful inside and out. May we always have good horses and good men."

"I'd settle for a good horse," Dani said.

CHAPTER SEVEN

Dani rubbed her aching head, wincing when she moved too quickly. Luckily Eve had helped with morning chores, so there was still plenty of time to drive to church. "Aren't you hung-over, just a little?" she asked, glancing at Eve.

Eve grinned, looking every bit as spunky as she had last night. "I'm fine. Just grateful to have a night off. I love little Joey dearly but it's always nice when Scott and Megan take him for the evening."

"You could stick around, come with me to church," Dani said hopefully. It would be nice to see a friendly face for a change.

"Sorry, not a churchgoer," Eve said. "And I have to get back. Don't forget to give me your divorce papers, and I'll ask Scott to check them out."

Dani nodded and hurried into her bedroom. The thick legal envelope was still in her bottom drawer, beneath the old scarves she never wore—where she had stuck it that horrible black day, two years ago.

She returned to the door, signaled Red to stay then followed Eve outside. "I'd like thirty percent of the proceeds," she said, passing Eve the envelope. "But I don't want to be greedy. Dex will need support when he gets out."

"Worry about yourself," Eve said. "I think it should be half. But let's see what Scott's lawyer thinks. Don't let Dex take you to the cleaners. He caused this mess."

Dani smoothed the front of her skirt, hating to see the sympathy on Eve's face. Part of her ached at the thought of giving up the ranch, but the other part looked forward to moving on.

"You look gorgeous, by the way," Eve said. "Too nice for a bunch of stuffy people at church."

"I'm meeting Jeffrey," Dani admitted. "We're going for lunch afterwards."

"Good," Eve said. "It's time to live a little." She pulled open the door of her car and slid behind the wheel. "I'll let you know what my boss says about taking Tizzy. Talk later."

Her car accelerated down the drive, kicking up a spiraling trail of dust, and it was obvious she drove as aggressively as she rode.

Smiling, Dani slipped into her faithful truck. It started reluctantly but once on the road, it stopped sputtering, the engine tick barely discernible. It was odd not to have Red riding shotgun, but it was too hot to leave him in the cab. Her father used to let the dog wait in the ministerial office during the service, but that was before Dex had gone to prison. Everything was different now.

The drive to town was just over half an hour, and she pulled into the church parking lot with minutes to spare.

She slid into a back pew. Her father was seated beside the pulpit. He didn't exactly nod but his eyes flickered in acknowledgement. And then a big smile creased his face as Jeffrey moved into the space beside her.

"Good morning," Jeffrey whispered. "You look beautiful. You should dress up more often."

"Not much need for that at the Double D," she said.

"Once you get rid of the place," he said, "you'll have time for a lot more things."

She nodded and picked up a hymnbook, ambushed by a wave of nostalgia. She'd been married in this building, only five years ago. Dex had said whatever made her happy was fine with him. The church had never seen so many leather-jacketed bikers, but it had been a joyful day. Sure, her father had been disapproving but at least he hadn't said anything. Not publicly anyway.

Now his sermons tended to take on a personal bent, and she'd become hardened to the swiveling heads staring in a mixture of sympathy and condescension. She forced her attention back to the sermon, then wished she hadn't.

"We must be role models for self-centered weaker people," her father said. "Our friends, our sons, our *daughters.*" His voice rose and he looked straight at her. "Young people often confuse sexual attraction with love. But if we set an example by living a life centered on the teachings of the bible, it's possible to start anew. Doing deeds intended for the accomplishment and growth of the church's views starts at home. Change can't help but spread."

"My own son, Matt," her father went on, "has chosen to devote his years to helping orphans in a third-world country. And there is nothing more admirable than giving oneself to others. To put another's needs over your own physical desires. So please, take the time to greet someone who needs support, or who perhaps has been seduced by pleasure and made poor life choices. We are all worthy in the eyes of God."

"But some are more worthy than others," Dani whispered to Jeffrey, who kept staring straight ahead. She folded her hands on her lap, trying to shield her embarrassment. She should be hardened by now. Her father had put Matt on a pedestal, understandable. But it still hurt when he constantly threw her beneath the bus.

And she needed to escape quickly. Otherwise two hundred well-meaning people would bolt to her side, keen to greet the minister's daughter who so obviously had been seduced by pleasure.

"I have to talk to your dad before we leave for lunch," Jeffrey said, rising slowly. "I'll meet you outside. We can take my car."

"No," she whispered, surprised that he was oblivious to her discomfort. "I'll drive my truck and meet you at the restaurant. I have to get out of here."

She didn't even wait for his nod, just scrambled from the pew and rushed toward the door. Too bad Red wasn't with her. He would have stuck by her side, providing unconditional approval. She almost beat the flood of people but a sweet old neighbor smiled a greeting, and Dani didn't have the heart to brush past.

"Are you still living alone at your ranch?" the woman asked, switching her cane to her left hand. "Someone told me they sent a horse to you for training and were very happy with the results."

"That's great to hear, thanks," Dani said, relaxing slightly. She generally remained on guard in public, but maybe after two years the scandal was fading. "I'll be selling the ranch soon," she said, "but I've always loved working with horses."

"Maybe you can find work at another stable." The woman gave a sympathetic smile. "It's too bad the money in those jobs is so low."

Dani gave a wry nod.

"Your father wants you to find a real job," Jeffrey said, coming up behind her. "So do I."

"I'll be considering all options," Dani said. She couldn't imagine life without horses or giving up Peppy. Jeffrey had told her the town hall had an opening for a receptionist. The job even had a benefit package. But no matter where she worked during the week, she'd try to find weekend work at a barn somewhere.

A woman with bluish-white hair tugged at Dani's arm. "Do you think you'd ever work with Matt in Africa?" she asked. "He's so selfless. Your father is extremely proud."

Dani nodded. "Yes, Matt is admirable."

"And so is this young man," another woman said, pushing forward and beaming up at Jeffrey. "Keeping our town safe from riffraff. Such an important job."

Jeffrey politely inclined his head. "Thank you, ladies. I do my best. And we have to get going," he said, addressing the growing cluster of faces. "Dani has finally agreed to join me for lunch."

"Oh, how lovely," someone said. Heads nodded in approval as people reluctantly shuffled sideways, clearing a path to the door.

Jeffrey clasped Dani's elbow and guided her toward his car. "Probably quicker if you ride in my car," he murmured, "now that everyone is hanging around the parking lot, waiting to speak to you. We can pick up your truck later."

"Okay." She cast a wistful look at her vehicle, but it was very clearly surrounded. "After a sermon like that, it's always a gauntlet. That's why I wanted to hurry," she added.

Jeffrey pulled open the passenger door. "This would all go away if you were with me. And I think your dad would approve. Aren't you a little tired of this constant attention?" He glanced over his shoulder at the people craning for a last look at the minister's daughter who had clearly been seduced by the dark side.

"Yes." Dani sighed and clipped on her seatbelt. "I am."

CHAPTER EIGHT

Dex adjusted the thin pillow, then folded his arms beneath his head, trying to block Tinker's prattle. Usually he had no difficulty shutting out his cellmate, no problem shutting out anyone, but the subject of conjugal visits always left Tinker effusive.

"I miss her smell, you know." Tinker sighed from the bunk below. "And the softness. Mighty fine woman. Gonna kill me to wait five months to do it again. Damn guards. I knew they were listening, jacking off. But for once, I got something they want. And that feels good."

"Don't let them know."

"What?" Tinker paused. "You finally say something, Tattrie?"

"If they know it's important, they'll find a way to take it away."

"Yeah, well, they can't have my woman," Tinker said. "And she's saving her loving for me. She tells me that all the time."

Dex closed his eyes. Half the inmates were divorced within the first year of incarceration. Tinker, however, remained optimistic. The man was a petty retailer of soft drugs and had done time before. But he never seemed to learn.

There was only one way to survive in prison. Hide your emotions. Never show fear, anger or pain. Yet Tinker's two main loves were his woman and basketball, and he always blew his mouth off to anyone who would listen. Unfortunately, for the last hour, that had been Dex.

"You have an opinion, best keep it to yourself," Dex said. "Now shut up."

Tinker muttered under his breath but silenced, and Dex was finally able to absorb the night sounds. Knowledge meant survival. Some men in the cells below were complaining about the Chicanos but nothing seemed to be cooking, at least nothing imminent. After last week's stabbing in the yard there would be repercussions, but nobody was in a hurry. In prison, time was relative.

In the adjacent cell, two prisoners bickered about who had plugged the toilet but they silenced when a guard's flashlight swept the door.

"Shut up, or I'll come in and shut you up," the guard growled.

Tank. Not a bad guy, for a guard. But it was dangerous to be seen talking friendly to the correctional officers. Dex closed his eyes, ignoring Tank's presence, straining to hear the inmates across the corridor. If trouble came, it would be from that direction.

Two men whispered in rapid-fire Spanish, but Dex was fluently bilingual and if the cell block was quiet enough, he could pick up more than the occasional word. Last week, they'd mentioned the Tattries, and not in an admiring way. His family had promised to lie low, maintain the status quo. However, most Tattries had short fuses. And when pushed, they shoved back. But dammit, he was almost eligible for parole.

The first year had been the longest. Some days Dex doubted he would ever make it out. He thought he'd been prepared, but the reality was jolting. Nothing could prepare him for the bleak and utter desolation of losing Dani. But he had no regrets. He'd destroyed three lives…and someone had to pay.

He hesitated for a moment, didn't want to prompt Tinker into talking again, but there might not be a chance in the morning. "Stay away from the nets tomorrow," he said.

"Yeah?" Tinker asked. "How do you know? You weren't in the yard since Sunday."

"Just keep an eye out," Dex said. "And next time pass the ball more to Road Hog."

"Okay. Thanks, bro. You working again this weekend?"

"Yes."

"Shaving your time?"

Dex grunted. He received one day off his sentence for each week of work assignment. But that wasn't the only reason he headed out every morning at six a.m. The prison work farm rehabbed horses. And the job had literally saved his life.

For eight hours each day, he could escape the numbing constriction, the pervasive stink of sweat and men. His cell was six feet across, nine feet deep, and if he held out his arms, he could touch the sides. The beds were mounted on the wall with two metal footlockers beneath the bottom bunk. Opposite the bunks sat two stark desks, also attached to the wall. At the back there was a chipped sink, a stained and temperamental toilet and a small metal mirror.

Below him, Tinker farted, his breathing slowing with sleep. Dex's tension eased. He liked his cellie, but resisted getting too close. Didn't want to worry about anyone else. Staying below the radar was critical, and it had been awhile since his last fight. He'd lost some, but won more, and the gangs now left him alone. It had been a taut balancing act, but street politics had always been a Tattrie way of life. And freedom was so close now, he could taste it.

CHAPTER NINE

Dex shuffled onto the morning transport bus, joining nineteen other offenders classified as non-violent. But he had a sharp eye for ink and some of the work crew's tattoos revealed their high status. Of course, what a man had done, and what he was convicted of doing, were two very different things. In fact, Carlos, the gimlet-eyed prisoner in the third row had ordered the shanking in the yard last week, and he still ran his East LA gang from the inside.

It was odd that Carlos even worked at the horse farm. Most inmates disliked the long hours and strenuous work, while others sneered at shoveling manure. A few genuinely feared the large animals, although they'd never admit it. The prisoners who volunteered seemed to have a real affection for the horses and except for the ashen-faced kid in the front, all the men had worked at the farm for months. Most worked five days a week. Dex was the only six-day man.

He kept his gaze forward, selecting a seat behind and to the right of Carlos. His caution was automatic. He doubted anything was going down, but for a man like Carlos it was political suicide to stay dormant. Alliances were always being tested, and if something happened on the outside, repercussions rippled inward. And knowledge meant survival.

Dex crossed his arms, using the motion as an excuse to check the guards. One of them was a fresh-faced newbie, unaware of any nuances, but the other two were seasoned pros and the wariness in their eyes was reassuring.

Nobody spoke. It wasn't permitted.

Generally Dex enjoyed the twenty-minute bus ride. But as they rumbled through the first perimeter gate, the sight of the electric fence topped with razor wire filled him with despair. He usually slapped down self-indulgent thoughts—tried to shut out most emotion. Sometimes though, it popped up when least expected. Last night, for the first time since his incarceration, he dared to believe he'd be released soon. He'd let himself think of Dani.

But bringing her into this place, if only in his thoughts, felt wrong. And she weakened him. She was the chink in his armor, the only woman he'd ever loved, while he was merely a dead weight dragging her into a churning cesspool. He'd always feared part of the reason she'd married him had been to escape her father—and to prove her dad's predictions wrong.

The minister's words were seared on Dex's soul: *The Tattries are nothing but trouble. They'll destroy this family.* Dex had been determined to disprove that statement. Unfortunately, Dani's father had been absolutely right.

Dex stared out the reinforced bus window, blocking his regrets. It was done. There was no going back. He didn't deserve a woman like Dani anyway.

Shots echoed from the firing range. A lone man in the segregation yard dropped from the parallel bars and gave a crude gesture. Officers often practiced their target shooting early in the morning, when high security inmates had their fifteen minutes of free time. No doubt, the gunfire had a psychological impact and was designed to keep the inmates in line.

Some of the cons had black souls while others, like Tinker, had never caught a break. It was a constant struggle not to be corroded by his surroundings, but Dex had mastered self discipline and instead he pictured the horses, awaiting their breakfast. They always nickered when the prison bus arrived, not caring that the men wore orange coveralls with 'So-Cal

State Prison' emblazoned on the back. And the horses' respect, although hard earned, was permanent.

The bus chugged along a winding road, the air turning sweeter the further they drove from the prison. Someone murmured that he was going to wash his horse today, and the guards didn't reprimand him for talking. The tightness between Dex's shoulder blades eased. Not completely. He was too cautious to ever totally relax. Even a work detail wasn't completely safe.

"There's my baby," the man across the aisle said, as a gray mare cantered along the fence line, eagerly following the bus. "The girls, they all love me."

One of the guards grimaced, but the inmate really did have a rapport with horses. He'd advanced to the riding detail, impressing Dex with how quickly he'd learned. The foreman had offered to put Dex in charge of the riders, but he'd declined. He didn't have Dani's patience for teaching and besides, some inmates didn't take direction well. Tempers were short and the possibility of inflaming someone's ire was too risky. There were others capable of teaching, and since it was a sought-after position, instructors were constantly rotated.

Instead, Dex had made sure he secured a permanent place on the equine work detail. He'd offered his services as a farrier.

Few convicts could properly shoe a horse. At first, his skills had been a little rough, barely enough to satisfy the foreman. But the library had some good how-to books and Dex had been able to order more as his skills developed. The pay was fifty cents an hour, the time reduced his sentence, and the only hard part was hiding how much he enjoyed the job.

The bus shuddered to a stop in front of the low-lying barn with its reinforced loading area, complete with surveillance cameras. Dex scanned the paddocks for Gypsy, his personal favorite. Like most of the cons, these horses were rejects. Many were off-the-track Thoroughbreds, horses that were injured or too old and slow to have much value. A few had been abused riding horses and consequently had developed some nasty habits, not out of meanness but from confusion or fear. Gypsy had been like that.

She'd been considered worthless, a pinto of dubious ancestry and temperament, weighing over twelve hundred pounds. The foreman kept her around as a tool. Whenever convicts turned too cocky, they were assigned Gypsy.

Fridays were the rodeo, a day of high entertainment, fun for all except the hapless rider climbing up on Gypsy's back. Dex had never known why he'd been chosen that Friday, two years ago, but when the foreman called Dex's name his hands had itched with eagerness. He would have paid a year's commissary funds for a shot at the big mare. For a precious moment he'd been back on the rodeo circuit, back when Dani jumped and cheered and smiled at him like he was a hero.

He shook his head, clearing the memories, and turned toward the window. And there was his horse. Gypsy was boss mare, too cool to chase the bus.

A path cleared as she strolled through the milling herd and toward the gate. She didn't flatten her ears; didn't have to. The other horses lined up behind her, in order of their status. Six horses back, there was a little pushing as a newly arrived gelding tried to challenge the pecking order. Gypsy snaked her head, showing her displeasure, and the new horse sidled away to stand on the fringe.

The men waited until Dex rose and stepped off the bus, followed by Carlos. No one could remove his horse until Dex led Gypsy out.

"Morning, boys," Quentin, the foreman called. "Bring them in, feed, then check your assignments. Tattrie, I have six coming to the secure area for shoeing."

Dex nodded. Quentin often arranged for outside horses to be shod, a mutually beneficial arrangement where the prison raised money and the extra work ensured Dex's position remained valuable. He scooped up Gypsy's halter and lead rope, and opened the gate. The mare nickered a greeting, then helpfully lowered her head and pushed her nose through the halter. Dex could feel Carlos's hooded gaze, but the man never spoke. Not to him.

Dex led Gypsy through the gate.

"Better wait," Quentin said.

Dex halted the big mare on the other side of the paddock. Horses were always eager for their morning grain and sometimes turned pushy if their pasture mates disappeared inside the barn. Some of the cons had trouble haltering their assigned horses and the mere presence of Gypsy kept the herd calm.

Carlos's horse was next in line but the tall chestnut kept throwing her head, making it difficult for him to buckle the halter. If a human had given Carlos that kind of trouble, they wouldn't be breathing by nightfall. But Carlos was surprisingly patient. His face remained impassive but his hand was gentle on the horse's neck. And of course, no one dared heckle Carlos. Even the watching guards were silent.

Carlos finally managed to halter the horse. It wasn't pretty but Dex caught a glint of well-deserved satisfaction in the man's eyes. Gypsy wasn't impressed, blowing out an impatient sigh. But the rest of the line moved swiftly, and soon the line of horses filed into the barn.

Gypsy had the first stall, where she could keep a watchful eye on both the barn and the pasture. Unless a horse was sick or injured, the animals remained outside and were only brought in for grain and grooming.

Dex checked her over, noting a tiny insect bite, then walked to the feed room and gathered her grain. One of the guards was already stuffed in a white plastic chair, enjoying a fresh coffee. Clearly this was a desirable work assignment for both inmates and guards.

"In my office, Tattrie," Quentin called. "Now!"

Dex dumped Gypsy's grain in her tub, gave her an affectionate pat, then followed the foreman down the aisle to the office.

Quentin closed the door and poured Dex a coffee. "Want a doughnut with that?" he asked, his voice much less authoritative now that nobody was listening.

Dex raised an eyebrow.

Quentin chuckled. "Sorry. Must have mixed you up with the guards." He pulled open his desk drawer and tossed over a protein bar and a carrot. "I thought the new kid could do some finishing on the little bay mare."

"She walked in a little sore on the left hind," Dex said. "But I'll check her out. Got a buyer?"

"If she's sound."

"Probably just a bruise," Dex said. "But what about the kid? He's only been here a week. Are you going to give him another horse?"

"No, this is his last day." Quentin picked up a red pen and jotted a notation in his book. "The warden wants to follow seniority. Too many inmates clamoring for this work assignment."

Dex took a pensive sip of coffee. The kid wouldn't last in the prison yard; he'd be chum in the water. Not that it was his concern. And he wasn't about to use up any favors for someone he didn't know. No way. He ordered himself to remain silent.

But seconds later he sighed and set down his cup, the sound loud in the cramped office.

"What?" Quentin glanced up. "I've got no room here. Really. I don't have a horse for him."

Dex just stared.

"I can't look after every lost kid," Quentin said, tossing aside his pen. "Neither can you."

"Nor do I want to," Dex said, his mind scrambling. There might be no horse to ride but many required shoeing. And there was no safer place than the ship-in area with the watchful guard and reinforced wiring.

"But I do need an assistant," Dex went on. "Little incident in the cell block last night left me with a sore wrist. Makes it tough to shoe alone… Impossible really."

"Bullshit." Quentin leaned back and crossed his arms. "I didn't see an injury report. And you better be healthy. We have horses booked six days a week. A couple of them are Thoroughbreds from the track, with tight schedules."

"Then it'll be unfortunate when I can't shoe them."

"Dammit, Tattrie." Quentin's jaw clenched and Dex knew he was pushing it.

"Look, it doesn't matter to me," Dex said, raising his palms, "but this kid knows horses. And he's teachable. You could increase outside bookings. More money would please the warden. Seems like a smart move to have a second farrier."

"I suppose," Quentin muttered, dragging a hand over his jaw. "The warden did commend me on the increased profits."

"No doubt you'll see a raise this year too," Dex said, "if you continue with the shoeing profits. I think it shows managerial foresight to bring in a trainee."

"And I think you're playing chess when everyone else is playing checkers," Quentin said. "Now get out. I'll send the kid to you later today."

Dex nodded and rose. He stuck the carrot up his sleeve before stepping into the aisle.

Gypsy shoved her head over the door, tracking his progress, knowing what a visit to the office meant. He entered her stall and pulled out the carrot. She gently lifted it from his hand, chewing rather daintily for such a big mare. Dex savored the morning carrot ritual as much as her, enjoying that he could do a little extra for the horse who meant so much to him.

"I'll be back," he said, eyeing her hooves. Gypsy didn't need shoes; he'd been doing a barefoot trim on many of the horses, especially the ones with good feet. But he didn't want to work himself out of a job either, so last year he'd sold Quentin on the idea of bringing in outside horses.

Now the work farm had developed an excellent reputation, shoeing hunters and jumpers as well as reiners and racehorses. Owners initially shipped their horses to take advantage of the rock bottom prices, but they sent their animals back because of the results.

The Thoroughbreds were the most challenging. Often they were thin-soled with brittle feet stressed from nail holes and excessive trimming. But Dex loved the job. If he could make a horse comfortable and better balanced, it generally showed in their race results. Sometimes he used glue-on shoes. They didn't last long and were more expensive, but the horses appreciated them. So did the trainers, and bettors.

He walked back to the feed room. The sullen guard lurched to his feet, pulled out a key and unlocked the adjoining supply room.

Dex walked in and gathered his shoeing apron and farrier tools.

"Sign here," the guard said, as if Dex didn't know the drill.

Dex bit back his reply and initialed the sign-out sheet, then headed to the secure visitor area at the far end of the barn. A trailer was already waiting with two horses peering curiously out their side windows.

A balding man led off a rangy gray Thoroughbred who picked his way tentatively over the rough gravel, clearly uncomfortable on all four feet.

"What's this horse used for?" Dex asked, picking up the horse's front left and studying his foot.

"My daughter jumps him," the man said. "Lately he's been refusing which is out of character because he always tries. She thinks it's because his feet are sore."

"She's right," Dex said. "I'm going to raise his heel and put some pads on him. It'll take a few trimmings to get him right, but she'll notice an improvement right away."

"Good." The father blew out a relieved sigh but didn't speak again, letting Dex work in peace.

Many new clients—even some of the returning ones—were intimidated by the orange jumpsuits. But Dex didn't need pointless chatter. This was the most treasured part of his day, a time when he was in charge, far from the prison drudgery where every decision was made for him. The job kept him sane…and it was all thanks to Gypsy.

She'd helped him earn Quentin's respect. And ironically if Dex hadn't been in prison, he never would have developed into such an accomplished farrier. Never would have studied so many books or had the chance to work with a variety of horses.

He enjoyed watching the animals walk back onto their trailer, happier and sounder than when they arrived. Regrettably there were some horses that couldn't be helped.

Like Dex's fifth animal of the day—a magnificent chestnut gelding.

"I'm sorry," he said, looking up at the black-haired woman who stared at him hopefully. "He has navicular syndrome. Have you seen a vet?"

"Yes." She squeezed her eyes shut, moisture glinting in the corners. "Two vets diagnosed navicular too. But I'd heard such amazing things about this place… Guess I hoped you could pull off a miracle."

"We can try to keep him comfortable," Dex said. "But that's the most I can do."

"He's only fourteen." The woman rubbed at her eyes. "I've had him since he was two. He used to run barrels. He was so good at it, and so smart. He always kept me safe."

The horse flicked an ear, watching with intelligent eyes as if sensing her distress.

"He looks smart." Dex cleared his throat. "And fast."

"Yes. One time we had a sixteen-second run."

"It takes a real partnership to do that," he said, the words flowing a little easier now. "My wife has a good old barrel horse. He's special to her too."

"That's right. They become so important. It helps that you understand." She stepped closer and gave him an impulsive hug. "Thank you," she whispered.

The hovering guard jerked forward, his hand reaching for his holster, his eyes widening with alarm.

"I've trimmed a little off his heel," Dex said, stepping away from her embrace. "You should cut back on his feed. Help him drop some weight. You could also try using a boot. That might help."

The lady sniffed and gave a grateful nod, then led her obliging horse toward a silver trailer, not even acknowledging the guard.

"What the hell, Tattrie," the guard snapped, once she was out of earshot. "Am I going to have to write you up?"

"I didn't touch her. She hugged me."

"You know the rules. And I notice there are a lot more women arriving with horses. What's with these bitches, coming here to sniff around a con?"

Dex ignored the man's comments and instead concentrated on re-arranging his tools. He'd need a new rasp soon. They didn't last long and had to be sharp. The spring farrier catalogue was out, and there were also some new clinch cutters he wanted to try. As long as profits for the work center continued to rise, Quentin was very obliging about ordering new products.

The guard wouldn't shut up though. "It pisses me off," he went on. "You're just an arrogant bastard who can barely talk. And a wife who barrel races? What kind of woman would marry someone like you?"

Dex's hand tightened around the rasp. He'd slipped up. Had mentioned Dani.

"I'm talking to you, Tattrie. Bet your wife's a hooker now. No doubt she's deep balling on the corner, enjoying the action while you're locked up."

"I'm divorced," Dex said.

"Yeah, well what do you expect?" The guard gave a knowing grunt and hitched up his gun belt. "Women never wait. Not even for big bad bikers."

Dex slid the long steel rasp onto the side of his tool box, portraying a calm he didn't feel. But the guard was right. Most women didn't wait. Couldn't be expected to. Even if they did, the men who left prison were vastly different from the ones who entered. Soiled forever. No woman should have to endure that. The stain was contagious, contaminating everything it touched.

"Here's your apprentice."

Dex jerked his head up, surprised he hadn't heard Quentin approach. Probably a measure of how he'd let the guard needle him. Something he didn't usually permit.

"This is Sandy," Quentin went on, gesturing at the inmate behind him. "He's green as grass but he's all yours."

"Hello, Sandy," Dex said to the nervous-looking kid. He looked like an upper class preppie with blue eyes, blond hair and baby-soft skin. And that was good reason to be nervous. "I saw you ride this week. You like horses?"

"Yes, sir." Sandy's head pumped in acknowledgement. "My dad owns horses and I've often ridden to hounds."

Dex sighed. This kid was going to need a lot of looking after. "Best keep that to yourself," he said. "In fact, any opinion, thought or belief, it's safest kept to yourself. And I'm not a sir," he added. "I'm a convict. Just like you."

CHAPTER TEN

Dani twisted the tap, staring in dismay as the water thinned to a trickle and disappeared. She kneeled down and peered into the faucet head, praying it was only plugged. Something simple, please. But other than a ring of rust, there was no obvious blockage.

"It's probably just a fuse," she said, glancing at Red, then at the long row of thirsty horses. *Please, be a fuse.*

She hurried back to the barn and scanned the electrical panel. Everything was neatly labeled in Dex's bold print: Barn Lights, Ring Lights, Water Pump. The fuse for the pump looked okay but she inserted a new one from the spares on the shelf then rushed back to the tap and turned the handle.

Nothing.

She dropped to the ground, groaning. The well shouldn't be dry; it was a drilled well and they'd always had plenty of water—one of the reasons Dex had chosen this property. But that meant it was either the submersible pump or a burst pipe, both of which would be costly to fix. And the horses needed water. Now.

Red whined and shoved his nose beneath her elbow. "It's okay, fellow," she said. The poor dog picked up on her stress and constantly worried. Every day more gray hairs prematurely dotted his muzzle.

"We still have water in the house," she said. "We'll fill buckets and carry them on the back of the truck. No problem."

Two hours later, she and Red slumped on the ground in front of the paddocks. Finally the horses were watered. But she'd have to repeat the laborious process again tonight. And the well that supplied the house could never keep up with the barn demand. The ranch would be dry within a week.

She tipped her head and rubbed her aching shoulder. She hadn't even ridden yet, and three of the horses were two-year-olds. Probably she should skip the training today. Their youthful shenanigans would definitely challenge her patience. Dex said it wasn't fair to work with horses if you couldn't block your emotions, but, unlike him, she wasn't so good at compartmentalizing.

And what was the sense anyway? Eve's boss might decide to train Tizzy, but the horse wouldn't be ready to sell for months. It seemed pointless to keep struggling. The ranch was doomed. The most she could do was spruce the place up so she'd receive a better price. She just needed to round up a little cash first.

She squared her shoulders, pulled out her phone and called the bank. It took twenty minutes and three people before she reached the proper department. And this person seemed incapable of grasping the point of her call.

"Yes, I'm aware I'm behind with a couple payments," Dani repeated. "But I just wanted to let you know I'm selling the ranch. And its market value is well over the amount owing. So if you could just suspend payments for a few months, I'll pay the entire amount when it's sold."

"I'm sorry," the bored voice said. "But your account is seriously delinquent. Therefore we need two months' payment along with interest and the incurred penalty fees."

"But you don't understand. I'll be repaying the entire amount soon. I just need some time."

"And we don't negotiate until delinquent accounts are brought up to date," the disapproving voice said.

"But that's the point of my call." Dani paced a circle around a concerned Red. "I just need a little help and then you'll get your money. Along with interest and any penalties you have to assess."

"We can't suspend your mortgage payment. It's bank policy. We might consider extending a consumer loan at eighteen percent, but only if you first pay the arrears."

"But that's why I need the money—"

"And both you and your husband will have to come into the bank and personally sign the papers," the woman continued.

"Thank you," Dani managed, squeezing her lower lip so tightly it hurt.

She cut the connection then sagged to the ground and wrapped her arms around Red. "No need to worry," she said. "Everything's okay." But her voice quavered and it felt like things would never be okay again.

"Looks like it's the pump." Jeffrey turned away from the fuse box, shaking his head. "You need to hire a plumber. I can give you the money."

"I'm grateful," Dani said. "But you know I can't accept it."

"Why?" He stepped closer and reached for her hand. "There's no reason to keep refusing. You know how I feel about you. And the quicker it's fixed, the quicker the ranch can be sold."

"I know," she said, blinking back her emotion. "I already called the bank and told them."

"You did! That's great." He squeezed her hand, his entire face lighting up. "I'll call a water truck," he said. "We'll fill that old holding tank until we can get a plumber. And you need to visit Dex and persuade him to sign the sale papers."

"I can't," she said. "He didn't put me on his approved visitor list."

Jeffrey jerked back. "What?"

She swallowed. "I haven't seen him in a while." Even after all this time, the reality hurt. She couldn't remember much of that fateful Saturday night, only that Dex had disappeared from their bedroom sometime after midnight. Hours later, the police arrested him at the hospital, just forty minutes after Tawny died. He hadn't even applied for bail.

"I only saw him a few minutes the day after he confessed," she said, her voice surprisingly level. "After that, he refused to see me." However, his words remained imprinted: *We should get a divorce. I didn't have sex with Tawny. I'm sorry.*

But he wouldn't look at her when he spoke and it was obvious he was lying. Her knees had buckled and she'd probably still be sitting dumbly at the police station if her father hadn't exploded and attacked Dex. "Worthless Tattrie scum!" he'd yelled. The police had intervened and pulled him away.

"I wasn't working that night," Jeffrey said. "But I heard that your father hit him. And we were all glad he did. Sometimes it's nice to cuff an asshole and put him in a private room."

"He wasn't cuffed," Dani said. "He just stood there and took it. Dad punched him so hard he broke a bone in his hand."

Jeffrey nodded sagely. "It's the guilt. I've seen it before. Dex could have squashed your dad. But he knew he deserved some shots in the face."

Dani winced, remembering the blood trickling from Dex's nose.

"Yeah," Jeffrey said, misreading her reaction. "He's a selfish bastard. Smart though. He's still yanking your chain. Makes it tough to finish things if you can't visit." His voice turned thoughtful. "I can probably get in to see him though. I know some guys who work there."

"I just need his signature on Tizzy's papers." Dani jammed her hands in her back pockets. "And to ask his agreement to sell."

"Don't ask him," Jeffrey said. "Tell him. You're selling, and you want a divorce."

"His lawyer sent divorce papers awhile back," she admitted. "There didn't seem to be any urgency. But I'll get moving on those too."

Jeffrey's eyes widened. "He already agreed? That's great. But you can't sign without advice first. Those Tattries are tricky. I better look them over."

"No need. I gave them to a friend who knows a lawyer."

"But this is fantastic." Jeffrey's smile returned and he slid his arm around her waist. "Soon you'll be rid of him. And I'll help you, I promise. You won't ever be alone again."

His head dipped, his mouth covering hers in a gentle kiss. Lately Jeffrey had been increasingly vocal about his feelings and while there were no stars, his kisses were pleasant enough. It was quite comforting to be held again. To have someone who was dependable and open.

He might not make her heart sing but she could trust him. She slipped her arms around his neck and kissed him back. Because the second time around, trust was really the only thing she wanted.

CHAPTER ELEVEN

"Sonofabitch! They're gone." Tinker smacked his fist in his palm, his voice rising with agitation. "You take my pictures, Tattrie?"

Dex rolled over on his upper bunk. "Remember when you first came? When we agreed to make this cell a place of quiet contemplation?"

"But my pictures are gone. And I don't know those big ten-dollar words. Just give my pictures back."

"Don't have them," Dex said.

Tinker stretched up, leaning over Dex. His nostrils flared and spots of red flagged his narrow cheeks. "I know you took them," he said. "You got no woman. No pictures. So you stole mine."

Dex gave a resigned sigh. But he couldn't let this go. His arm shot out and wrapped around Tinker's neck. He yanked Tinker off his feet, jamming his head against the steel mattress frame. "I don't have them," Dex said. "Understand?"

"Goddamn—"

Dex tightened his hold, cutting off Tinker's curse and pressing the man's face into the steel. "Let me know when you understand," he said, applying more pressure.

Thirty seconds later Tinker slapped the mattress. Dex dropped him and the man fell to the concrete, sputtering for breath.

"Am I going to have to come down from my bunk?" Dex asked. "And talk some more?"

"No, man," Tinker said, his voice ragged.

"Good." Dex closed his eyes. The man was a constant soap opera, and he suspected the guards had paired them together as some sort of joke.

Still, this time his cellie's distress seemed very real. Dex cracked open an eyelid and peered down. Tinker rocked on the floor, groaning, his head in his hands.

Dex waited until he couldn't stand it any longer. "Go ahead and tell me," he said.

"Someone stole my pictures. Not you," Tinker said quickly. "But someone."

"When?"

"Came back from supper and they were gone." Tinker groaned again. "Someone's jerking off right now. That's my woman. And it's not right."

"You talk to anyone about your conjugal? Besides me," Dex added dryly.

"No... Well, maybe a few of the homeboys. And Fat Tony and a couple guys on the court."

"So the whole yard then."

Tinker shook his head back and forth. "Should have kept my mouth shut," he said. "But I finally had something good, you know." He banged the back of his head against the wall. "I can't do this no more. Need my pictures."

"I'll take care of it."

Tinker stopped wailing. His head shot up. "You will?"

"Yes. But give me a little quiet so I can think."

Tinker nodded and instantly quit moaning. Dex closed his eyes, relishing the blessed silence. An additional benefit of working six days at week at the horse farm meant he was exhausted at the end of the day, unlike many of the inmates who were bored silly. Like Tinker.

And while Dex understood the temptation to bring family pictures inside, it only meant you had more things to worry about. To protect. The less that could be taken from you, the simpler it was to survive. And he'd warned Tinker about shooting his mouth off. The man never listened.

At least, the guards hadn't seen Tinker smashing his head. Some of the more aggressive ones were quick to throw an inmate into the hole, claiming solitary was for the prisoner's protection.

A guard's steps sounded. "Pig walking," someone shouted. The call relayed along the block in a chorus of deep and hostile voices.

Moments later, the cell door clanged open. The guard with the barrel chest filled the doorway. "Tattrie. Come with me."

Dex steeled his face against any telltale emotion. Being pulled from your cell was never a good thing. But as long as everyone was fine on the outside, he could handle it on the inside. More than likely the farm guard had reported him for improper contact with the horse owner yesterday.

He swung his legs over the bunk and slid to the floor, not too quickly but not slow enough to be accused of insolence either.

"You the Tat Man!" Tinker said, igniting a show of solidarity from fellow inmates.

"Tattrie in the hole," someone else called. And another, "Make 'em suck your dick, Tattrie."

Dex walked down the steel corridor, flanked by two guards, barely aware of the ribald calls from fellow inmates. *Just make it not about Dani. Make her be okay.* He realized his fists were clenched and pressed them against his orange chambray pants, trying to loosen his fingers.

They passed through three steel doors. The air turned fresher, cleaner, and a smoothly whirring air conditioner maintained a comfortable temperature.

His escort stopped and pulled open a door. "In there," he grunted, inclining his head.

Dex walked into the room. Jeffrey Nicholson, one of Dani's old friends, sat at the table, his gaze assessing. His police uniform was crisp and blue. Dex remained standing, surprised and silent.

"Have a seat," Jeffrey said. "Dani sent me."

Which meant she was just fine. Dex kept his face impassive but his entire chest bumped with relief. He settled into the cramped chair.

"How have you been?" Jeffrey asked. "Looks like you bulked up."

Dex simply stared. He wasn't a big fan of Jeffrey Nicholson. The man was an acquaintance and a cop, but he'd always been a suck-up, especially around Dani's father. And clearly he'd pulled some strings to visit. Dex certainly hadn't mailed him a visitor application.

"You're probably wondering why I'm here." Jeffrey shifted uncomfortably. "It's about Dani. She's finally ready to move on. She wants a divorce."

Dex kept his face impassive. He'd assumed they were divorced. That she had moved on.

"She's kept the place running for over two years," Jeffrey continued, talking faster now. "Been making the mortgage payments. I feel she should get sixty percent of the proceeds."

Dex leaned back an inch. This was confusing as hell. "She's still on the ranch?" he asked. "Still training?"

"Yes," Jeffrey said, "but it's getting harder. Economy is down. People are broke. Just last week some client from Santa Clara came in the middle of the night and sneaked his horse out. Didn't pay a dime for a three-month job."

Dex's mouth tightened. "What's his name?"

"Mr. Richard Higgins and Spunky was all the information she had." Jeffrey gave a condescending eye roll. "You know Dani. She assumes everyone is honest."

"No reason for her to think a client would sneak in and take his horse," Dex said, resenting the man's smug superiority.

"Of course not," Jeffrey said quickly. "I wasn't criticizing. Just explaining why her cash flow is hurting."

"What do you want?"

"Dani wants to send a Thoroughbred called Tizzy for some race training and evaluation. Maybe you remember that horse?"

"I do."

"And she needs a record of ownership before he's allowed on the track. The horse probably isn't going to be worth much and it's Dani who's taking all the risk. She's trying to raise money to pay for ranch repairs, so there's no reason for you not to sign—"

Dex lifted a finger, stopping the man's blather. This whole ownership thing seemed redundant but if it made things easier for Dani, of course he'd sign. "Do you have the papers?"

Jeffrey whipped out Tizzy's registration papers along with a pen and pushed them across the table.

Dex flipped the paper over and signed his name. He didn't understand the man's satisfied exhale.

"She's also going to need you to sign some bank papers concerning the mortgage," Jeffrey said. "The documents will be ready soon, including the divorce agreement." He tucked the paper and pen into his side pocket, then slid his chair back a few inches. "And just so you know, I'm not going to stand by and let you take advantage." He paused a beat. "You need to know Dani and I are together."

A muscle twitched on the side of Dex's jaw. He was able to keep his hands still but he couldn't resist measuring the man's neck, imagining giving it a good throttle. It was inevitable this day would come—in actuality, he'd assumed she'd already moved on—but he'd blocked the knowledge. Taking one hour at a time, keeping his thoughts carefully controlled, was the only way to prevent hopelessness from rotting his soul. However, he hadn't been prepared for this visit or the spiteful glint in Jeffrey's eyes.

And what was this prick thinking, to even talk about Dani in this wretched place?

"Before I go," Jeffrey added, as if emboldened by Dex's silence, "I need to be assured of your cooperation. This process needs to go smoothly...or else my next visit won't be as neighborly."

Dex crossed his arms.

Jeffrey's gaze darted to the door, as if reassuring himself that reinforcements were still standing beyond the mesh window. "You seem to be a model prisoner," he said, "but everyone hates a snitch. Your parole is coming up. Be a shame if any rumors started."

Dex abruptly leaned forward, flattening his hands over the table. Jeffrey shrunk back.

"We finished?" Dex asked.

Jeffrey flushed as if embarrassed by his reaction. "Guard," he called, scraping back his chair.

But his voice lowered as he passed Dex. "Just remember," he whispered. "I have friends here. And you really don't want me coming back."

CHAPTER TWELVE

'This phone call has originated from a California state prison.'

Dex waited for the irritating recording to stop, then continued talking, aware the alert would replay every fifteen seconds. And that all calls were monitored. "Be nice to have a visitor," he said into the mouthpiece. "Everything's good. Just need to see my family."

"I'll make an appointment," his cousin, Cindy, said. "You working six days?"

"Yes, so Sunday is best." Dex cut the connection. A burly inmate at the back of the line rushed forward and grabbed the phone from his hand.

Dex glowered and the man paused. "You finished?" the inmate asked.

"No," Dex said, pulling back the phone. Every word, every gesture could have repercussions, and a man lived on his reputation. It had been over a year since he'd been forced to fight, and he liked it that way. But constant vigilance was necessary. And pushing in line couldn't be tolerated. Already three cons grumbled. But the last twenty-four hours he'd been preoccupied, thinking of Dani. And that was dangerous.

"Stand at the back," Dex said, jabbing the man in the shoulder. "Wait your turn."

The man shifted, rocking on his toes, his eyes assessing. Dex gave him his coldest stare. A taut moment later, the man's eyes flickered downward. He turned and shuffled to the end of the line.

"Yeah, punk, back of the line," someone said, while another man with a tattooed forehead gave Dex an approving nod.

Dex ignored them and replaced the receiver, then returned to the line of prisoners awaiting escort back to their cells. Right now, his status was more or less established. But Jeffrey's whispered threat was very real. When an inmate met with a uniform, at night in a private room, rumors could spread like wildfire. And life could turn ugly. Especially if Jeffrey knew guards who could fan the innuendos.

But at least the man had brought news of Dani. Dex had walled himself off from the outside world, accepting that his life had permanently changed. Sometimes, in a moment of weakness, he'd let himself question his choice. But his course was set and there was no room for regret. Dani deserved a better life, a better man, and he wanted to make it as easy as possible.

But she's still on the Double D.

He shook his head in disbelief, unable to imagine how she'd kept the ranch going. His cousin said she hadn't once called. Of course, Dani probably didn't want to accept help from the Tattries. Her father certainly wouldn't be eager for any relationship; he'd always said Dex would bring nothing but grief.

"Got 'em."

A man's low growl yanked back Dex's attention. He hadn't even heard Icepick approach. Not a healthy state of mind when surrounded by felons.

"You'd go to the mat for this?" Icepick asked, the white scar on his forehead puckering in confusion. "People will think Tinker is your bottom bunk bitch. Why you always looking after these punks?"

"Nothing to do with Tinker," Dex said. "Someone stole from my house."

Icepick grunted but slipped Dex the pictures. "She's ugly anyway. No tits or ass. No one be taking them again. Everything good?"

Dex nodded and stuck Tinker's recovered photos up his sleeve. Seconds later, the guard hollered for Block D, and Dex followed the line back to his cell.

He stepped inside. Tinker lay on the lower bunk, his arms tightly folded, a bible pressed over his chest. The man had been uncommonly quiet the last forty-eight hours, and while Dex appreciated the lack of chatter, he worried about his cellie.

"I'm ready," Tinker mumbled, without opening his eyes. "The boys are waiting for you."

The yard had parallel bars but weights could be used as weapons, so weren't available. Dex worked at the horse farm all day but most inmates—and many guards—followed a strict fitness regime. To compensate for his missed yard time, Dex had organized evening sessions where inmates took turns lifting their cellies. It fostered solidarity and during the repetitions, the entire aisle echoed with encouragement.

But it didn't appear Tinker was too enthused about the upcoming workout. He hadn't opened his eyes, and his body language resembled a whipped pup.

"I can do pushups," Dex said. "Just rest. I don't need to lift you tonight."

"Whatever. Your dime, boss."

Dex shook out his sleeve and dropped the photos on Tinker's chest. The man jackknifed up, clutching at them in disbelief. "You got them? I was hoping, praying." He pressed the photos to his face, crowing in delight, smiling and kissing each one.

Dex turned away, embarrassed by Tinker's emotion. He planted himself in front of the cell door, staring outward and blocking the view. Knowledge gave inmates and guards more power; it exposed vulnerabilities. And dragging family into prison, even in the form of a photo, was a risk Dex would never take.

Tinker, though, saw it differently. The pictures were his crutch and helped him get through each day. And now the man was ecstatic. He hopped around the cell, waving the photos in one hand, his bible in the other. "Thank you, Lord. Thank you, Tattrie."

"That's enough," Dex said. However, even though he rarely indulged in a smile, the side of his mouth twitched. Tinker's euphoria lifted the entire cell, coloring it a brighter shade of gray.

"Let's go." Tinker bounced on his toes. "Signal the homies. Tonight I'm gonna raise you five times."

Dex lifted an eyebrow. He hit twenty repetitions, but Tinker only weighed one eighty. Dex weighed over two hundred and thirty pounds, and Tinker struggled with lifting him even twice. However, it would be healthy if Tinker had a goal. And it might help his status with the boys.

"All right," Dex said, gesturing at the concrete floor. "And if you're shooting for five reps, tonight you can lift me first."

Tinker gave an enthusiastic fist pump and stretched out on the concrete. Dex positioned himself above Tinker's shoulders, then called out the countdown. Moments later the aisle echoed as inmates began their weight training, yelling out numbers as they lifted their cellies.

Tinker huffed and puffed, struggling to lift Dex. One, two, three. The man was definitely inspired by the return of his photos. His mouth was set in gritty determination, his breath laboring as he fought to hit another rep.

And Dex shared Tinker's achievement, punching his cellie's thin shoulder in jubilation, when—for the first time ever—Tinker didn't put Dex down until the count reached five.

CHAPTER THIRTEEN

Dani paced around the kitchen, watching the driveway for the investigator's car. She rather regretted letting Eve take the divorce papers to her brother-in-law. Dani hadn't expected that Scott Taylor would request a personal meeting, and she was terrified of the cost. Even Eve had been surprised that Scott wanted a face-to-face.

Dani grabbed a wet cloth and rewiped the kitchen table. She should have just signed the papers, no matter how the assets were divided. Besides, Dex had raised the down payment. The Double D was mostly his. Granted, the horses were more difficult to split. Both she and Dex had put their hearts and souls into building up the training business. He definitely should have the proceeds from Tizzy though; he'd picked that colt out at a Thoroughbred sale.

Dex had winked and promised that Tizzy's race winnings would buy them either a bigger tractor...or a case of beer. But that at any rate, he'd be fun to watch. Unfortunately, the last couple years hadn't been fun at all.

Red whined, picking up on her turbulence, and she patted his head. The dog was another problem. Who would get Red? And at the rate he was aging would he even be alive by the time Dex was released? That thought was so depressing, she sank into the chair. Beneath his cool exterior, Dex was the kindest man she'd ever met. He'd be devastated if he never saw Red again.

Red abruptly turned and trotted to the front door, his ears pricked. Seconds later a gray Mercedes cruised up her driveway. A broad-shouldered man stepped out, carrying a thick leather case.

She pressed her palms against her jeans, then pulled in a deep breath and opened the door.

"Dani?" he asked. At her nod, he thrust out his hand. "I'm Scott Taylor, Eve's brother-in-law. Thanks for making time to see me."

She shook his hand, instantly liking the man. His smile was deep and sincere and put her at ease. She liked him even more when he stooped and held out the back of his hand for Red to examine. The dog sniffed his fingers, then wagged his tail and turned toward the kitchen, as if granting house privileges. And Red was a first-class judge of character.

"Thank you for coming," she said. "I'm not sure if it's really necessary though. Eve thought a lawyer should check the papers before I signed."

"Yes," Scott said. "It's an interesting document. Our company lawyer is still reviewing it."

Her shoulders slumped. Judging by Scott's cautious tone, it was a good decision to send it to a lawyer first. But still, her disappointment welled. Despite everyone's reminder that Dex was a convicted felon, deep down she'd expected his agreement to be fair.

"I see," she said. "Would you like some coffee?"

Scott's assessing eyes swept the counter. "I'd love some," he said, but she guessed he spotted the fresh coffee and was only trying to make her relax.

Not that she was nervous, or sad. Of course not. She'd postponed signing the divorce papers only because she'd been busy. She wanted a split as much as Dex. But her hand quivered as she poured the coffee.

"Nice-looking horses you have," Scott said. "Is the bay in the end paddock a Thoroughbred?"

"Yes," she said, appreciating the distraction. "That's Tizzy, the horse Eve is helping me with. He's the full brother to a stakes winner. A friend was going to meet with Dex last night and have him sign the registration papers. Not that I think I should own Tizzy," she added hurriedly. "It's just so I can make some decisions. We're rather in limbo until the divorce is finalized."

Scott picked up his coffee, studying her over the rim. "Your husband's lawyer prepared this package when Dex was first incarcerated. Have you ever had time to sit down and take a good look?"

She flushed. She remembered receiving the thick package in the mail but she'd been in shock. And denial. Dex had mentioned a divorce but she never dreamed he'd follow up so quickly. She had shoved the envelope in the bottom drawer, resolving to deal with it later…after she'd accepted the shock of his infidelity, drug involvement and lies.

"I scanned the front page," she admitted. "But I was rather upset."

Scott nodded. He reached into a legal-sized manila envelope and pulled out several sheets of paper. "Your husband pleaded guilty to unlawful possession of heroin, but not to dealing. The sex worker was an obvious heroin user. Unfortunately this was a bad batch, heavily laced with fentanyl. They tried to throw the book at Dex. Wanted to charge him in her death."

Dani squeezed her eyes shut. The thought of that poor woman writhing on the floor still gave her nightmares. And despite her husband's cheating, she knew it must have been even more horrible for Dex. She couldn't stop imagining how he felt. "He tried to help," she said, her voice wobbling. "I heard he gave CPR."

"Yes." Scott's voice softened. "And that was a mitigating factor in the judge's sentencing. Both the motel clerk and the ambulance attendants testified he tried valiantly to save her. Police threatened to charge him with her death. But it's obvious they were really after the dealer. In these cases, they want to take out the supply chain, not low-level users." Scott gave a wry smile. "California prisons are crowded enough."

Dani's fingers relaxed around the handle of the mug. He spoke so matter-of-factly about the case, unlike her father who blamed the Tattries for every evil in California.

"The woman's name was Tawny Dunn," Scott said. "The clerk remembers a car arriving about thirty minutes after Dex paid for the room. Investigators suspect the driver was the dealer. But only two people saw him. And one of them is dead."

Scott frowned. "Dex wouldn't tell them anything. It really was a wrong place, wrong time, but the judge still gave him five years. If he'd given up the dealer, it would have gone easier legally, but it wouldn't have been good for Dex. As it is, I'm surprised he made it through the first six months."

"What do you mean?" Dani shot forward, her heart hammering. "Is he in danger?"

"Not anymore. But this heroin was linked to a cartel. And they don't like people walking around who can implicate them in a high-profile drug death. Obviously the dealer trusts your husband not to talk. And now I have to ask you... Is Dex related to the Tattrie family, the motorcycle club?"

"Yes," she said, hating the defensiveness in her voice. "But he sold his bike. Stopped riding with them about five years ago."

"That connection explains why he's alive though," Scott said. "The Tattries are rumored to be solid. They stand behind their word. Although it's apparent even Dex suspected he might not make it out of prison."

Dani set down her mug, blinking in dismay. Dex had seemed so casual at his sentencing, almost bored with the proceedings. Her father said he was probably keen to relax in prison, that it was really a country club where inmates were coddled with taxpayers' hard-earned money.

"I must admit the reason I wanted to talk to you was because of your husband's background," Scott said. "This has critical implications for a case I'm working on. Is there any chance he'd provide a description of the dealer? To you maybe? I promise it would be off the record. If you were to assure him the next time you visit—"

"But we don't talk," Dani said. "He doesn't let me visit. And if he wouldn't give a description before, there's no sense asking again. He's not the type to change his mind. Sorry to waste your time," she added.

"Not a waste at all," Scott said. However, his voice was heavy with disappointment. "This heroin has killed eight people. There are still many questions."

Dani sighed. There certainly were questions. She'd always found Dex's abrupt rejection bewildering. They'd been friends long before they were lovers. The fact that he'd been with another woman had been crushing, but losing her partner and best friend had been devastating. She'd been in a fog the first eighteen months.

"The fog is what gets people through it," Scott said, and she realized she'd been speaking aloud.

"Eve said you've been running the ranch on your own," he went on. "That's a big job for one person."

"It wasn't too bad." Dani forced a shrug. "But it's time to sell. I appreciate that your lawyer will check out the agreement."

"It shouldn't take much longer," Scott said. "Did Dex own this ranch before you married him?"

"No, he worked at the Tattrie garage just ten miles down the road. He had an apartment there."

Scott nodded. "I remember passing it on the way. There were some big bikes outside. A few I'd like to own."

Dani made an agreeable sound, trying not to wiggle beneath his astute gaze. She wanted him to leave now, didn't want to talk about the bike club. He was clearly after Dex.

Unfortunately Scott still had a full cup of coffee, although he certainly didn't appear to be drinking it.

"I do appreciate you coming." She slid back her chair. "And that you'll have your lawyer check those papers."

"Don't you find it curious that Dex doesn't want you to visit?" Scott asked, not moving. "Even as a friend?"

"Not really," she said, hoping private investigators didn't charge by the hour. "My father is very religious and never approved of our marriage. Dex was always aware of that."

"I see." Scott's voice hardened. "Because it almost seems as though your husband is protecting something. The club perhaps?"

Dani swallowed, still perched on the edge of her chair. Scott didn't look so friendly now. Rather he appeared scarily implacable; the steel in his voice reminded her of Dex.

I'm not sure," she said stiffly. "I do know I have a lot of horses to ride. May I pay your bill after the ranch is sold?"

His expression instantly softened. "There's no charge for our lawyer's opinion," he said. "I already gave him your divorce papers. And this visit was more about you helping me than anything else. The Tattries are a complicated bunch. I do appreciate your time." He placed a business card on the table and rose.

She followed him to the door, her mind whirling. He spoke about the Tattries with a grudging respect. And hearing Dex's name always made her heart quicken.

She hadn't spoken to Jeffrey since he'd driven to the prison last night. He was coming for dinner though. And while yesterday she'd wanted to ride horses instead of staying inside and preparing a fancy meal, now she could barely wait for his arrival.

Because in a few short hours she'd hear about Dex. How he looked, how he felt, and more importantly...if he had asked about her.

CHAPTER FOURTEEN

Jeffrey showed up promptly at six with flowers in one hand and a bottle of red wine in the other. "I have three days off," he said, pushing past a growling Red and kissing her on the cheek. "So I can be here when the plumber comes... What is wrong with that dog?"

"It's the way you walk in," she said. "Kind of aggressive. And maybe it's the kiss. He's not used to seeing people touch me."

"Then I'll have to touch you a lot more." Jeffrey grinned, splaying his hand around her waist and coaxing her closer. "In my opinion, it's about time."

"These flowers need water." She pivoted from his arms and gathered a vase. "Have a seat," she called over her shoulder. "The corkscrew is on the table."

She arranged the flowers in the container, determined not to ask about his prison visit. It was strange she was so jumpy. She'd known Jeffrey since grade school, and he'd been helping out with odd jobs since the day Dex was arrested. Even when Dex was here he used to drop in for neighborly visits. One time his car had broken down and Dex had towed him, and a couple times Jeffrey had popped by for coffee.

Dex had winked and said the local lawman wasn't coming to the Double D to look at horses. But neither she nor Dex had cared one way or the other; their world had been complete. At least she'd thought so. But she couldn't hide behind a broken-down marriage for ever.

"I have some good news from last night," Jeffrey called.

She rushed back into the kitchen, carrying the vase, unable to hide her eagerness.

Jeffrey reached into his inside pocket and waved some papers in the air. "*He* signed them. Not only will you be able to send the horse to the track, but you'll get all the proceeds when you sell. When's the first race?"

"Not for at least six months," Dani said. "They'll pick him up this week and see how he gallops. And Tizzy is still Dex's horse." Her gaze locked on the registration papers in Jeffrey's hand. Dex had touched them, signed his name. Maybe even sent a note.

"He didn't ask any questions," Jeffrey went on. "Didn't seem to care what was happening."

"Oh." Dani set down the vase, her hands stilling over the flowers. She bit her lip, determined not to ask, but the question popped out anyway. "How is he?"

"Big. Most people look smaller in prison clothes but not him. Those Tattries are so damn arrogant. Didn't matter though." Jeffrey filled two glasses with wine, his voice triumphant. "I've taken more than one course on dealing with felons. Told him you were selling and insisted you wanted sixty percent."

"You discussed our divorce?" Her throat tightened. "But you went to talk about Tizzy."

"He brought it up." Jeffrey clinked his glass against hers. "He wants this business finished as much as you."

"But did he agree to see me? Just one last time?"

"No." Jeffrey set down his glass and tugged her onto his lap. "I know it's difficult. Just remember, none of this is your fault. You're the one who was suckered."

Dani's eyes pricked and she turned her face into Jeffrey's chest, needing a second to blink back the sting. *He still didn't want to see her.* She hadn't wanted to admit, even to herself, but there was a reason she hadn't filed for divorce. Deep down, she'd harbored a tiny seed of hope. And she despised herself for it. She seemed to have no pride where Dex was concerned. And that had to change.

Jeffrey slid his hand beneath her hair and kneaded the back of her neck. "Just relax. You were young and impressionable. You moved from your dad's house to Dex's. But a man like him is accustomed to a variety of women. He probably cared for you and the ranch, in his own way, but it was never going to be enough."

"He told me he didn't have sex with her," she said, remembering Dex's last words.

Jeffrey's chest moved in an exasperated sigh. "A naked prostitute in a flop motel. It wasn't a church meeting. No doubt there were other women too. If she hadn't overdosed, you might never have known."

Dani stared at the shiny buttons on Jeffrey's shirt. She'd been a stubborn fool for hanging on, for hoping. And suddenly she was exhausted, as if the source of her strength had drained away, carrying with it every last bit of energy.

"It's okay, honey," Jeffrey whispered, his breath skimming her neck. "The last few years have been hell. But I can prove all men aren't the same. If you let me."

"It's going to take some time," she whispered, her voice rusty.

"That's all right." His thumb grazed the underside of her breast, then slipped higher, cupping her. "I've been waiting so long, I can wait a little longer. In the meantime, we can get to know each other." His hand slid around and unhooked her bra then returned to her breasts, stroking, touching, exploring. Not an unpleasant feeling. And she was so tired, his hands were almost comforting. Soothing even.

The kissing was nice too. Even the feel of his tongue was okay. And he was quite skilled at slipping his hand down her jeans… When had he lowered her zipper?

But naturally she was going to be a little clinical about things. And the first time was bound to be awkward. She kept her eyes shut, knowing it was best to get it over with and prove to herself, to everyone, that she could get along fine without Dex.

As he had without her.

But she couldn't stop analyzing Jeffrey's technique. It wasn't bad really. He'd adjusted her on his lap and definitely seemed turned on. His breathing was almost as thick as his arousal.

She shouldn't let that irritate her but it sounded annoyingly loud in the quiet kitchen. He pressed against her thigh and she knew it was decision time. They should probably move into the bedroom. Eat dinner later. But then he simply stopped…his touch, his mouth, even his heavy breathing.

She cracked her eyes open, rather puzzled.

Red's front feet were on the chair, his jaws clamped around Jeffrey's head.

"Red! No!" She jerked sideways. "It's okay."

The dog opened his mouth and dropped reluctantly to the floor. Jeffrey's face looked an unhealthy gray, but there were no teeth marks.

She stood up and adjusted her clothing, trying not to giggle. "Guess Red thinks we should move a little slower. He's probably right."

Jeffrey said nothing. He still looked rather pale.

"I'm surprised his mouth was big enough to fit around your head," she said, studying Red with a tinge of admiration.

The dog had returned to his mat by the door, but his intent eyes remained locked on Jeffrey. "We were never sure of his breeding," she added. "Only guessed he had some Aussie and shepherd. His jaw is definitely big like a shepherd's."

Jeffrey remained silent, still sitting, obviously not so interested in discussing Red's ancestry. "Next time I'll lock him in the barn," he finally said. "How much longer do you think he'll live?"

She stepped back, folding her arms. "Years and years, I hope. And this is his home. He sleeps by the door. And he'll continue to do so."

"Of course. I didn't mean it like that," Jeffrey said quickly. "Maybe I'll start bringing treats. That will help. But one way or another, I'm going to soften up your dog." He gave a determined smile and picked up his wine glass.

"And then you," he added.

CHAPTER FIFTEEN

Dex walked into the visiting room and spotted Cindy seated at a square table at the opposite end of the control booth. She knew the routine and had already purchased a variety of snacks from the vending machine.

She greeted him with an exuberant hug, one of the two they were permitted during the visit. Her hair smelled fresh and clean and flowery, and he held her a bit too long, earning a rebuke from the hovering correctional officer and his sniffer dog.

"Short hair looks good on you, cuz," she said. Her smile was big and white, but her throat moved convulsively.

"Thanks for making the drive," he said, still absorbing her presence, the normalcy of her street clothes, even the whiff of feminine perfume. He'd anticipated this would be tough but wasn't quite prepared for the aching reminder of all that he'd lost.

"Are you kidding?" she asked, regaining her composure and sitting back in the chair. "We'd visit every week if you'd let us. Well, except for Jimmie and Luther. Doubt they'd pass the background check."

"Probably not. How's everyone doing?"

"The garage is busy. Always booked a week ahead. Boomie bought a new tow truck and Sarah is pregnant again. Jimmie won the Barrels on Bikes class at the valley rodeo. And we did the diabetes poker rally again this year. Raised over six thousand dollars."

She tilted forward, her voice lifting with hope. "This is the first time you've asked for news. Are you coming up for parole?"

"I've had a prelim. Still waiting for a date."

"But you have good time. Luther's guys say you're working six days, going to church, even met with the prison councilors. It has to look good."

Dex picked up a bag of chips and ripped it open. The prison news line was remarkably effective; Luther probably knew how many eggs he had for breakfast.

"Luther thinks it's time to push," she added. "The lawyer can shine it up for the hearing. You'll be coming out to a good job, a home above the garage and we also hired a cop as a part-time mechanic. That'll be reassuring. Even the parole officer was impressed."

Dex broke a chip in half, watching as Cindy fiddled with her wedding band. It was difficult not to reach out and still her twitchy fingers. Her nervousness was contagious. And uncharacteristic. "What else does Luther think?" he asked.

Cindy hesitated for a moment, then lifted her head. "That we need to get you out, quickly," she admitted. "While you're still a model prisoner."

He blew out a resigned breath. There had been undercurrents. The guards were hassling him more than usual, Jeffrey's influence, no doubt. At least he now knew it wasn't his imagination. "Do you think Luther could arrange a friendly chat with someone?" he asked. "Just to explain the importance of a man's word."

"Of course." Cindy's voice hardened. "You want someone to talk to that cop who visited you last week?"

"No," Dex said. "To a Mr. Higgins and Spunky in Santa Clara."

***

The cinder-block classroom at the edge of the prison yard was almost full. A burly pastor reached out and pumped Dex's hand, greeting him with a welcoming smile. The Sunday afternoon service was always popular and it wasn't just because the pastor was an ex-NFL football player.

Dex grabbed the last vacant chair at the back. Despite the fellowship here, it was folly to totally relax. Worship service was a safer place than the recreational yard though. And the hour and a half of spiritual peace was always uplifting. This was a combined service for all Christians and despite that the prison was unofficially segregated, here everyone seemed to get along.

"They're giving out soap today," the Hispanic man seated next to Dex said. "Hope they don't run out."

"Should be enough," Dex said. "Looks like over a hundred bars in those boxes."

"Maybe we'll get two then." The man spread his tattooed hands, dwarfing the hymnbook.

"Maybe," Dex said. His visit with Cindy had left him too late to snag a hymnbook, but it had infused him with hope. Everything he'd done had been geared to making early parole but conversely, he couldn't depend on early release. Prison life was too fluid, with many factors beyond his control. But with Luther pushing…

Baritone voices lifted in song. The tattooed man next to him helpfully held out his hymnbook. Dex blanked his mind and joined in the singing.

The pastor was actually quite good. Sometimes Dex's mind drifted, but that was generally when he couldn't hear the words. Dani's father had always used a microphone at his service, but this man didn't need help. No doubt, he was used to talking over the crowd at noisy sports stadiums.

"Keep on seeking and you'll find God," the pastor said, raising his hands to mark the completion of the service.

"Thanks for coming. We have three bars of soap for everyone today."

"Hallelujah," the man next to Dex said, raising his fist. "My canteen money was getting low."

"Mine too," Dex said agreeably. He always spoke more on Sundays, softened by the mood in the room.

"See you next week," the Hispanic said. He glanced over his shoulder at the two officers. His voice lowered. "Heard a couple dirty guards are gunning for you."

Dex nodded. The Whites, Blacks, Hispanics and Asians all had different information networks, and having access to a cross channel of news was invaluable and another bonus of Sunday's service.

Unfortunately, the news wasn't at all good.

CHAPTER SIXTEEN

"Try it now," the plumber said.

Dani turned the tap, sighing with relief when water spurted from the faucet.

"That should last another ten years," the plumber said, wiping his hands on his coveralls.

"As long as it lasts for the sale," Jeffrey said. "Hard to sell a ranch without water."

"Hard to sell a ranch *with* water," the plumber said, dropping his tools into his kit. "Prices are rock bottom." He must have noticed the dismayed look on Dani's face. "But this is a pretty spot," he added. "Looks like you have a smart irrigation system. Fix the fences, add some paint and you should get some offers." He picked up his tool kit and turned toward his van. "I'll load up and be back with your bill."

Jeffrey laid a comforting arm over Dani's shoulders. "Wish I had more days off to help with the fences," he said. "But maybe we can hire someone to paint."

Dani forced a smile. She had no money to hire anybody, but it was definitely reassuring to have Jeffrey's support. To share the worry as well as the tough decisions. And he was nice, attractive and dependable. Maybe he wasn't so good at plumbing—and he was never able to start the tractor—but he was plenty good at other things. At least her father would finally stop harping about daughters and bad choices.

Jeffrey was a police officer, certainly a respectable profession in her father's eyes. He wasn't saving lost souls like

Matt, but he was known to be fair. More importantly, he'd always been the first to show up whenever she needed help.

She'd married Dex for love—love and earth-shaking passion. But that had brought nothing but heartache. This time she wanted dependability. She didn't have the strength to endure another breakup. She needed someone safe.

Red growled low in his throat and trotted toward the road, his ears pricked. A blue truck, pulling a matching trailer, rolled cautiously up the driveway. Dani stepped forward, shading her eyes and studying the rig. It looked vaguely familiar but she couldn't place the driver.

A man stepped out and lowered the ramp. He disappeared inside the trailer, then led out a chestnut gelding with distinctively high head carriage.

"Spunky," she breathed. She flung her arms around Jeffrey and impulsively kissed his cheek. "You're amazing. I don't know how you did it, but thank you. If Mr. Higgins is here, he probably plans to pay. And now I'll be able to afford the plumber."

She gave Jeffrey's hand a grateful squeeze. Spunky had been important to her, and Jeffrey must have sensed it. "I can't believe you tracked that man down," she went on. "I hope you didn't have to call in too many favors."

Jeffrey hesitated. "Not at all," he said, clearing his throat. "It was worth the effort." His hand tightened around hers. "So does this mean I'm invited to your dad's tomorrow?"

"Sure. If you really want to come." They both knew Dani's father would be ecstatic if she finally brought a man to his Thursday night dinners. A suitable man. She didn't know why she'd been so reluctant to invite Jeffrey, especially when he'd been angling for an invitation for months.

"I have to talk to Mr. Higgins now," she said, giving his fingers an apologetic squeeze before freeing her hand. "Do you work tonight?"

"Yes. But I have tomorrow off." He gave a meaningful pause. "And the morning after as well."

Her stomach gave a nervous kick. But what the heck. It would be a perfect night for him to sleep over. It wasn't as if she'd be breaking any vows. The divorce wasn't final but both she and Dex wanted one. Besides, marriage certainly hadn't stopped Dex. "I need to talk to Mr. Higgins now," she said, nodding and backing away.

She walked toward Mr. Higgins, curious how he'd justify taking Spunky in the middle of the night. He'd been so arrogant on the phone and might still argue about the bonus. But even if he only paid half the bill, it would be a big help. She'd be able to cover the mortgage as well as the plumber. Maybe buy some posts and paint.

Spunky danced around, head and tail high, excited to see old friends, and for a minute Mr. Higgins was occupied with controlling the horse. Red didn't help matters. He was always interested in the new arrivals and darted in and out, nipping Spunky on the heels, eager to greet his old nemesis.

"Red," she called, giving a stern shake of her head. Sometimes the dog still acted like the foolish pup Dex had rescued on the rodeo grounds. She pointed at the ground and Red trotted over and sat by her side, his expression rather sheepish.

Mr. Higgins finally calmed Spunky enough to step forward and press a thick envelope in Dani's hands. "Here," he said. "Thirty-five hundred dollars. I meant to leave the money when I picked him up, but I was in a hurry."

Dani gawked at the envelope. She'd been prepared to battle for full payment, yet settle for half. This was too easy.

"Sorry for the inconvenience," Mr. Higgins went on, shuffling his boot in the dirt. "I wanted to tell you it was a good training job. No, not just good, excellent. And I want your lesson. If you can fit me in today, that's fine. Otherwise, I'll leave the horse and come back."

"A lesson is included in the training price, Mr. Higgins."

"Oh, but I don't want...anyone to think I'm taking advantage. I'll pay sixty dollars an hour, or whatever your price. And I can drive back when it's convenient. Just let me know."

Dani fiddled with Red's collar, needing a moment to absorb the man's strange turnaround. He was nervous, almost laughable in his need to make amends. It had been three years since she'd witnessed such groveling, and that was back when the feed man had accused her of underpaying the bill.

Jeffrey must be as persuasive as Dex. And she'd always been quick to forgive.

"I'm just glad you're back," she said, sticking the envelope in her back pocket. "And I'd be happy to give you that lesson now."

"Good. My saddle's in the truck. As everyone can see," he glanced over his shoulder at the deserted road, "I'm here. And eager to learn."

"Yes, I see that," she said, still rather stunned at his changed attitude. "Go ahead and saddle Spunky. I'll be back in about twenty minutes and we can start then. He can use his old paddock." She gave a wry smile. "I believe you know where that is."

Mr. Higgins had the grace to flush, but his head was still nodding when she turned away.

Dani hurried back to Jeffrey. "What the heck did you say to him?" She checked the contents of the envelope then shook her head in disbelief. It was all there. He'd paid his full training bill, even including extra for the lesson. "You deserve some of this money," she said. "He's a different man. Much nicer."

Jeffrey gave a modest shrug. "It wasn't a big deal. I didn't see Mr. Higgins personally. I sent...someone."

"But it made all the difference," she said. "And I appreciate it so much." Jeffrey wasn't a horseman and she'd assumed he wouldn't understand how much time, love and energy was put into training. That he wouldn't realize how devastating it was to have a three-month job disappear into the night. But obviously she'd underestimated him.

"My feelings are no secret," Jeffrey said. "We're a team now and I want to look after you." His voice hardened. "I'll do whatever it takes."

His 'team' references were a little irritating, but it meant a lot that he was trying. And he'd certainly stepped up when it was important. The last of her reservations faded. Even the butterflies in her stomach disappeared.

She rose on her toes and kissed his cheek, then sank back to the ground, still smiling. "I'm going to be busy with Mr. Higgins now. But thanks for your help. I'll see you tomorrow night. And be prepared for a computer chat with Matt," she added. "It's the highlight of Dad's week."

"I hear a lot about Matt on Sundays," Jeffrey said, squeezing her hand, "but it'll be great to talk with him."

Dani rolled her eyes. Her father constantly preached about Matt's missionary work. She loved her younger brother but was rather tired of the never-ending praise fest. "Don't you find it irritating? How Dad goes on about him?"

"No," Jeffrey said. "The world needs more people like Matt. He's a great example. Giving up his life, not earning a cent, all to help others. Your father should be proud. You should be too. We all just do what we can in this world."

"Exactly." She gave a mischievous smile, amused at how Jeffrey parroted her father's sermon. "And now I'm going to go help this horse. You do realize," she said, copying her father's pompous tone, "I'm just changing the equine world, one rider at a time."

But Jeffrey didn't laugh, didn't seem to realize she was making a joke. "You won't have to rush around so much," he said, still holding her hand, "when the horses are gone and this place is sold. You'll make a good receptionist. Then you'll feel better about your life."

Dani's smile faded. "But I like my life. Especially when I can help horses like Spunky."

"That isn't a real job though. More like a hobby. An impractical and expensive one."

"I suppose," she muttered, tugging away her hand. "I have to go."

She trudged back to Spunky's paddock. However, her earlier exuberance was gone, replaced with an odd melancholy. She loved riding, loved teaching. Yet this might be the last rider she ever instructed.

Mr. Higgins was already mounted and walking Spunky along the driveway. He had a tight hold on the bit, his legs clamped against the horse's sides. Spunky swished his tail, protesting the pressure, his ears flat with resentment.

"Let's move to the ring," Dani said, "where you can loosen the reins and let him stretch his neck. How long was he on the trailer?"

"About an hour or two," Mr. Higgins said. "Yeah, guess I should let him limber him up first."

They walked into the ring where he cautiously loosened the reins a notch. Dani gave an encouraging nod and then showed him some stretching exercises. It was always best to let adults arrive at the correct decision. The lessons were more about how to work effectively with their horses once they were home. And much of this man's riding habits were based on fear and self-preservation.

Twenty minutes later, both Spunky and his rider were more relaxed. Mr. Higgins sat deep in the saddle, his left hand on the looped reins, acting like he trusted his horse not to buck or bolt. Spunky's head was low, his face vertical and he was using his hindquarters well.

"Good job," Dani said. "You have him set up, mentally and physically, and he's listening to you. Now look at the big oak tree on the left side of the field and move your hand slightly."

Mr. Higgins moved his hand a half inch to the left and Spunky lowered his head and smoothly veered to the left. Mr. Higgins's face creased in a big smile. "If I could get him to behave like this at a show, I'd be ecstatic."

"What warm-up routine do you use?"

"Warm-up? Well, you know. Nothing specific." He fiddled with the brim of his cowboy hat. "There're so many horses in the ring, and Spunky's always excited and misbehaving. But maybe I should take twenty minutes and do this warm-up every time," he added. "Yes, think I'll do that."

"And release the pressure when he listens," Dani said. "Like you're doing now."

"Yeah, the last couple times, I just raised my hand and he framed up. I barely touched the bit. It's like riding a big cat that's ready to pounce."

"A big cat is a good analogy," Dani said. If the rider felt the difference between a collected horse and an artificial frame, it made her lesson much easier. "All Spunky wants is a release from the pressure. And if he knows how to get that, he'll give you his best, every time."

Mr. Higgins nodded and gave Spunky's neck an affectionate pat. "This is great. I might even try a milder bit when I get him home. The last couple maneuvers he responded just to me turning my head."

Dani smiled. The success of connecting riders with their horses always left her elated. Dex said she was a born teacher although she wasn't sure what she enjoyed most, training horses or people. Luckily the Double D enabled her to do both. Or it had.

Unfortunately that was about to change.

CHAPTER SEVENTEEN

Dex brushed Gypsy's spotless hindquarters, absorbing the comforting smell of horses and hay. Being with the big mare, alone in her stall, was always a treasured escape. Gypsy didn't care about gangs or prison politics or that he would be forever branded a felon. She wasn't trying to stab him in the back either. The mare respected him.

Their relationship was based on the immediacy—not what he could do for her tomorrow or what he'd done in the past. For this hour, it was just the two of them, and the time was treasured. Dex had always appreciated his solitude. But it was impossible to be alone in prison. The place was a writhing mass of humans, and sub-humans.

The work farm, however, was a relative oasis of serenity. And Gypsy was the best therapist of all.

"You saved me, sweetheart," he whispered, scratching the top of her muscled rump. It wasn't surprising she could buck. She had excellent conformation, with an athleticism and competitive nature that matched any of the horses he'd ridden on the circuit. She had the optimal size and build too, solid boned and more than sixteen hands high.

He flicked the brush over her gleaming coat, happy for any excuse to linger. Whenever he had spare time, he hung out with Gypsy. Quentin didn't bother him. As long as Dex finished his shoeing jobs, the foreman was happy. And the guards knew little about horses. If they peered over the stall door, he merely pulled out his hoof gauge and pretended to be checking the angles of her feet. They always assumed he was engrossed in important farrier work and moved on to hassle some other con.

Today he only had three horses to shoe and two to trim. It was slow going, trying to teach the new kid about the complexities of the foot and the importance of keeping horses balanced. However, he still had all afternoon to be with Gypsy. Most of the cons were outside, working with their horses in the paddock, but he avoided watching the riding sessions.

The current instructor was a bully, with both the horses and men. And after Dani's knowledgeable touch, the well-meaning yanks and kicks of the convicts made Dex shudder.

He still remembered her gentle admonishment. 'A horse can feel a fly on their side. Do you really think you need to kick that hard?'

'But I have to make him listen,' Dex had said.

'Just ask nicely. Then let him know when he does it right,' Dani said. 'You might be surprised.'

And she'd been right. He loved the adrenaline rush of sticking eight seconds on a rodeo horse and his spurring action had always been topnotch. But he'd never known how to really ride—how to form a willing partnership with a horse—until she'd taught him. Ironically clients sent their horses to the Double D believing he was the expert. Yet it was Dani who was the elite trainer. She always had been.

"You horses ought to be real grateful there are people out there like her," he said, straightening Gypsy's forelock and staring into her soulful brown eyes. His throat felt a little tight, and he automatically coughed. *Don't think of her.*

But Jeffrey's visit had kicked up too much emotion. Dani and Jeffrey. It was inevitable she'd hook up with someone, but he wished she'd found a better man. He'd always thought Jeffrey had an inner asshole tucked beneath that crisp blue uniform. No doubt the liaison would please Dani's father though. Maybe now the minister would cease his endless sniping and give Dani some peace.

Thud. Gypsy's ears shot forward. Dex stoically increased his pressure on the brush, trying not to listen. The oil was really coming out from her skin now, giving her coat a beautiful shine. He'd been adding a little flax seed to her grain and the results were gratifying.

The noise sounded again, along with a muffled cry. Gypsy turned her head and stared at Dex, as if questioning why he wasn't concerned. He tightened his grip on the brush. "Not my herd," he muttered.

But a horse churned in agitation, and Gypsy clearly felt it was her business. She stepped forward and stared over the door, nostrils flaring, concern radiating from every inch of her taut body.

"Pay attention." He gave her shoulder a slap and she immediately backed up, but the look she shot him was full of reproach. "The guards will look after it," he said, determined to ignore the ruckus.

But the surly guard never left the supply room and the other two guards remained conveniently out of earshot, either by accident or design.

Someone yelped, and this time there was no mistaking the sound of pain. "Dammit, all right." Dex tossed the brush aside, opened the door and stalked down the long aisle.

A bay gelding stuck his head over a stall door. White rimmed his eyes and he tossed his head in agitation. It took a moment to push him back and look inside. Juan, one of Carlos's gang, stood at the back of the stall, his clothes draped around his ankles. Sandy kneeled at his feet. Blood trickled from the kid's nose.

Juan glanced over his shoulder, his voice thick with arousal. "Get out of here, Tattrie."

"No."

"What the fuck! Beat it. This is none of your business."

Sandy stared beseechingly up at Dex, his face full of terror.

"I need the kid for shoeing," Dex said.

"Yeah, well I need him too. Give me five minutes. Carlos is okay with it."

"But I'm not." Dex clicked open the latch and stepped inside.

"What the fuck? You walking into my bone yard? You crazy, man?"

Dex flexed his fists, his adrenaline rushing. He knew he should walk away. He couldn't take on Carlos and the entire Hispanic gang. And his parole was coming up. But his voice seemed to be operating independently from his thoughts. "Leave the kid alone," he said. "He works with me."

Juan glowered. "You're a dead man. Maybe I'll stick it in your mouth instead—"

Dex shot forward. He smashed Juan in the jaw, brought his knee sharply into the man's naked groin then picked him up and tossed him headfirst into the wall.

"Come on," he muttered to the kid.

A wide-eyed Sandy scrambled to his feet and fled from the stall. Dex latched the door and walked down the aisle. "Gypsy needs a trim," he said. "I'll gather my tools."

He walked to the supply room, signed out his tools from the surly guard, and led Gypsy from her stall. The entire time, Sandy remained locked at his hip.

"Grab a bucket and wash the blood off your face," Dex said. "Juan won't say anything and neither will you. Why weren't you outside with the other riders?"

"They told me to go inside and get a helmet. I should have known better. The prep course said not to be caught alone."

Dex clipped Gypsy on the cross ties, then paused. "You took a course? On surviving prison?"

Sandy's breath was still ragged but he managed a nod. "My dad hired a couple people. To teach me how to talk, how to act, how to fight. One of the instructors said it would be tempting to join a gang…to counteract other gangs, but that it would be a mistake."

Dex nodded. Gangs didn't care about parole dates. And they forced members to do acts of loyalty that merely added time to their original sentence. Unfortunately Juan was ganged up. And Carlos was merciless.

"They told me to get all my vaccinations and build up some muscle," Sandy said, studying the cut on his knuckles. "I gained sixteen pounds before I came in. But Juan was too big."

Dex rifled through his tools and pulled out his dullest rasp. The new one was too sharp and awkward for a newbie.

"That was amazing how you flung him across the stall like that," Sandy went on. "I owe you."

Dex pressed the steel rasp into Sandy's hand, wishing the kid would just stop talking. It only reminded him that he'd jumped into a snake pit. Gypsy pressed her nose against his chest and blew out a sympathetic sigh, as if sensing his agitation. To her, rules were simple. The horses followed a pecking order and every animal knew their place. If they stepped out of line, she administered strict and quick punishment. Unfortunately, Dex had challenged gang authority. And there would be repercussions.

"Remember to rasp from heel to toe," Dex said. "Get rid of that chip on the toe and round the corners in a mustang roll."

"Will Carlos be gunning for me now?" Sandy asked, staring blankly at the rasp, as if he'd already forgotten his morning lesson.

"Just be aware," Dex said. "Know where the guards are. Try not to make enemies."

"But you did. And my cellmate said the Hispanics are the most powerful gang in here."

Dex picked up Gypsy's front leg and cleaned the dirt from her foot. "That's why," he said, "you shouldn't make any long-term plans. It's not fair to the people waiting outside."

Sandy glanced down the aisle, scanning for movement. His shoulders hunched and he gripped the rasp, clutching it in front of him like a shield. "Guess there's no safe place here."

"No," Dex said grimly. "There isn't."

CHAPTER EIGHTEEN

"It's Thursday," Dani said, packing up a casserole, wine, salad, dessert and even some brightly colored napkins. "You have to stay home."

Red flattened his ears, his tail drooping. The dog may not know every day of the week but he definitely understood Thursday. He'd never been welcome at her father's family meals. There were many reasons—allergies, hair, damage to the wood floor. However, Dani suspected the dog was a reminder of her first major rebellion. Knowing Dex was temporarily keeping Red had spurred her to move from her father's house and find an apartment. And admittedly, she'd wanted a place to be alone with Dex.

"It's okay," she said to Red. "I won't be long."

She scratched his head, sighing at the tangled hair that matted his neck. His nails needed clipping too. Maybe next week she'd find time to give him a thorough brushing. Lately the only grooming he ever received was an absent-minded rub with a horse brush. And she'd never been good at clipping his nails. He always protested, turning it into an unpleasant ordeal for both of them. With Dex though, the dog had flopped on his side and offered his paws.

"And please be nice to Jeffrey," she said as his beige car cruised up the driveway. "He might sleep here tonight."

She'd changed the sheets, scrubbed the bathroom, and stocked the fridge—all the while resentful because she'd rather be in the barn, and the shortened day had resulted in hurrying her rides. In fact, her last horse of the day, an Appendix Quarter Horse sent for barrel training, had actually regressed. The horse had picked up on her agitation and she'd dismounted after fifteen minutes, electing to put him back in the paddock rather than make the situation worse.

She brushed a piece of Red's hair from the front of her dress but couldn't shake the persistent knot in her stomach. Tucking clean sheets into the bed she'd shared with Dex, preparing to share such an intimate place with another man, seemed wrong. After all, she was still legally married. And that status was no one's fault but her own.

Dex had made a divorce easy. She was the one who'd procrastinated. She hadn't been ready to make the leap. But she was now.

She pulled open the door before Jeffrey could even knock. "Hi," she said.

"Wow." His eyes widened. "If you ever wore that dress to church, I don't think any man would be able to listen to the sermon." His appreciation turned to puzzlement. "We are going to your dad's, right?"

"It's probably a bit of a rebellion," she admitted. "He hasn't approved of me since I turned eighteen, and he doesn't like slinky cocktail dresses. But Thursday is the one night I clean up." She picked up the bag containing the wine. "Can you carry some of this stuff?"

Jeffrey's gaze remained locked on her body. "You're stunning." He visibly swallowed. "Let's cancel dinner. Just stay here."

Dani thrust the bag into his arms. "About that," she said, "you can't sleep here tonight. I wouldn't feel right about it, not until the divorce is finalized. But Dex signed a settlement agreement. I just need the lawyer to check it over before it goes to a judge. It shouldn't take long." She paused. "At least that's what the private investigator said."

"You hired an investigator as well as a lawyer?" Jeffrey's brow furrowed. "Why pay money when I can do the same thing?"

"I didn't hire an investigator," she said. "I'm just using Scott's lawyer. And it didn't cost anything. Scott's related to Eve so he's doing it as a favor."

"But maybe we should get a second opinion," Jeffrey said. "You can't rashly sign when property is involved."

"It's fine, Jeffrey." She added a loaf of bread to the bag in his arms. "I'm not being rash. And I'm sure Scott's lawyer is very capable."

"Who's Scott?"

"Eve's investigator friend," Dani said. "An in-law."

"I just hope the guy has a good lawyer," Jeffrey said, shuffling the bag to his other arm. "What is all this food?"

"Tonight's dinner," Dani said. She always brought the meal to her dad's; it was family tradition. There used to be four of them but with Dex and Matt gone, now there were only two.

"Looks like a lot of work," Jeffrey said. He pulled out a dog treat with his free hand and waved it in front of Red's nose. "Wouldn't it be simpler for your dad to come here?"

"It's the way he wants it," she said, picking up the warm casserole. "And he's my dad."

Jeffrey shrugged, concentrating now on Red. "Won't your dog bark or roll over or something?" he asked, still waving the treat.

"He doesn't do silly tricks," Dani said, a tad impatient. She pressed her mouth shut. She'd been edgy all day and it wasn't fair to take her mood out on Jeffrey. The man was trying. In fact, it was rather sweet he'd brought Red a treat.

"I have three other flavors in my car," Jeffrey said. "Along with some rawhide chews. Maybe we can renegotiate the end of the night?" He glanced toward the bedroom, his voice turning hopeful. "If I can keep your dog happy with food?"

Red turned and flopped on his mat, completely ignoring the treat in Jeffrey's hand.

Dani smiled. "Looks like both Red and I need a little more time."

"He's definitely a hard sell." Jeffrey shook his head and tossed the dog treat on the floor. "But I'm in this for the long haul. And hopefully your dad is easier to charm."

"This meal is delicious," Jeffrey said, folding his napkin and leaning back on his chair. "Thanks very much."

"You're certainly welcome," Dani's father said. "I hope you'll come again."

Dani took another sip of wine and refrained from checking the time. She usually fed evening hay at nine, but it would be a little late tonight. Her father loved having an audience, and she didn't want to spoil his fun by yanking Jeffrey away too early.

Matt had always been the more talkative child, as well as the more favored. She and Dex would simply nod at appropriate intervals and exchange grins when her brother and father weren't looking.

"Your dad acts like he cooked the meal himself," Dex had once said, his dark eyes glinting with amusement. "But as long as it doesn't bother you, I won't let it irritate me."

"We don't have to go every Thursday if you don't want to," Dani had said, wringing her hands and feeling torn.

Dex had picked up her hand and gently kissed her fingers. "It's three hours a week when you can give back. I understand family loyalty. He's your dad. And you love him."

And that had been enough. Occasionally Dex had nudged her foot beneath the table or winked at one of her dad's more pompous statements. And Matt wasn't much better. He thought their dad was perfect. She suspected Matt's volunteer work in Zimbabwe was based on her father's unachieved dream of working abroad. But raising two children involved sacrifices, especially when the daughter was a stubborn kid who refused to leave her horse.

"Ten more minutes and we'll call Matt," her father said, yanking back her attention.

"You Skype Matt every Thursday?" Jeffrey asked, leaning forward and acting like her father's reply was of the utmost importance.

Her father gave a smug nod. "Yes, our family remains close, even with Matt abroad. The church has always strengthened our bonds and kept them tight...even through some unfortunate missteps." His accusing gaze shot to Dani.

His barbs no longer hurt and she calmly began removing the plates. "He's referring to my marriage to Dex," she said to Jeffrey. "Were there any other missteps, Dad?"

"That was the worst." Her father grimaced and passed over his empty plate. "I still don't understand your infatuation with horses though. Aren't you a little old to keep playing around with them?"

"If I could make a living at it," she said, "I'd keep *playing* around with them the rest of my life. But you'll be relieved to know I'm selling the ranch." Despite the pain that sliced her chest, she was able to keep her voice light.

"She just has to get the paperwork in order," Jeffrey said, "and do some cosmetic work."

"But that's excellent news. We should celebrate." Her father reached for the wine bottle and topped up the glasses. "A ranch is no place for a single woman. And it was always a poor idea, partnering with a Tattrie. They bring nothing but trouble."

"Actually we don't have too many problems with the Tattries," Jeffrey said. "They're a good buffer between some of the more violent gangs. And their reputation is rather overblown."

Dani gave Jeffrey a grateful smile. She'd met most of Dex's relatives and they were all very polite. If they blamed her for Dex leaving the motorcycle club, they'd hidden it well. Most seemed confused but genuinely happy that Dex had turned to ranching. Dex's uncle, Luther, had even given them a tractor for their wedding present.

However, Dani's father crossed his arms and glared at Jeffrey, as if resenting his comment. "You're a policeman," he said. "My children aren't used to that kind of people. Dani was young and impressionable and fancied herself in love. Even Matt was changing, hanging out at the garage and driving a sinful car. I told Dex he was ruining our family."

"Dessert anyone?" Dani asked, shaking her head slightly at Jeffrey who looked like he was about to speak. However, it was too emotionally draining to argue with her father; it only extended his rants and wasted precious energy.

Her father pushed back his chair and headed toward his office. "No dessert for me," he said over his shoulder. "I don't want to miss Matt."

Jeffrey waited until he left the room, then looked at Dani. "I gather he doesn't just preach in church. Does he ever shut up?"

Dani's mouth tightened. It was okay for her and Matt to criticize their dad— Jeffrey, not so much. "My mother walked out when I was four," she said. "Matt was six months old. I think if Dad wants to rant a little, I'm big enough to take it."

"And I think you're a beautiful and loyal woman." Jeffrey reached up and squeezed her hand. Then he grinned. "Even though you've been permanently sullied by the wicked Tattries."

Dani laughed. She'd never thought Jeffrey had a sense of humor but he was really a very nice guy. She should have invited him to dinner months ago. And he deserved an explanation.

"My mom ran off with a guy on a motorcycle," she said, lowering her voice. "Dad considers them all home wreckers. Dex promised to change his mind." She lifted her shoulders in a deliberately casual shrug. "And now you know all our secrets."

Jeffrey rose to stand beside her. "I'm just glad she didn't leave with a cop in a car," he said.

Dani set the dishes back on the table, carefully studying his face. "My dad isn't going to change. Are you sure he won't drive you away?"

"Not a chance." Jeffrey squeezed her shoulders. "I just want...*need* you to finish that paperwork so we can move forward. I doubt your father would want us living together so I guess it'll be a fall wedding."

She stiffened.

"Or not," he said quickly. "If you don't want to get married now, that's okay. I thought you'd want to please your dad."

"Just because I let him rant," she said, "doesn't mean I listen to him."

"No, I guess that's already established."

"Come and talk to Matt," her father called.

Dani scooped up the plates, for once grateful for her father's imperious summons. She might live with Jeffrey, but the word 'marriage' left a bitter taste in her mouth. And that would take a few years to change.

"Hurry," her father called, his voice edged with impatience. "He doesn't have much time."

Matt worked the desk at the orphanage on Wednesday mornings. Because of the ten-hour time difference between California and Zimbabwe, Thursday evenings had turned into the scheduled family calls.

Dani placed the dishes on the kitchen counter and followed Jeffrey into the office.

Matt's face was on the screen, his voice enthused. "We've developed a seed bank and now the orphanage is self-sufficient. We even have extra food to sell at the market. It's awesome, Dad."

"I'm proud of you, son." Dani's father leaned closer to the computer. "Of how you're dedicating your time and energy to such an impoverished nation. But we have good causes here. Isn't it time to come home?"

Dani smiled. Every week her father asked Matt when he was coming home. And every week Matt hedged. He finally seemed to be developing a backbone.

Her father motioned at Dani and she leaned in front of the screen. "Hi, Matt. How is the little boy who had appendicitis? Is he okay?"

"He's doing fine. We rushed him to an emergency center. He had ice cream for the first time and loved it. How are all your horses?"

"Good. The bucker really settled and the owner is going to be able to handle him." She tugged Jeffrey in front of the screen. "Look who's here."

"Hi, Jeffrey," Matt said. "What's up?"

"Jeffrey is helping Dani sell the ranch," her father said.

"Sell the ranch?" Matt's eyes widened. "Is Dex out of prison?"

"No," Dani said. "But I can't keep the place running any longer."

"But you can't just sell it," Matt said. "Not while he's locked up. That's not right."

Dani gripped the sides of the desk. Her brother was usually so caught up in his orphanage work, he barely listened to news from home. "I can't make the mortgage payments," she admitted.

"Sell my Camaro," Matt said. "Use that money. I can't believe you'd be so selfish. It's Dex's ranch too."

Dani blinked and backed away from the screen. Matt's opinion seldom deviated from her father's. While she'd always hoped her brother would become a little more independent, to demonstrate it now was rather inconvenient. And was she being selfish?

"I'm not kidding," Matt said. "Sell my car. It should bring ten grand, at least. Take it to the Tattrie garage and get a tune-up first."

"We don't use that garage anymore," her father said, his voice clipped. "We go to a nice mechanic who joins us for church on Sunday evenings. He does excellent work at fair rates."

Matt rubbed his forehead. "I thought you were doing fine, Dani," he said, his voice troubled. "I didn't know you had no money."

Dani shrugged. These weekly calls had always been about Matt and his work in Africa. They rarely discussed problems back home. Matt's struggle with AIDS orphans made her own problems shrivel in comparison. The few times she'd mentioned Dex, way back when her heart was breaking, Matt had silenced, and it was obvious he shared their dad's embarrassment about Dex's prison sentence.

"Tell me about the fundraising," her father said. "I talk about your mission every Sunday and how you're doing the Lord's work. We're all very proud."

Matt instantly switched to an enthusiastic recital about the money they'd raised. Dani slipped from the room. She yanked open the dishwasher and began stacking dishes, the clinking noise discordant in the quiet kitchen. Jeffrey passed her the rinsed plates but didn't speak.

"Am I being selfish?" she finally asked.

Jeffrey jammed a spoon into the cutlery container, his mouth twisting with exasperation. "Your husband picked up a known prostitute and holed up with her in a flop motel for two hours. They bought fifteen grams of laced heroin from a supplier who is criminally responsible for her death. Dex refused to cooperate and swore he didn't see the dealer. The scandal left you publicly humiliated and stuck alone on a ranch with twenty needy horses, ten of them sent for training. No, Dani," he said, "you're not the selfish one."

"But maybe I should give Dex the chance to buy the ranch?"

Jeffrey snorted. "He doesn't have any money. He works six days a week shoeing horses. Probably makes fifty cents an hour."

"He's doing farrier work? How do you know?"

"Saw his file," Jeffrey admitted. "Like I told you, I have friends there."

"That's good," she said. "So they'll look after him?"

"Yes." Jeffrey's mouth flattened. "They'll give him very special attention."

CHAPTER NINETEEN

Dani swept the brush over Tizzy's neck one last time, then stepped back to admire his shiny coat. "If you run as well as you look," she said, "you're going to do great."

The colt nosed around the ground, hunting for a last stalk of hay, blithely oblivious about his upcoming trip to the track. His calm temperament would help but she couldn't stop worrying. She'd never sent a horse to the racetrack before, where his entire care would be overseen by a trainer she'd never even met. Luckily Eve would be around. But Tizzy was Dex's horse, and Dani couldn't help wondering what he was thinking.

According to Jeffrey, Dex had signed Tizzy's papers without a single question. He hadn't asked about the horse, about the dog, about her. And the last piece of her heart shriveled.

"Don't you worry," she whispered to Tizzy. "Horses from broken homes can do just fine."

Hopefully he'd be good enough to enter the starting gate. Eve said that would be a triumph in itself since most Thoroughbreds never even make it to the track. Still, it felt a bit like she was sending a naive kid off to university. She'd done everything possible to prepare him, even leading Tizzy in and out of an old cattle chute, trying to simulate a starting gate. But nothing could compare to the hustle and bustle of a racetrack. And Tizzy was a country boy.

She abruptly flung her arms around the surprised horse's neck, wondering if she'd ever see him again. "Just do your best," she said. "Maybe someday Dex will see you race."

Tizzy endured her hug. But the instant she stepped back, he dropped his head to the ground, more interested in his search for hay.

Her phone buzzed, signaling a text. She scanned Eve's short message. *Trailer is ten minutes away. See you soon.*

Dani squared her shoulders and tightened the buckle on Tizzy's halter. Eve said to use a cheap nylon halter because it wouldn't be returned. However, first impressions were important so Dani had pulled out the nicest leather halter the Double D owned.

"He looks like a racehorse, doesn't he?" She looked at Red who wagged his tail in staunch agreement.

A truck rumbled in the distance and she checked the envelope for the third time: vet history, registration papers, emergency number. It was all there, even his feeding schedule which she knew was totally over the top. The trainer would feed according to Tizzy's new energy requirements. She and Dex had always grinned when clients gave them a two-page sheet detailing their horse's habits and preferences. Yet here she was doing the exact same thing, even noting that his favorite treat was a peanut butter and jam sandwich, something Dex had discovered when Tizzy was a yearling.

Eve's Civic pulled into the driveway followed by a huge van that looked capable of carrying ten horses. Dani's mouth dropped. She'd never had such a fancy rig in her yard. At least Tizzy would be traveling in style.

Eve stepped out with a big smile. "All ready? These guys don't like to wait."

"Wrapped and ready," Dani said. She snapped the lead on Tizzy who raised his head and coolly studied the trailer, not nearly as impressed as Dani.

"He's a calm one," Eve said, nodding with satisfaction. "That makes it easier. My boss is looking forward to meeting him."

A driver and attendant climbed down from the cab and opened a side door. A ramp silently lowered. Inside a horse nickered, and some of Dani's nervousness disappeared. At least Tizzy would have company.

"Stay, Red," she said, then led Tizzy toward the trailer. The horse didn't hesitate. He followed her up the ramp and into a spacious stall complete with a hay net full of sweet-smelling alfalfa. He immediately started chewing, flattening his ears only once while asserting his claim to the hay, but otherwise totally ignoring the other three horses. Dani gave Tizzy's neck an affectionate pat then resolutely walked away. She passed the envelope to the driver and joined Eve and Red at the side of the gravel.

The van circled the driveway, picking up speed as it rumbled back down the drive and onto the road.

"Don't worry," Eve said, "I'll keep an eye on Tizzy. I already offered to gallop him in the morning."

"Thanks," Dani said, crossing her arms. "I know it had to be done. All the horses have to be sold before the move." But she was giving up on Dex's dream of owning a racehorse and she blinked a little too rapidly, struggling to hide her turmoil.

Eve gave her shoulder a comforting pat. "Tizzy was bred to race. You're giving him a chance. And in a few months, his value might triple. Now we'll feed your horses and then I'm taking you out for supper."

Forty minutes later, they zipped down the highway in Eve's compact car. "Wow, you drive like you ride," Dani said, adjusting her seatbelt. She rarely went out, except to her dad's, and the best thing about a horse friend was that they understood the unrelenting demand of animal care. Eve had helped with water, grain and hay, even refilling the shavings bin, and it had cut the work in half.

"Where are we going?" Dani asked.

"To a skuzzy little bar, or maybe two or three," Eve said. "Anywhere with cheap food and drinks, where you can forget your troubles for a while."

"Sounds good," Dani said "But I didn't think jockeys could drink. Aren't you always watching your weight?"

"Yes." Eve gave a rueful smile. "That's why I'm an excellent designated driver."

The first bar they entered was one Dani had passed but never visited. And she couldn't understand why. The food was cheap and plentiful, and the smiling bartender was extremely attentive, keeping their bowl full of salty pretzels and even giving her a complimentary drink, with an umbrella and cherry on the side.

"I'm definitely coming back here," she said, draining her glass.

"How about later tonight?" the bartender asked. "I get off work at two."

"Sorry," Eve said, tugging at Dani's arm. "We have to go. We only have a few hours and this girl needs to see the world."

"Or at least the town," Dani said, smiling at the bartender. His jokes had turned funnier with every drink, and he looked genuinely disappointed that they were leaving. "Maybe we should stay here," she whispered to Eve. "It'll save on gas and he's giving us free drinks…and he's kind of nice."

"Four places minimum," Eve said, urging Dani outside and toward the car. "You need to see what you're missing. You can't settle for the first guy that comes along."

"You're right," Dani said. She sank back onto the passenger seat as Eve propelled the car out of the lot and back onto the road. "But I didn't settle for Dex."

"I'm not talking about Dex," Eve said.

A light flashed red. She yanked the wheel to the right and the little car squealed around the corner.

"Holy smoke," Dani said. "You drive like a hellion. Wait." She peered out the window at a paint-peeling building with a gaudy neon sign. "Can we stop there?"

"At that dingy dive? Sure." Eve obligingly swerved into the rutted parking lot. Blinking red letters proclaimed cheap rooms, rented by the hour.

Dani clenched her hands on her lap. "The Starlight Bar and Motel. That's where Dex was."

"With the prostitute?"

"Yes." Dani sighed. "With...Tawny." She generally avoided saying the woman's name. It made Tawny seem less real, her death less tragic. "I don't really have it so bad," she added. "Neither does Dex. At least we're still alive." She pressed her face closer to the car window, studying the low building. "They were in room one hundred and thirteen."

"That explains it," Eve said. "Certainly a damn unlucky number. Want to go in?"

"Is the bar even open?" Dani asked. "The windows are dark."

"Let's find out."

The Starlight was indeed open. It had an attached bar with subdued lighting, and three bourbons later Dani had completely relaxed. Service was fast, liquor was cheap and the atmosphere congenial. A wide range of patrons drifted in and out, most of them grinning. The wide-eyed boys whispering in the corner were definitely underage, and she was quite certain the nice lady next to her was a hooker.

"I wish I could walk in shoes like that," Dani said, wistfully eyeing the woman's six-inch heels. "Your legs look gorgeous. That black fishnet is so pretty."

The woman gave a throaty laugh. "I'd give it all up to look like you, sweetie. You don't have to dress up to get a man's attention."

"Maybe I should have dressed up though," Dani said. "My husband might not have strayed." She blinked, surprised she'd even voiced the thought. It had been lying beneath the surface for years but she'd always kept it suppressed.

The woman patted her hand. "Just add heels. Wear them in the bedroom. You won't have to walk far. Your husband will love them."

"He's in jail. Three more years." Dani hiccupped and tilted on her stool. "Have you been hooking long? Maybe you knew him?" She felt Eve's elbow in her ribs and turned around. "What?" she asked.

"It's okay." The woman leaned forward and nodded at Eve. "I like your friend. And to answer the question, I've been in this business for five years. Feels like fifty. But I don't remember my clients. It's healthier that way."

"Healthier?" Dani wrinkled her nose. "What do you mean?"

"Just that it's safer not to talk. My handlers trust me, no matter what I see or hear. I wouldn't last long if I had a big mouth. Those border boys are ruthless."

Dani nodded but her eyesight was a little blurry and she had no idea what this nice lady was talking about. "I still think you'd remember my husband if you had sex with him," she said stubbornly. "He was good...really good."

"I think we should call it a night," Eve said, laughing and rising from her stool.

"But this is only two bars," Dani said, holding up her hand, trying to wave two fingers. "You promised we'd visit four."

"That was before you starting talking about Dex's prowess," Eve said. "No man is going to like hearing that, no matter how pretty you are—"

"Dex?" the woman asked. "Dex Tattrie? He's your husband?" At Dani's nod, the woman gestured at the bartender, her bright red nails flashing with authority. "Bring this lady another drink," she said. "My tab."

"See," Dani said happily. "I told you he was good." She paused, guessing she shouldn't be quite so delighted that a prostitute remembered her virile husband. However, she liked talking about Dex. And the warm glow that filled her chest felt much nicer than the usual bitterness and hurt.

"I didn't know him personally," the prostitute went on. "But he's certainly looking after Tawny's sister."

"What?" Dani asked, her inner glow suddenly turning cold.

"He sent her money. Made sure she was looked after."

Dani squeezed her eyes shut. She'd had more liquor than she usually consumed in a year but suddenly she was stone cold sober. And aching again. Because Dex certainly wasn't sending *her* money. Maybe it wouldn't hurt so much if she hadn't just led Tizzy onto a trailer; if she hadn't been chewing her nails trying to figure out how to pay the mortgage; if he had just shown a little concern. But the reality was that he was a selfish jerk.

She pushed her glass away. "It was nice meeting you," she said to the woman. "But Eve's right. It's time to go."

"But that's a full drink," the woman said. "You can't waste it."

"You drink it," Eve said, and even though she was barely five feet tall, the whip in her voice was unmistakable. "Let's go, Dani."

Neither Dani nor Eve spoke until they'd driven three blocks.

"Last night," Dani said slowly, "my brother accused me of being selfish. Said I shouldn't sell Dex's ranch. And admittedly I had misgivings. I was even ambivalent about signing the divorce papers and sending his horse away. But he isn't thinking of me. So I have to stop worrying about him."

"That's right." Eve's angry eyes flashed beneath the glow from the streetlights. "Your husband's a first-class prick. When I think of how you've been struggling…" She stopped talking and simply shook her head.

Dani clasped her arms over her chest, feeling cold and worthless and empty. Perhaps Dex hadn't been as deliriously happy as her, but he'd always been supportive. She'd thought they shared a good marriage.

But he hadn't just paid a prostitute; he'd sent her family money. Yet he'd never once permitted Dani to visit. Had barely spoken to her before he went to prison. Had never called or written, or even sent a message back with Jeffrey.

"We should hire Scott to rough him up a bit," Eve said, shooting Dani a sideways glance.

Dani forced a smile. "Does Scott's company do that?"

"Not generally. But he has a guy called Snake who can get down and dirty. And Scott detests drug dealers. His first wife died of an overdose."

"That explains his interest in the heroin," Dani said, clenching her arms tighter to her chest.

"Well, there's been some problems with fentanyl-laced heroin," Eve said. "They want to charge the dealer with manslaughter. But witnesses either disappear or won't talk. And I don't blame them. It's all connected to the cartel, and those people are ruthless."

The sadness in Eve's voice was wrenching and for a moment, Dani forgot her own problems. She reached over and patted her friend's shoulder. Eve's son, Joey, would never know his father; the man had been a talented jockey who'd been shot in the head simply because he'd stumbled into the middle of a drug deal.

But he'd been totally innocent. Dex wasn't. Dex deserved his sentence. And Dani had been the fool who stubbornly waited.

She squared her shoulders. "Next time we go out, it's your turn to drink. You relax and I'll drive. Better still, we'll both drink. I'll ask Jeffrey to pick us up."

"Sounds like a plan," Eve said.

CHAPTER TWENTY

"Good job," Dex said, studying Sandy's work with a critical eye. "But take a little more off the left toe."

"You two still fiddling with the same horse?" the guard growled.

Dex ignored the man, pushing the bay gelding back a step and adjusting the animal's position. Sandy had made huge progress in the last two weeks, and the kid was brimming with confidence. Maybe too much. The guards tended to slap inmates down if they were too happy.

Although perhaps the hostility wasn't directed at Sandy. There had been a marked attitude change in a couple other guards—the night guard in Block D as well as the guard who'd made Dex squat and cough before the bus ride yesterday.

Dex turned and looked at the guard. "Seen Quentin around?" he asked mildly.

"I'm not your errand boy, Tattrie." The guard scowled. "And no unnecessary conversation is permitted. Break the rules again and I'll write you up."

Sandy's eyes widened and he looked at Dex. The guards always relaxed away from the prison gates and even though technically the same rules were in force, they were never followed. The guard's admonishment was unusual. And definitely worrisome.

Dex handed the rasp to Sandy, his mind whirling. This probably wasn't coming from Carlos who would settle the

stall incident in his own time, his own way. But the guards'
animosity at the work farm was a wild card, rather
unexpected and almost as troubling.

He'd been planning to take a break after this horse and
join Quentin for a coffee but technically that was against the
rules. On the other hand, Quentin might be able to shed
some light. Dex needed to talk to him, alone.

"I'm not sure about this foot," Dex said, bending down
and picking up the left front. "See the quarter crack starting."

Sandy nodded, his eyes meeting Dex's over the horse's
perfect foot. "It sure is a mess," Sandy said helpfully.

"What's the problem?" the guard asked, still glowering.

"This horse needs shoes," Dex said.

"To protect his feet," Sandy added. "But the work order
only calls for a barefoot trim."

"Well, go ask Quentin," the guard snapped. "Don't act like
idiots."

"I'll stay and watch him," Sandy said. "He's probably too
sore to lead back to his stall."

Dex nodded. The kid caught on quickly. Not only had he
picked up on Dex's need to see Quentin, but he'd also
positioned himself so he'd remain close to a guard. And safe
from Carlos and his gang.

Dex passed him a hoof gauge. "Practice eyeballing the
angles, then measure them. I'm not sure how long I'll have to
wait…to see Quentin."

Dex walked down the aisle but Quentin's office was
empty. The guard sitting in front of the supply room
immediately rose and stalked toward him. "What do you
want?" he asked. "You already checked out two sets of farrier
tools."

"I have a shoeing question for the foreman," Dex said.

"Outside." The guard gestured with his thumb.

Dex nodded and walked toward the door, keeping his
expression impassive. The supply room guard was always

morose so it was difficult to gauge if there was any change from that quarter.

He stepped outside, pausing for a moment to let his vision adjust to the bright sun.

Quentin and a guard stood at the far end of the dirt ring, watching as eight inmates walked their horses around an instructor. Dex's eyes automatically swept to the animals' feet. All eight horses stepped out nicely, clearly relaxed and comfortable. A few of them might need front shoes though, now that the ground was hardening.

He stepped closer to the rail, his eyes narrowing on a chestnut's legs. He stopped a lot of problems before they developed, simply by watching the horses move, and knowing the needs of the rider. Dex lifted his eyes to the man in the saddle.

Carlos stared down, his dark eyes full of such venom Dex almost recoiled.

"Everyone jog," the instructor called. "And keep your ass in the saddle. Don't jab your horse in the mouth. If you do, you'll be kicked off the riding squad."

Dex kept his face impassive, but the instructor was a bully and enjoyed his authority. The riders didn't give him much respect though and unfortunately didn't seem to be learning much either. They looked stiff, bouncing around the saddle with various degrees of awkwardness, all except Carlos. His signal to his horse was almost imperceptible, and his mare moved into an easy trot.

The horse in front of Carlos, a Roman-nosed mare, clearly resented the rider's heels on her ribs. She crow hopped, then followed up with a jarring buck. The rider sailed over her head, hitting the ground with a thud.

"You forget how to ride a woman?" another rider snickered. Everyone hooted, even the guard. But the guard's smile turned to a glower when he spotted Dex.

Damn. Something was going on. Dex hadn't expected that the guards at the horse farm could be so easily influenced by Jeffrey. Obviously the deputy sheriff really did have contacts within the prison.

Quentin's gaze flickered to Dex and the foreman gave an imperceptible nod. "Have them dismount," Quentin called to the instructor, "and give the horses a break. Most of them have been lugging around dead weight. Well done, Carlos."

Carlos ignored Quentin's praise. However, he patted his horse's neck and the affection he held for the mare was obvious.

"I need to see you in my office, Tattrie," Quentin bellowed, as if spotting Dex for the first time.

Dex followed the foreman into the office. Quentin closed the door and immediately poured two cups of coffee. He frowned and pushed one over to Dex. "You pissed off somebody. They wanted you removed from the work detail. But we need a farrier so I refused. And I saw your name on the Board's schedule when they requested my report. Were you even going to tell me you're up for parole?"

"I'm up for parole," Dex said. "Doesn't mean it'll be approved."

"You like to play your cards close to your chest," Quentin said, "but you better walk a tight line between now and the hearing. Looks like they intend to make your life miserable." He rubbed his forehead, his voice turning plaintive. "If you get out, will the new kid even be ready to take over the shoeing? This really isn't very convenient."

"You're right," Dex said. "Maybe I should hang around here and shoe the rest of my life."

Quentin had the grace to look embarrassed. "I only want to keep the place profitable. I gave the Board a good report. Said there was a real rapport between you and the renegade mare, and that I've never seen anyone with more patience."

He shuffled a stack of papers. "I asked for client statements too, and they're all glowing. They love how you help their horses. More important to the Board is the frequent mention of your professionalism. But something's wrong. Jamie, the fat guard, said I couldn't give you coffee anymore. Quoted some bullshit about inappropriate fraternization with cons."

Quentin shook his head, his voice troubled. "How did you manage to piss off someone outside when you're locked up?"

"A Tattrie gift," Dex said, cupping the warm coffee. He always appreciated the glass mug. With Quentin, he could pretend life was normal, that he wasn't a threatening inmate necessarily restricted to paper cups. "Thanks for the heads-up," he added. "I'll be careful to follow protocol."

"There's more, I'm afraid." Quentin paused. His gaze skipped around the office, studiously avoiding Dex's face.

Obviously it was bad. Dex concentrated on keeping his breath even, on hiding any twitch.

Quentin pulled in a heavy sigh and finally looked at Dex. "I received a notice this morning," he said, "directing that Gypsy be sold."

The coffee in Dex's cup rippled, tiny movements that covered the surface and then spread to the side of the mug. He set his coffee down, his fingers cold and clumsy.

"A stock contractor with a Born to Buck program is looking for mares," Quentin went on. "Someone must have suggested Gypsy."

"She's probably a good candidate." Dex finally managed to speak over the painful lump in his throat.

"But this is personal and vindictive." Even Quentin's voice sounded ragged. "And it's a damn shame. Besides, that mare's a valuable tool for straightening out inmates. She helps them understand that horses should be treated with respect. Just like people."

Dex stared down at his empty hands, his insides splintering. Gypsy was the one good thing in his life. Like Dani, she was pure and brave and honest. She'd been his main support, and now it seemed as if his legs had been kicked out from underneath him.

"When does she go?" he asked, clearing his throat.

"Tonight."

Dex gulped. He'd only have forty more minutes with his horse. "Might be a good life," he managed. "Do you know the operation?"

"Skyview Buckers, west of Santa Clarita. I visited a couple times. Good people. Lots of grass and shade. Mares are always sleek and happy."

"So a cool breeze and no flies." Dex forced a smile, appreciating Quentin's attempt to make him feel better.

"Exactly," Quentin said, smiling back. "And there really is lots of grass."

Dex dragged a hand over his jaw. "What happens if she's barren? If they try to ride her, someone could get hurt."

"I'll note she's unrideable," Quentin said, "except by a PGA cowboy."

Dex swallowed. Gypsy would love the life, ruling a herd of mares, knee deep in grass. At least she wouldn't have to deal with ignorant cons anymore. All in all, it was a step up. Fortunately it wasn't his choice to make.

"Look," Quentin said. "I always follow these recommendations but you've done a remarkable job here. And we owe you. Maybe I could say she's barren. If the Board turns down your parole, you're going to need that horse."

A muscle convulsed in Dex's jaw. Here, the herd was crammed on two acres of shriveled grass. They were led inside to be fed, groomed and saddled but otherwise stood beneath the blazing sun with only a tiny apple tree for shade.

If they were sick, a vet wasn't called. They either rebounded, or a bullet put them out of their misery.

But he needed Gypsy. Badly. Needed to see her regal head when he stepped off that bus, to hear her welcoming nicker when she spotted him. She was the thread that kept him connected, lifting him above the prison rat race and keeping him human. He'd had many horses come in and out of his life, and he appreciated them all. But he loved Gypsy.

He swallowed, warring with indecision, knowing he'd never be able to look after her the way she deserved. Sure, he brought her inside so she could stay in the shade and munch hay. He kept her immaculately groomed and her feet trimmed. But every Friday, he had to saddle her up and watch an angry con wrap his legs around her barrel and try to stick to her back. They yanked her around and yelled and cursed and called her a bitch. And when her reproachful eyes found his, he always felt slightly ashamed. As if he wasn't doing his best for her, like she always did for him.

"No, let her go." He forced the words through stiff lips. "It'd be a good move."

"For her," Quentin said. "Not for you."

"No problem," Dex said. "She's just a horse."

He wanted to throw the desk through the window and let the shattering glass match the fragmenting inside his chest. But he squared his shoulders and pasted on a bored expression.

"I don't understand you." Quentin frowned. "We can try to keep her. She won't know she missed out."

"Yes," Dex said. "But I'd know."

CHAPTER TWENTY-ONE

Dex reached down from his bunk and clicked off the blaring radio. Tinker immediately protested. "Hey man. I was singing."

"Don't," Dex said.

"Can't talk. Can't sing," Tinker grumbled. "What kind of house is this?"

"A silent one." Dex propped his arms behind his head, waiting for his morning call to the work bus.

"Something wrong, Tattrie?" Tinker asked. "The last couple days you've been quieter than usual. And that's saying something. Hey." His voice lifted with enthusiasm. "I brought some sugar packets back from breakfast. You can have them. Horses like sugar, don't they?"

"Yeah, they do," Dex said. A sad smile twisted his mouth. Gypsy had loved sugar.

"You can have it all. Three packs. The old guard never checks my sleeves." Tinker paused, his voice lowering. "Look, I'm your cellie. And I hear whispers. If something's going down, I need to know."

Dex rubbed his forehead. He didn't want to drag Tinker into anything but the man had a valid point. The campaign to goad Dex had already affected his roomie. Just today, their soap and toilet paper had disappeared, a feather had been placed in Dex's scrambled eggs, and a guard had tripped him on the steps. The incidents were escalating even as his parole hearing inched closer. Ironically he was more affected by

Gypsy's departure than the forces that conspired to keep him behind bars.

"What did you hear?" Dex asked.

"That a couple guards want to write you up. Guess they like you so much they want you to stay." Tinker cleared his throat. "The other rumor is worse."

"Carlos?"

"Yeah. You're on his list. Don't know what you did, but he took it personally."

Dex stared at the chipped ceiling. The guards clearly wanted to provoke him but their actions weren't life-threatening, merely ineffectual attempts to make him lose his temper, no doubt at the request of Dani's cop boyfriend. Carlos, however, dealt in more permanent solutions.

"Might be safer in the SHU," Tinker said. "Until your date."

Dex winced at the thought of solitary housing and no more trips to the horse farm. And if the Parole Board turned him down, he'd still have three years to go and no farrier job. Besides, he couldn't leave Sandy alone to face Carlos and his gang.

"I'll think of something," he said, rubbing his jaw. "If I get out, I want you to have my radio. There's a hidden compartment in the front, behind the volume button. A little cash too."

"Cool," Tinker said, his voice bouncing with glee. His wife tried to send money for Tinker's canteen fund, but the woman was constantly struggling.

"It's time, Tattrie," a guard called.

Dex rose and stepped down from his bunk.

Tinker reached out and punched the top of Dex's hand with his fist. "Watch your back, bro," he said.

Dex followed the guard down the corridor. A correctional officer slipped in behind him, walking so closely Dex could smell the man's onion breath. But there were no brazen incidents, and he safely joined the line of men waiting to board the bus.

His tension eased a notch when he spotted Carlos and his three gang members already in line. It was always desirable to stand behind the gang, where he could keep them in sight. He checked his back, but the only person behind him was Sandy.

"Sure is windy," Sandy said, raising his voice so he could be heard over the loud gusts. "It's hard to tell the weather when you're inside."

Dex checked the flapping flag. Another westerly. The horses would be skittish with the powerful winds. Probably best if Sandy used the dull rasp today. The kid had already cut his hand on Dex's rasp when a horse had unexpectedly spooked and pulled his foot away.

"You doing okay?" Dex asked, keeping an eye on the guards and talking between tight lips, a skill he'd perfected in grade school. "Anyone giving you a hard time?"

"Seems good," Sandy said, covering his mouth with his hand. "Following all your tips. Glad I'm not in the yard though."

Dex inclined his head, stepped forward and lifted his arms. The guard patted him down, then gestured at the bus.

Dex climbed the steps. Carlos was in row four on the left but two of his men were seated at the very back. Dex chose a seat in the middle, on the opposite side of Carlos. He doubted anybody had a shank, not unless it had been placed under a seat prior to boarding. And Carlos only had a six-year sentence. It would be one of his men assigned the messy work.

The drive started quietly but as usual, the men loosened up as they approached the farm. Today though, more than one horse ran along the fence. In fact the entire herd galloped in a nervous circle, heads and tails high, eyes rimmed with white.

"They look loco," the inmate seated beside Dex said. The man's leathery forehead wrinkled in confusion. "What's their problem?"

"The wind," Dex said. "They can't hear approaching danger. There's also an overload of smells." He could empathize with their spookiness. Sweat tickled his forehead and the back of his neck felt itchy, vulnerable. It wasn't easy being a prey animal. Predators lurked everywhere.

Two of the horses were in a complete lather but still, the galloping herd was a beautiful sight. Even the guards stared. Carlos took advantage of their inattention. He abruptly turned. His eyes raked over Dex and Sandy, and he made a slashing gesture across his throat.

Dex kept his hands loose on his lap. Clearly Carlos was playing with them. He had something planned but it wouldn't happen on the bus. The guards remained oblivious. All three uniforms watched the milling horses with varying degrees of interest. The bus driver also craned his neck, glancing from the road to the hillside field.

Dex looked away. It hurt to see the horses without Gypsy. And clearly the herd missed her too. Some of their agitation was related to her absence. Carlos's horse, the second in the hierarchy, didn't carry the same authority, and the herd was spooked.

One of the convicts rose, obviously concerned about his horse.

"Back in your seat," a guard snapped. The man reluctantly sat.

The bus bumped along the dirt drive, finally stopping by the main entrance. The men filed off the bus and hurried to the gate. They were going to have fun leading their horses today, Dex thought.

"Will it be harder to shoe?" Sandy asked.

"Yes. We'll give the horses time to settle." Dex paused. "Carlos wants payback. This feels like the day."

Sandy's face paled. "I knew it was coming. My dad is working hard to get me some protection, but it won't be in time." He gave Dex a weak smile. "Bet you're sorry you helped me."

"No, kid. It's fine. And he might be gunning more for me than you."

Sandy peered over his shoulder. "This sucks. Maybe we could tell the guards?"

"That would make it worse."

"My course instructor said that too," Sandy said. "But it's a little different when you're in the moment. Nothing can prepare for this. Will they...kill us?"

"Depends where it hits," Dex said, absently fingering a scar on his ribs. "Might just be a little stab."

"A little stab?" Sandy gulped, reminding Dex so much of Dani's little brother, he wanted to reach out and rumple the kid's hair.

"It's not like we don't have a say in this," Dex said.

"But our voice isn't as loud as Carlos and his gang."

"No," Dex said. "It's not."

"Damn." Sandy dropped the rasp, staring at the reddening blotch at the base of his thumb. This was the third time he'd cut his hand, largely due to the freaky winds and the skittishness of the mare.

It was tempting to step in and help, but Dex merely gave an encouraging nod. If he made parole, Sandy would be responsible for the animals. And if he didn't please Quentin, he wouldn't keep the position. Luckily, the kid was a fast learner.

The owner of the mare stopped talking to the guard and hurried over to the horse, almost bumping Sandy's hip. "Did you cut my horse's sole?" the man asked, his tone accusing.

"No, it's *my* blood," Sandy said. "When she pulled her foot away, the rasp cut my hand."

"Oh, that's good then," the man said. Reassured, he wandered back to talk to the guard.

"Switch to your duller rasp," Dex said. "It's shorter and easier to handle. We don't want to worry our customers," he added dryly.

"I'd like to switch," Sandy said, peering up over the horse's foot. "But I couldn't find the little rasp."

"You signed it out this morning." Dex frowned and flipped through the contents of the shoeing kit: clinchers, nippers, hoof knife, hammer, pullers, wire brush, hoof gauge, tester, steel tongs. No rasp.

"I signed out the farrier kit," Sandy said, still wiping the blood from his hand, "but I didn't count every tool."

Dex's mouth tightened in frustration. This kid was so damn green. "You need to count. And stay near the guard," he warned, before turning and heading down the aisle.

Most of the stalls were vacant, the horses turned back out in the pasture. It looked like the riding session had been cancelled, probably because of the high winds. A few inmates brushed their horses while two more lingered in the aisle, cleaning tack. Gypsy's stall was empty, stripped of hay, bedding and bucket. Dex averted his head.

The guard sitting outside the supply room scowled. "What do you want now, Tattrie?"

"Pair of shoeing gloves for my apprentice," Dex said.

The man rose and unlocked the door. "Be quick," he grumbled, following him into the room. Dex made a show of looking for the least cumbersome pair of gloves while he scanned the shelves. Plastic pitchforks, hammer, first aid kit and a wrinkled Sports Illustrated Magazine, swimwear edition. But no missing rasp.

He picked up the pen and signed for the gloves, checking the short list of signatures. Only his and Sandy, along with

Quentin. The supply room was strictly monitored... Usually. He glanced at the guard who refused to meet his gaze, and a sick feeling churned in Dex's stomach.

He rushed back down the aisle, cold with fear. Clearly this was a distraction. But surely they couldn't get to Sandy now, not if he stayed in the secure area. But sometimes the kid didn't listen. And a rasp was a powerful weapon. The handle had a sharp point while the blunt end could easily dent a man's scalp.

He hurried into the visitors' area and his breath oozed with relief. Sandy was bent over the mare's hind leg, still healthy, still alive. The guard stood only ten feet away, still chatting with the horse owner.

"Find it?" Sandy asked, his attention on the mare's foot.

"No," Dex said.

Something in Dex's voice must have alerted Sandy. He glanced up, then dropped the mare's foot. "What's wrong?" He gulped, his face turning so white his freckles sharply contrasted to his skin. "You think Carlos has the rasp?"

"Afraid so," Dex said.

CHAPTER TWENTY-TWO

"Take a look at the white line. We need to correct this or he won't be able to walk." Dex ran a finger along the sole, trying to pull back Sandy's attention. The kid was usually an avid student but the last few hours he'd been distracted, constantly checking over his shoulder.

"Nothing will happen here," Dex said quietly. "Not with a guard at the entrance."

Sandy nodded but his forehead gleamed with perspiration. "When, do you think?" he asked, his voice squeaking.

"Before we get on the bus. Or they'll hide the rasp here and use it another day."

Carlos wouldn't wait too long though. Dex's parole hearing was scheduled for next week. Dex dropped the horse's hoof to the ground. There was another scenario, but one he didn't want to voice. Sandy was already squirrelly with fear, and there was no sense worrying the kid anymore.

"If I were Carlos," Sandy said, "I'd use the rasp on me and frame you. That would be a two for one."

Dex gave a wry nod. Exactly what he'd been thinking. The kid was definitely a fast learner. "I imagine there's going to be a disturbance soon," Dex said, turning his attention back to the horse's leg. "Now take another look at the toe. We'll have to cut away part of the hoof. It'll look bad but it will grow—"

Someone yelled in Spanish, the voice high and excited, words indiscernible over the blowing wind.

"Keep working," Dex said.

The guard pushed past them and peered down the gloomy aisle. "What's wrong?" he called. "Where's Quentin?"

"Busy," a man called. "Sick horse."

The guard frowned, wrinkles furrowing his forehead. "You two stay here," he said to Dex. "Don't even think of stepping outside." He walked down the aisle, his hand palming his holster.

Sandy spun around and fumbled in the farrier's kit then straightened, brandishing the tongs. "Are they making a run at us? I'm ready."

Dex motioned for him to be quiet, still straining to hear the conversation. It had all the ingredients of a setup. However, the vibes he picked up seemed truly panicked, and he'd learned to trust his instincts much more than words. His shoulders slowly relaxed and he turned back to the job. "I think we'll have time to finish this horse," he said.

"But the guard's gone." Sandy's knuckles whitened around the handle of the tongs. "This is the perfect time for Carlos."

"They really do have a sick horse," Dex said.

"Oh. No wonder they sound worried." Sandy nodded in complete understanding and dropped the tongs back in the box. Despite the rough nature of the inmates, every one of them genuinely cared for their assigned horse. "How long will it take for the vet to come?"

"There won't be a vet," Dex said. "No money." Quentin would do what he could, of course. But the first aid kit was limited and so were the foreman's skills. Dex blew out a resigned breath. At least it wasn't Gypsy who was ailing. It would kill him to see something he loved in pain, and yet be powerless to help.

"Bummer for the horse," Sandy said, his troubled gaze drifting down the aisle. "Wonder whose it is?"

"Don't know. Don't care." Dex's voice hardened. "It buys us time. Stay here and finish your job."

"But maybe we can help."

"There's plenty of men milling around that poor horse right now," Dex said. "They'll figure it out. And if the animal dies, you don't want to be in the blame radius. Sometimes people don't think straight…especially here."

Comprehension colored Sandy's eyes. "So it's a lose, lose?"

"Yes," Dex said, lowering his voice so the returning guard wouldn't hear. "Let me take over now. I'm going to cut a little higher."

Thirty minutes later, the gelding's hoof was cut away. It looked drastic and regrowth would take months, but the infection had been removed. Even better, the animal's prognosis was good so Quentin could be persuaded to keep the horse.

Dex unclipped the cross ties and nodded at the guard. The guard bellowed and a convict hurried down the aisle to collect his horse.

"Is King going to be okay?" the man asked, swiping at his brow. His eyes widened with horror when he spotted the cut-away hoof. "Goddammit, Tattrie! What the hell did you do?"

"Removed the infected portion," Dex said calmly. "The hoof layers separated from the toe to the coronary band. That's why he was lame. The foot will grow out and he should be fine."

"He better be," the man spat, so aggressively that spittle formed at the corners of his mouth. "Or we'll be talking."

"And I'll recommend to Quentin that King remain here with you," Dex added. "Since he'll be sound in about six months."

The man's eyes widened with hope. "So they won't get rid of him as planned? All right then." He cleared his throat, even shooting Dex a grateful nod.

Dex watched him walk down the aisle. Already the inmate's gruff voice had turned to a childish singsong as he encouraged King to follow. Certainly no one could question the man's affection for the horse. Dex felt a bittersweet pang. Gypsy was gone, but at least King was staying. And that inmate would be better for it.

"Guess we're done for the day," Dex said, rubbing his back. The aisle looked quiet. Safe. Several of the men were already lined up for the bus. "We're going to turn our tools in now," Dex called to the guard who gave a curt nod of permission.

Dex readjusted the kit so the steel tongs were in easy reach. Sandy's eyes widened but he gulped and quickly rearranged his tools as well.

They walked down the aisle in single file. Horses contentedly munched hay but the aisle was eerily deserted.

Not so when they rounded the corner. Quentin, eight inmates and a guard ringed a single stall. They all looked concerned except for Carlos whose face, as usual, was impassive.

Quentin glanced at Dex. "Come back after you check your tools," he said, his voice somber. "I want your opinion."

Dex nodded, stealing a glance at the mare as he walked past. Her neck was wet with sweat and her flanks heaved. But she lay quietly, not thrashing or trying to roll.

He returned his tool kit to the supply room then stopped at the sign-out table.

"Carlos thinks someone poisoned his horse," the supply guard said, sneering at Dex and Sandy. He shoved a pen across the table, his fleshy eyes glinting with malice. "Bet you know something about that."

"We wouldn't poison a horse," Sandy said hotly.

"Doesn't matter." The guard smirked. "I just hope we can shoot her outside. It's more work if they stiffen and you have to break their legs to get them out the door. Kind of fun though. Weird how you cons get so squeamish about these stupid animals."

Dex tossed the pen back to the guard, aiming for the gap at the top of his shirt. The man stuck his hand up, trying to catch it before it disappeared above his swollen gut. His face flushed as he struggled vainly to retrieve the pen. "You're a prick, Tattrie," he said. "And you ain't going to make parole."

Dex turned and walked back to the cluster of men surrounding the ailing horse's stall.

"She's been down for two hours," Quentin said to Dex. "Temperature and respiration are high. Elevated pulse. I gave her a shot of Banomine with no relief. Seems like colic but I can't figure out the cause. Carlos said she didn't eat any hay or grain when she came in."

Dex studied the mare. She looked in pain, her eyes dull and listless. "Did you check the pasture?" he asked. "Wind probably blew down a lot of apples. She's top mare now. Would have eaten the most."

Carlos gestured with his head, and Juan immediately rushed out the door to check the pasture. The guard didn't say a word to stop him.

Five minutes later, Juan reappeared, nodding and talking and even waving a half-eaten green apple. Dex eased backwards. At least Carlos now realized it wasn't a malicious poisoning although that wouldn't help his horse.

The mare abruptly bit at her stomach then twisted on her back. Dex didn't intend to get involved but he couldn't stand by and watch her suffer. He stepped forward and grabbed her halter. "We can't let her roll," he muttered. "Get a lead line and help me get her up."

Quentin grabbed the mare's tail, his voice regretful. "But the bus is leaving. It's probably best to put her back in the pasture. Then just hope she makes it through the night."

"She won't," Dex said, clipping on a lead line. "Not if she rolls and twists her gut. And rolling is all she wants to do right now."

Quentin gave a helpless shrug. "This is a prison barn. It shuts down. Every inmate has to be on that bus."

"She'll live if she doesn't roll?" Carlos's gruff question surprised Dex. He'd never heard the man speak before.

"Maybe not," Dex said, "but she definitely won't live if she twists her intestines."

Carlos turned and looked at Quentin. "*Por favor,*" he said, his voice tight.

"I'll do what I can," Quentin said. "But it's hard to keep them on their feet when they're hurting. Might be kinder to put her down while the guards are here."

The mare groaned, her eyes flashing in pain. Carlos crossed his arms, his face suddenly as stricken as the mare's.

"Come on, baby." Dex pulled on her halter, almost single-handedly lifting her to her feet. "Don't give up."

The mare resisted, then finally stood, swaying on trembling legs. But she lowered her head, trying to roll again, desperate to relieve the pain in her belly. Only Dex's strength kept her standing.

"I can't stand this." The waiting guard unclipped his holster. "You men get on the bus. I'll take care of the horse."

"There's a clause covering farrier work at the farm," Dex said, looking over the mare's back at Quentin. "Section 29.6. Extraordinary circumstances. With your permission and presence, I could stay and help."

"That's not farrier work," the guard said, but he raised an eyebrow at Quentin. "Unless you call it that?"

Quentin looked at Dex for a long moment, then nodded.

"All right," the guard said. "Call for a van when he's ready to go back. Everyone else load up."

Carlos lingered in the doorway, his inky eyes shooting from the mare to Dex. "She better live," he said.

Dex concentrated on the mare. It had been a mistake to step forward. Carlos would blame him if she died. But he'd never been able to ignore suffering. She was sitting back on her hindquarters now, fighting once again to roll.

"Sometimes trotting helps," he said to Quentin. "Come behind us and get her moving. You'll need a whip."

"No," Carlos snapped. "She's hurting. Don't make her move."

The mare rocked forward, bending her knees, intent on rolling in the aisle. "We have to, Quentin," Dex said urgently. "It's do or die."

"On the bus, Carlos," the guard said, his voice almost respectful.

Carlos turned and trudged down the aisle. He gave one last threatening stare before disappearing through the side door.

"I wish you hadn't used that do or die term," Quentin said. "I worry for you. It would have been safer to let the guard shoot her."

"Slap her rump," Dex said. "Get her moving."

Quentin sighed but swung a lead rope and the protesting mare followed Dex out the end door. He urged her into a trot, with Quentin following and waving the rope.

The bus pulled away. Every inmate's face was pressed to the window, including Carlos and his hate-filled eyes. But Dex couldn't worry about Carlos now. Besides he was already on the man's hit list. Nothing changed if he were listed twice.

Twenty minutes later, Dex and Quentin were both dripping with sweat and gasping for breath. The mare, however, stood quietly.

"She's not trying to roll anymore," Quentin said, his breath labored. "Think she'll make it?"

Dex loosened the lead, letting her head drop. She seemed much less agitated, no longer desperate to rid herself of the ache in her belly. Now, she merely looked exhausted, eyeing the ground as if she wanted to stretch out.

"Are you going to let her go down?" Quentin's voice sharpened. "After all that work?"

"It's different now," Dex said, keeping his voice low. "She just wants to rest."

He stroked her neck, murmuring encouragement. She seemed to understand and bent her knees, lowering herself heavily to the ground. But her ears flicked toward the curious horses milling by the fence, and her interest in the herd was reassuring.

"I've got some beer in the office," Quentin said, turning toward the barn. "We deserve some. I'll be back."

Dex sat down by the mare. She seemed comforted by his presence, even moving her head closer so that her warm breath fanned his knee. A fly buzzed around her rump and she swished her tail. She clearly was feeling better, her ears flicking sideways as she tracked Quentin's return.

"Here," Quentin said, walking up and tossing Dex a frosty can of beer. "This is much better than your prison hooch."

Dex snapped open the can and took a long and appreciative swallow. "Thanks," he said. "But we better listen for that van. The guards won't like this."

"Maybe beer is covered under the extraordinary circumstances clause."

"Doubt it," Dex said. "I made up that clause."

Quentin smiled. "Knew you did."

CHAPTER TWENTY-THREE

"How did the mare make out last night?" Sandy asked. He slid onto the bus seat beside Dex, his eyes concerned.

"Okay." Dex stifled a yawn. "We had a rough bit but were able to keep her moving. When I left last night, she was back in the pasture with her buddies."

Sandy tilted his head, his eyes narrowing. "You look like you had a party. Like you're hung over."

"But alcohol isn't permitted in prison," Dex said. "You know that. I stayed late…helping Quentin pick apples."

Sandy gave a wistful sigh. "Sounds like fun…picking apples."

Dex lowered his voice. "Quentin and I had a chat. You'll be the new farrier when I go. No more probation. He'll keep your schedule light while you're learning."

"Thanks, man," Sandy said, pumping his fist in the air.

"No talking," the guard behind them snapped.

Sandy lowered his fist, clutching his hands sedately on his lap. But his grin didn't fade and he was still smiling as the bus approached the work farm. Carlos rose and scanned the field. No one corrected him for leaving his seat.

"Does he know about his horse?" Sandy asked, keeping his voice low.

Dex shrugged. Carlos had his own pipeline. Besides, no inmate spoke directly to Carlos, not unless given permission. Hopefully, the mare was okay. She'd seemed fine when he left shortly after midnight. But colic was tricky and horses could be achingly fragile. She'd certainly been a good drinking companion though.

Someone in the front hollered. Seconds later cheers broke out. The usual gray horse chased them along the fence line but today she was ignored. All eyes were on Carlos's chestnut mare who cantered down the hill, followed by the rest of the herd. The mare's tail was up and her white blaze flashed. She lacked Gypsy's regal air, but she looked beautiful, happy and healthy. *Thank, God.*

"Too bad Carlos won't give you credit for saving her," Sandy said, his voice slightly bitter. "Only trouble if she'd died."

Dex shrugged. Carlos wasn't known to be a charitable man. And it was impossible to cross a gang member without repercussions.

"Why'd you do it?" Sandy twisted sideways. "Why'd you help me in the stall that day? You must have known Carlos would retaliate."

Dex shifted uncomfortably. The kid was okay, but he talked too much.

"My course instructor said that prison reduces people," Sandy went on. "It forces them to look out for number one. But you went out of your way to help me, and that mare, even when there was only a downside. And all the horses trust you. You look tough but they must sense what's underneath."

Dex scowled and folded his arms. "You should sense I want you to shut up."

"But I'm not scared of you anymore," Sandy said.

The kid even had the audacity to smile, and Dex had a hard time keeping a grim face. Besides, Sandy's words left him feeling buoyant, even human. Maybe, just maybe, he was going to leave here with his soul unscathed. Maybe Dani hadn't filed for that divorce yet. He only had to last a couple more weeks.

He stared straight ahead, but it seemed his world had tilted. Before, he'd only hoped to survive, to make it through one day at a time. But now an odd warmth kindled in his chest. He hadn't felt the emotion for so long, he barely recognized it as hope.

He'd seen cons when they walked out of prison, hardened disillusioned men who dragged their families down with them. Dani didn't need that. He cared too much to saddle her with a broken and bitter man. But now, he was only ten days away from his parole hearing. And he didn't feel broken. He felt…optimistic.

He rocked forward on his seat. "We need to find that rasp," he said urgently. "Before they have a chance to use it. Who was the last person on the bus last night?"

"Carlos," Sandy said. "And then the guy you threw across the stall."

Dex rubbed his jaw. If he were hiding a weapon, he'd probably bury it in the manure pile. Or possibly his stall. However, a horse might kick aside their bedding, leaving it exposed. Carlos's men used the stalls halfway down the aisle. The walls were smooth and the rafters high.

Juan had checked the apple tree when everyone was worrying about the sick mare, but he hadn't been gone long. The sandy riding ring was on the way to the pasture but it wasn't a great hiding spot. If a horse's shoe hit a buried rasp, the telltale clink would grab a guard's attention.

"Maybe we should report it," Sandy went on. "Then at least we won't get written up. And you'll be clean for your hearing."

Dex squeezed his eyes shut. He'd been tempted to tell Quentin last night, after downing a case of beer with the man. But a missing rasp would warrant a shakedown and the entire prison population would know they'd ratted. Sandy's life wouldn't be worth a nickel, and with Dex paroled, the kid would be stuck facing the backlash alone.

"Oh," Sandy said, the freckles on his nose turning more prominent. "I just remembered what my instructor said happened to snitches."

The bus jerked to a stop in front of the barn. Dex rose but Sandy remained seated, his eyes wide with remorse. "I bet you wish we hadn't met. I've been nothing but trouble."

"God gives everyone trials, kid," Dex said. He impulsively reached out to rumple Sandy's hair then jerked his hand back. "Come on," he said, his voice gruff. "We have a lot to do today."

CHAPTER TWENTY-FOUR

Dex uncovered another section of manure, his fingers gripping the plastic pitchfork. The front end of the pit was fresh but further back the manure had bleached and dried beneath the sun. A truck hauled it away every month but judging by the size of the pile, pickup was overdue. It seemed a risky place to hide a rasp, especially with the floater guard hovering in the doorway.

"What are you doing, Tattrie?" the guard called, his voice suspicious.

"Looking for a missing shoe," Dex said, brushing away a buzzing fly. "Think it went out with the manure when the stalls were cleaned."

The guard shrugged, somewhat appeased, and wandered off. Dex watched the doorway. If any of Carlos's men appeared, he'd keep checking the manure. Otherwise, this search was way off base. Voices rumbled from inside the barn and a horse kicked the stall wall, but there was no movement in the doorway.

Damn. He'd searched the stalls while Carlos and his men were riding, even finding an excuse to check the dusty corners of the supply room. But with no success. There weren't many other places to look. Possibly they'd attached it to the bottom of the bus and already removed it from the farm. However, inmates passed through a metal detector upon return, and smuggling it back to the cell block would be difficult.

Difficult but not impossible.

Dex grimaced, hating to think of the carnage a rasp could inflict. It was the ultimate gift weapon, like Christmas for Carlos. And Sandy's name was on the sign-out sheet. On the bright side, it meant they didn't intend to kill Sandy but instead wanted the rasp in the prison yard.

Either way, as the farrier in charge of the tools, Dex would certainly be held responsible. He scooped the manure faster, fighting an edge of desperation. He'd almost made it. However, he could be on his best behavior over the next few weeks, even smile at the guards' clumsy provocation attempts. But the rasp remained a ticking bomb.

And Carlos had a devious mind. If he could knock off a rival gang member and implicate Dex at the same time, it would be vintage Carlos—a man who always paid back his enemies in spades.

Juan walked around the side of the manure pit, carrying a bucket. "Lose something, Tattrie?" He gave a taunting sneer then sloshed the contents of his dirty bucket over Dex's legs.

Dex wheeled, balancing the pitchfork in both hands, measuring the vulnerable expanse of Juan's throat.

Juan smacked his hand against the bottom of the bucket but backed away. "You won't look so tough soon," he spat.

"Hey, keep moving," the guard called.

Juan swaggered away, clearly unconcerned about Dex finding the rasp in the manure. And the guy was too stupid to pretend. He hadn't looked anywhere but at Dex. That meant the only place left to search was the ring.

Dex gave a final half-hearted stab with the fork then turned toward the guard lounging in the doorway. "Didn't find the shoe," he said. "It must have come off in the ring."

The guard frowned. "Is it so important? Can't you just use another?"

"This was an expensive aluminum one, good for navicular. Corrective shoeing takes a lot longer. I need a natural balance shoe."

The guard's eyes glazed over as Dex knew they would. "Go and check the ring then," he said, gesturing impatiently. "No longer than ten minutes."

"That's all I need," Dex said.

He walked over to the ring, carrying the pitchfork over his shoulder, his pants already drying around his legs. Ten horses and riders trotted in a circle. The ground was packed along the rail but the corners looked deeper, the sandy ground undisturbed by hoof prints. If they'd buried the rasp in the ring, it would be in one of the corners.

"Remember, we're training some of these horses for resale," the instructor called. "They need a good stop and to stay in gait. If your horse slows or speeds up, make the correction." He paused, his gaze flickering over to Dex. "What the hell are you doing out here, Tattrie? If you're looking for Quentin, he's holed up in his office."

"No, I'm looking for a lost shoe," Dex said.

The instructor waved a hand, not even questioning the story. "Just don't get in the way," he said, turning back to the riders.

Carlos trotted past on his mare. As usual, the man stared straight ahead. But the horse slowed, her eyes flashing with recognition. Dex stiffened, surprised to see the mare working. Quentin must be hung over and not as alert. It was risky to send her for a riding session after her bout with colic less than twelve hours earlier. And laminitis was always a threat.

She looked as if she was struggling. Sweat covered her neck and flanks, and white lather caked her hind legs. He itched to feel her hooves and check her digital pulse.

But he turned and trudged to the corner of the ring, accepting his influence was limited. Both the instructor and

Carlos would resent his interference, and Quentin was out of reach.

He sifted through the deep sand. But his gaze kept shooting back to the mare. She moved evenly but her head carriage was low and she lacked her usual energy. Worse, she seemed to be looking at him with pleading eyes, as if aware he'd helped her last night and she'd appreciate a little more assistance today.

Dex flattened his mouth and walked to the second corner of the ring. He pulled the fork through the sand, feeling for the rasp and trying not to watch the struggling horse. But there was no escaping the heavy sound of her steps, the way she dragged her toes, and even though there were two corners of the ring left to search, he couldn't ignore her distress.

He walked to the center of the ring and stopped in front of the surprised instructor. "I wonder if that mare might need some time off. She coliced last night and looks a little beat. Maybe put her feet in some cold water—"

"Who the hell do you think you are?" the instructor snapped. "I'd certainly notice if there were something wrong. And you're disrupting my session."

"Something wrong out there?" the guard called.

"Yes." The instructor's face reddened and cords stood out on his neck. "Escort this inmate back to the barn. Make sure he remains in his designated work area."

The guard gestured with his thumb. "Get your ass back inside, Tattrie."

Dammit. Dex's gaze shot to the far end of the ring but he turned and trudged toward the barn. He shouldn't have spoken until he'd checked the remaining two corners. The riding instructor was insecure and on a power trip. Besides, his attempt to help the mare had been futile anyway. She still had an hour of lesson left, and the sun was blazing hot.

Juan gloated as Dex walked into the barn. "You ain't going to find it. You're dog meat, Tattrie."

Dex ignored him and continued down the aisle, rejoining Sandy who was trimming a compact gray gelding. Sandy immediately set down the foot, his gaze sweeping Dex's sleeve. "Did you find it?" he whispered.

"Not in the stalls," Dex said. "Not in the manure pile. Not in the left half of the ring."

"What about the right half?"

"I was ordered back," Dex said. No need to tell the kid he'd been impulsive. It seemed the closer he inched toward his parole date, the softer he was turning. And that was folly. He had to harden his heart—to horses, to inmates, to Dani. This wasn't Boy Scouts. One had to be tough and merciless, or the other convicts would skin you alive. Carlos hadn't become top dog by succumbing to sentiment.

"Could we pay the supply guard to say we returned it?" Sandy asked.

"Do you have enough money?" Dex snapped.

"Well, no, just my commissary fund." Sandy's eyes flashed with hurt. "Money's not allowed here."

"And that's the reason it's not allowed," Dex said. "Prisons run on fear."

"So what do we do?" Sandy gulped. "We have two hours before the bus. Should I try to check the ring?"

Dex shook his head. It wasn't safe for Sandy to wander around. At least there was a guard in the shoeing area. And horses were walking into the far end of the barn now so Carlos and his men were afoot. The lesson must have ended early, luckily for the mare.

He shook his head in disgust. He had more important things to worry about than a tired and vulnerable horse. And even though he accepted he was sentimental, it was vital not to reveal that weakness. Carlos and his gang were probably still snickering about his blunder in the ring.

The guard murmured into his radio, his voice drifting as he spoke to another guard. Dex edged closer, straining to hear the conversation. Apparently Carlos had demanded the lesson be ended, and it only underscored the man's scary power that the riding instructor had listened.

"The horse in stall seven?" the guard said, speaking into his radio. "I'll send someone down." He paused. "The young one?" He replaced his radio on his belt and looked at Sandy. "They want you to collect a horse from stall seven, just returned from a riding lesson. Needs his feet trimmed."

Sandy gave a reluctant nod. Stall seven was at the far end, and the same stall where Juan had accosted him last month.

"That horse is a handful," Dex said. "I'll collect him."

"No," the guard said. "The kid should go."

Dex stared at the guard, hiding his consternation. This was a stark reminder of Carlos's insidious control. The voice on the other end had been a guard, and yet somehow Carlos had exerted his influence.

"It'll take two handlers," Dex said. "I'll return this gray to his stall and help out."

"Why does he need two handlers?" the guard snapped.

"That horse has studs on his shoes," Dex said. "And he strikes out. We don't need any more trips to the infirmary."

The guard fingered his radio, then gave a dismissive shrug. "Okay then. You can both go."

Dex tightened the gray's halter, waiting until the guard moved away before slipping the steel tongs up his left sleeve. He unclipped the horse from the cross ties, watching while Sandy concealed a hammer.

He led the horse down the aisle with Sandy following five paces back. They rounded the corner. To the far right, the supply room door was locked and the guard's chair vacant.

Dex balanced on the balls of his toes, every one of his senses screaming. Several cons peered out from behind the meshed screen of their stalls. They'd holed up, and he didn't blame them. It was a vital survival skill not to get involved in other people's grudges.

Behind him, Sandy's breath escaped in ragged gasps. The kid wasn't going to be much good in a fight if he couldn't settle his breathing.

A stall door opened and Juan stepped out. "Finished with that horse?" he asked, not looking at Dex.

Dex nodded. "And picking up one in stall seven."

Juan reached out, taking the gray's lead line. "I'll take him for you," he said.

Dex's fingers coiled over the tip of the tongs, but Juan merely turned and led the gray down the aisle and into his stall.

Juan closed the door and then moved to stall seven. Seconds later, he led out the bay gelding and passed the lead line to Sandy.

Two stalls down, a chestnut mare with a blazed face stood with her front feet immersed in a tub of water. She stretched her neck toward Dex and nickered a friendly greeting. Carlos walked from the side of the stall to stand beside his horse. They both stared at Dex; the mare's eyes were soft and liquid while Carlos's remained dark and expressionless. But Carlos nodded, his head moving an entire inch.

Dex loosened his death grip on the tongs. He nodded back, just as curtly, then turned and walked up the aisle. Sandy followed, leading the bay gelding.

Neither of them spoke until Sandy clipped the horse in the cross ties. "Why didn't they do anything?" he whispered. "There were four of them. And no guards."

"We don't have to worry about Carlos anymore," Dex said. He tried not to smile but his relief was overpowering. "Seems he holds his mare in very high regard. And she's grateful. So he is too."

"Does that mean he won't use the rasp until after your parole hearing?"

"Means he won't use it all," Dex said. He bent and scooped up the missing rasp, magically returned to his farrier kit. And this time he didn't stop himself. He reached out and rumpled Sandy's hair, not caring who saw.

CHAPTER TWENTY-FIVE

"Thanks for taking my horse," Dani's neighbor said, lifting his right wrist and waving a gleaming white cast. "My bones are too brittle for a horse like that. Too bad Dex isn't here."

"I can handle him," Dani said, squaring her shoulders.

"Yes, of course you can." The man fiddled with the brim of his cowboy hat, belying the sincerity of his words. "But Cracker has a nasty streak. I don't usually send horses out for training, but he's too good looking not to invest some money. Maybe I can run him through a sale." He shook his graying head, not looking at all hopeful. "I'll give him away if I have to. But I don't want anyone else getting hurt."

Dani nodded. Cracker was certainly an eye-catching buckskin with a flashy black mane and tail. His head was a little coarse but he looked balanced and powerful, certainly an animal many people would be eager to own.

The man turned toward his pickup. "Just be alert," he called over his shoulder. "He's sneaky."

She sighed and tossed Cracker a flake of hay. Good looking and sneaky seemed to go hand in hand, at least with the males of a species. She still couldn't absorb that Dex was sending money to another woman while she struggled to keep their ranch afloat. It didn't matter any longer though. The 'For Sale' sign would go up as soon as the place was presentable.

She rejoined the two people by the far paddock. Jeffrey hadn't wasted any time calling a real estate agent, and the lady seemed very eager to secure the listing. However, Lorna Thompson didn't look as if she had much experience selling country properties; her high heels and short white skirt were glaringly unsuitable for walking around a ranch. But she had won numerous sales awards and Jeffrey highly recommended her.

"Fresh paint will hide the rundown appearance," Lorna said. She gave Dani a dismissive glance then turned back to Jeffrey. "You need new fence posts and a stall door repaired in the barn. Trim the grass and harrow the ring and track. I've made the house recommendations separately." She passed a file folder to Jeffrey. "Just some basic things like installing a new shower and toilet. If you can't do it yourself, our agency has a list of recommended contractors."

Lorna angled her camera and snapped a picture of the horses eating hay then another of Red scratching his ear. "I like to show contented animals," she said, "especially for the acreages." She glanced down at her shoes and gave Jeffrey a rueful moue. "I'll have to come back and take more pictures. I'm on my way to a meeting but wanted to assess this property immediately."

Jeffrey nodded, his gaze drifting over Lorna's legs. "Come back anytime," he said. "Hopefully I'll be here. But if I'm busy with police work, Dani is always available."

Dani's mouth tightened. Jeffrey made it sound as if she lounged around all day, doing nothing. "I'm busy training horses in the morning," she said, feeling like an outsider. "And I have chores in the afternoon," she went on, "so evenings are best. If that time doesn't work for you, maybe there's another agency who'd like to sell my ranch."

"Evenings are fine," Lorna said, her gaze finally including Dani. "But I'd like to take the pictures during the day. I'll also need your signature on the listing agreement once the papers are prepared. See you both next week," she said, turning toward her car. "Good luck with the repairs."

"What a nice lady," Jeffrey said, watching as Lorna walked back to her car. "She sold the chief's house in one day."

"Seems to know her business," Dani said, more impressed at how Lorna had managed to keep her skirt clean. Maybe the woman had some ranch experience after all.

She brushed a hay stalk off her faded jeans, painfully aware of the contrast in their appearances. No wonder Jeffrey couldn't take his eyes off the agent. No wonder Dex had turned to a hooker.

Other than church and Thursday night dinners, she rarely dressed up. Hadn't felt the need. She'd never noticed Dex looking at other women, unlike Jeffrey who openly watched while Lorna slipped into her cherry-red sports car. But his openness was better than Dex's blindside. At least they could joke about it.

"Maybe you should have taken off your jacket and put it down over the manure," Dani teased. "Help keep her shoes clean."

"There's definitely too much manure around," Jeffrey said, still watching Lorna. "Can you clean it up for her next visit?"

"Horses shit approximately twelve times a day," Dani said crisply. "So, no, I think she'll have to manage."

Jeffrey turned back to Dani, as if aware he'd been staring. "I'm just glad you have a good agent," he said. "Soon you'll be able to live a normal life. Go out at night, take vacations. Imagine, no more worrying about having enough money for hay."

"I can't really imagine that," Dani said. She certainly couldn't imagine not riding every day. "Guess I'll start painting rails this afternoon. And start work with the new horse tomorrow."

"Did that owner pay in advance?" Jeffrey asked, frowning at the buckskin gelding now happily chewing hay.

"Yes." Dani patted her back pocket. "Although it's not really a concern. You've already proven to be an excellent bill collector."

Jeffrey stared, then gave a humble shrug. "Don't mention it. I'll do whatever it takes to make you happy. Just give me a chance, okay?"

She nodded and when his mouth lowered over hers, she kissed him back. And while her enthusiasm didn't match Jeffrey's, it was enough that Red whined in protest.

"I'm making progress with your dog too," Jeffrey said, glancing at Red but keeping his arm looped around Dani. He reached in his pocket and pulled out a treat. Red sniffed it suspiciously then crunched it between his teeth.

"You're going to make him fat," Dani said.

"But the treats are working. He didn't bark when I drove in this morning. I think he's starting to accept me. He looks way more relaxed."

"You're right." She tilted her head. Red looked unusually happy, his coat bright and shiny. Even his muzzle looked less gray. The last few days he'd had a bounce in his step, almost like he was a puppy again. "Guess he likes having a man around," she said. "Less for him to worry about. You even brushed out his tangles. How sweet."

Jeffrey didn't speak for a moment. "So it looks like your dog is okay with us," he said. "Now it's just the lawyer." His voice thickened. "I can't wait for his go-ahead."

"Me either. I'm seeing Eve tonight. Maybe she'll have an update."

"At least a lawyer will keep Dex from ripping you off." Jeffrey's phone buzzed. He checked the display then gave an apologetic smile. "I have to take this. Police business."

Still smiling, he pressed the phone to his ear. But his smile quickly faded. "How the hell did that happen?" he asked. "You were supposed to stop it."

He dropped his arm and shuffled sideways, his voice hardening. "Powerful friends? But they can't just move dates. Yeah, thanks for nothing. I'll call you from the station."

He shoved the phone in his pocket and turned back to Dani. "It's probably easiest if I come back after my shift," he said. "I'll put the new toilet in tonight. In fact, why don't I sleep on the sofa this week? That way I can take care of more repairs."

"But I'm going out with Eve tonight," Dani said. "I won't even be here."

"No problem. Just give me a key and I'll start on the spare bathroom."

"All right," Dani said, still hesitating. She didn't want to hurt his feelings and she appreciated his eagerness to help, but sometimes it seemed she knew more about plumbing than Jeffrey. "Have you ever installed a toilet before?" she asked.

Jeffrey shrugged. "It's not rocket science. I'll move some of my clothes over and work here anytime I don't have a shift. Red can keep me company."

Dani nodded. At least Red wouldn't be locked up and it was nice that Jeffrey was thinking of her dog. "He'll like that," she said. "And thanks for helping. I really appreciate it."

"My pleasure," Jeffrey said.

And this time when he tugged her into his embrace, she ignored Red's whining and enthusiastically kissed Jeffrey back.

CHAPTER TWENTY-SIX

"What are those white spots on your hand?" Eve asked. She tilted on the bar stool, gesturing at Dani's fingers.

"Paint," Dani said, taking another appreciative sip of her drink. Bourbon was good, but she'd forgotten how much she loved the sweet tang of a properly mixed margarita. "I started the south side this afternoon," she added. "That fence is never ending. What a boring job. Even Red disappeared."

"What about your boyfriend?"

"Jeffrey was working." Dani hesitated, playing the word over in her mind. *Boyfriend.* The concept seemed foreign. Not quite right. But Jeffrey was doing all the boyfriend things. He'd driven them here and even offered to return at the end of the night. Now she and Eve could drink together, making for a more relaxing evening.

"He seems okay," Eve said grudgingly, "for a cop. But I didn't realize you lived together."

"We don't," Dani said.

"Sure looks that way. His uniform is there and both his cars are parked in your driveway."

"He takes the police car home so he doesn't have to pick it up at the station." Dani cradled her drink, studying Eve's face. "Why do you dislike the police?"

"They weren't at all helpful when Joey disappeared." Eve's pert nose wrinkled. "If it wasn't for Megan and Scott, I'd still be waiting for Joey to come home. You just can't trust cops. They make their own rules."

"But Scott used to work for the LAPD. So he was police."

"That doesn't count," Eve said, "since he's a private investigator now. All those jobs are like a club. Men have codes that make perfect sense to them...not so much to women. And some cops abuse their power. The others are just lazy, or stupid."

"Tell me more about Tizzy," Dani said hastily, hoping to deflect any more criticism of Jeffrey. "Does your boss really like him?"

"Loves him," Eve said, her smile returning. "This morning we galloped in company and Tizzy finished strong. He wanted to be in front, but you can put him where you want." She clinked her glass against Dani's. "Congratulations. That's because of your excellent training. It makes him easy to rate, even though he's fiercely competitive. He's already a favorite of the exercise riders."

Dani straightened on her stool. Praise from a successful jockey like Eve meant a lot. And the fact that the exercise riders liked to gallop Tizzy was even more significant. "Wish I didn't have to sell him," she said. "It would be great to own a racehorse. Even if he didn't win, it would be fun to stand by the rail and cheer."

"Don't sell him yet," Eve said. "His value is only rising."

"I don't know how long I can wait," Dani admitted. "I had a new horse come in today for training but already spent most of that money on paint. And the real estate agent gave us a big list of recommended repairs."

"Which is why I'm buying the drinks tonight," Eve said.

"No, it's my turn. Besides, that bartender won't take any money. He's very sweet."

"I don't know how sweet he is," Eve said dryly, "but being with you makes for an inexpensive night. I wish he wouldn't hover though. It's difficult to talk. Let's go to another bar."

"But Jeffrey is picking us up here once his shift is over."

"Text him," Eve said, draining her glass. "We'll grab a cab and choose a place on the way."

Dani finished her drink and smiled at the bartender. He was sticking a little too close but no wonder; the place only had six customers. And she and Eve were the only women.

"Hope you come back soon," he said, rushing toward them. "Was that your brother with you earlier? The guy in uniform?"

"No. He's my boyfriend." Dani slid off her stool, realizing she'd finally said the word aloud.

The bartender gave a rueful shrug. "That figures," he said.

"This looks perfect," Eve said, nodding her approval as they walked into a popular lounge the taxi driver had recommended.

The place seemed to have a universal appeal. Bodies writhed on the dance floor while at the bar scantily dressed women flirted with men in leather jackets. In the far corner a hanging light illuminated a busy pool table. There were cowboy hats and suits and everything in between. Yet the music wasn't so loud it would prevent talking.

"I'll get the drinks," Dani said, squeezing between a red-haired woman and a man in a hard hat who kept checking his phone. It took about five minutes to be served but she was pleasantly surprised at the liquor prices—little wonder the place was crowded.

She glanced around for Eve, finally spotting her chatting with a handsome man in a blazer and white T-shirt. Dani wove through the crowd, carefully balancing the drinks.

"Thanks," Eve said, accepting her glass. "This is Shane from the track. He's kicking up his heels tonight too."

Shane gave a friendly smile and continued talking about the weather. However, when he discovered Dani was also in the horse industry, his conversation immediately livened, and they proceeded to take turns talking about the best and worst animals they'd ever ridden, along with the many horses in between.

"That blockheaded chestnut wasn't the smartest horse I ever rode," Shane went on. "But he was the most dependable. He stood over me while the bull pawed and snorted. It was unbelievable. Of course, he was my favorite after that."

Dani nodded, loving all the stories. She couldn't remember how many drinks they'd downed or who had told the wildest horse tales, but she did know it was the nicest time she'd had in years. Since Dex left, she hadn't hung out with many horse people— not committed ones anyway.

She smiled with contentment, rather glad Jeffrey hadn't arrived yet. He would have pretended to enjoy the horse talk, but his eyes would have glazed and she would have felt obliged to change the subject.

"You ever run into a real mean one, Dani?" Shane asked. "A horse that is rotten to the core?"

Dani pursed her lips. "No. Don't think I have."

"Be careful," Shane said. "There aren't many but just like people, they're out there."

A possessive arm slid around her waist. "Who's out there?" Jeffrey asked.

"Bad horses," Dani said, swinging around to greet him. She quickly made the introductions, shocked to realize it was after midnight and Jeffrey's shift was over. He'd even had time to change into street clothes. Part of her wished he hadn't shown up yet, then she immediately felt guilty about harboring such a selfish thought, especially since he was so nice to come and drive them home.

Shane nodded at Jeffrey, then launched into a story about how his usually steady mare had freaked when a loose saddle slipped. He was just getting into the good part when Jeffrey leaned down.

"Let's dance," he said, pulling her onto the dance floor.

It was a slow song and only a few couples were dancing. However, the mood was mellow and once on the floor, she slowly relaxed. Jeffrey tugged her closer, cradling her between his arms and legs, his hand stroking her hair.

She rested her cheek against his chest. It had been a lovely night. Tomorrow, she'd start groundwork with Cracker, then ride the other six horses. The fence painting remained a distasteful task, but for now it was a luxury to simply close her eyes and enjoy the night. And she couldn't stop smiling at Shane's story of the bull. It might have been wildly embellished, but it had definitely been entertaining.

When she opened her eyes, she saw Dex.

She squeezed them shut, accepting that she'd been drinking. And she wasn't accustomed to much alcohol. But when she opened her eyes again, Dex was staring at her.

So much happiness burst in her chest, she could barely breathe. And then hurt and white-hot anger replaced the joy. Jeffrey's mouth skimmed over her neck but all she could do was stare at her cheating husband. The man who didn't care enough to even let her know he'd been released.

He looked good. His hair was shorter than usual, his handsome face even more chiseled, and she didn't remember his shoulders being so broad. His T-shirt clung to the ripples on his chest. Obviously other ladies found him attractive. Already two women fluttered around him, like moths to a flame, their lips bright and inviting. One of the women arched provocatively, rubbing her breast against his arm.

Jeffrey stiffened. Clearly he'd spotted Dex and was also shocked. She jerked her head away, willing her legs not to collapse. It was great Dex was out. But pain coiled in her chest, stunning her with its intensity.

He hadn't even bothered to call.

Her ears pounded and her mind seemed trapped in a thick fog. She gripped Jeffrey's shoulders, struggling to remain upright, struggling simply to breathe. The dance would be over soon. She'd have to say something to Dex, even though her dry throat would make conversation difficult.

Maybe she'd start by asking how long he'd been out. Perhaps join him in a drink and congratulate him on his early parole…then inquire why he hadn't bothered to let her know.

Of course, he had no reason to call. He'd signed all the papers she needed, even turning over Tizzy. But they'd been married once and surely after all that time away, he'd want to talk. If only to check on Red.

She wet her lips, aware her heart was thudding almost as loudly as the music, aware also of a traitorous tingle of anticipation. It was always like this when Dex was around. And maybe he had good reason not to call. Perhaps he'd just been paroled and wanted to surprise everyone. Surprise her.

He had to know she'd be happy about his release. Even with all her hurt and anger and despair, she'd never stopped thinking about him.

The music stopped. She gulped and turned, her lips quivering in a hesitant smile. But there was only a gap at the bar where his big body had been, and her chest split with such horrible pain she feared she was having a heart attack.

She couldn't be dreaming. Or was she? She wheeled, desperately scanning the exit. But there was Dex, already halfway out the door closely followed by a man in a yellow hard hat. The door slammed shut. And her heart shattered.

"Were you talking to him?" Jeffrey asked. "Did you see him? Before I arrived?"

She couldn't speak, could barely manage to shake her head.

"I didn't see him either," Jeffrey went on. "But I'll check with his parole officer. He's supposed to stay away from bars. That's usually a condition."

Jeffrey was still talking about rules and regulations and penalties, his arm supporting her, but Dani couldn't absorb his words. She could barely shuffle back to Eve and Shane. She'd been wondering what to say, how to act. Yet Dex hadn't even wanted to talk.

Maybe he didn't recognize me. She grabbed the thought like a lifeline. That would explain why he'd left. Although she didn't know what was worse: the possibility that he didn't recognize her or that he cared too little to say hello.

Eve's eyes widened on Dani. "You're pale," she said. "Are you sick? Let's go to the bathroom."

Dani nodded, concentrating on putting one foot in front of the other as she followed Eve across the room. Her chest felt odd, empty, as if there was a hole where her heart had been. The last time she'd felt such pain had been when Dex refused to put her on his visitors' list. She'd promised herself she wouldn't let him hurt her, wouldn't agonize over his constant rejections, but now it was happening all over again.

Eve wheeled inside the bathroom, anger sparking her eyes. "I knew that cop was a mistake. What the hell did he do?"

Dani leaned numbly against the sink. "It wasn't Jeffrey," she mumbled. She eyed a toilet stall, wondering if she might be sick. But that felt too much like a victim and she didn't want to be one of those. She turned back to the sink, struggled with a tap, then shoved her entire face beneath the spray of cold water.

When she lifted her head, Eve passed her a wad of paper towel then helped wipe her face.

"Your eye makeup is messed," Eve said with a smile, "but you're still a knockout."

"You and I met two years ago," Dani said. "Do I look the same? Would you recognize me?"

"Of course."

"Dex was here," Dani continued, her voice monotone. "He didn't even say hello."

"I thought he was locked up."

"I did too," Dani said.

Eve frowned. "He didn't even ask about Tizzy?"

"No," Dani said. "Or Red. And he loved that dog. Red still waits for him by the front d-door." Her voice broke, thinking of Red's faithfulness and the man who most certainly didn't deserve it.

"What a prick." Eve shook her head with indignation. "I can understand quitting on a wife but what sort of man deserts a dog?"

Eve's righteous anger made Dani feel better. "Not a nice one," Dani said. She splashed more water on her face, then raised her head. "I really have to get over him, don't I?"

"Yes," Eve said. "And Jeffrey isn't so bad, for a cop."

"He's steady. That's what I want. Someone safe."

"I'll call Scott tomorrow," Eve said, clumsily dabbing at Dani's cheeks. "Find out if his lawyer checked those divorce papers yet. It's time for you to get out of this mess."

"Yes." Dani squared her shoulders. "It's definitely time."

CHAPTER TWENTY-SEVEN

Dex sighed and took another appreciative sip of coffee. For the last three days he'd been spending his lunch hour on the ridge overlooking the Double D. After being deprived of freedom for so long, it was utter bliss to absorb the blue expanse of sky, the smell of fresh grass, the cheeky scolding of the squirrels.

And the solitude was rejuvenating. No steel doors clanged, no guards shouted orders and no lurking inmates tried to stab sharp objects in his ribs. Just having the freedom to climb into the tow truck was exhilarating. The boys at the garage understood. Most of them knew someone who had done time and having a mechanic's job waiting had certainly swayed the Parole Board. Thank God for Luther and the club...although it was the Tattrie connections that had sucked him into this mess.

He shook his head. Didn't matter now. It was over. He was still shocked Dani hadn't sold the ranch and couldn't quite understand how or why she'd kept it going. It needed some solid man hours of work but everything looked functional.

He dragged his gaze away from the sagging posts. The compulsion to roll up the front driveway and grab a hammer was almost overwhelming, but he fought the itch. He'd seen Dani reach up and kiss Jeffrey, saw the cop car parked by the house every morning. It was clear she'd started a new life, just as Jeffrey claimed.

Part of him had hoped that wasn't true. The last few weeks in prison he'd entertained the faint hope clause, that maybe there was a way to win her back. But he'd seen her face in the bar when she was dancing. Her eyes had been closed, her head pressed against Jeffrey's chest, and she'd looked utterly happy. She deserved happiness, even if the sight ripped at his gut.

His fists clenched at the haunting image. He hadn't expected to see her last night, hadn't been ready. He wasn't even supposed to be in a public bar, not while on parole. Had only entered to find the owner who'd called for the tow. But when he spotted Dani dancing, he'd fought the urge to rush across the floor and pound in Jeffrey's pretty face. The man had caused him a lot of flak in prison, but that could be forgiven. It was seeing Jeffrey's hand flattened over her ass that had blown his mind. And he had to be a bigger man than that.

Dani was innocent in all this.

He pulled out his phone and checked the time. Red was late. Maybe he wouldn't come today. The dog seemed to sense when Dex was on the ridge, but perhaps he was busy with Dani and Jeffrey.

Brush rustled behind him. Dex set aside his coffee just before Red launched against his chest. The dog's wet tongue slopped over his face, his body quivering in such ecstasy that Dex's throat tightened. For a moment he couldn't speak.

"Hey, fellow," he finally whispered, his voice raspy. "How've you been?"

He gently pulled his fingers through the long ruff around Red's neck. No more knots. The first day it had taken him forty-five minutes to untangle the hair. Yesterday he'd trimmed Red's toenails, something the dog always hated. However, Red was clearly forgiving, his glowing eyes following Dex with complete devotion.

"Ready for lunch?" Dex reached into his bag. "I've been waiting."

He pulled out his peanut butter and jam sandwich, ripped off a piece and passed it to the dog, then took a smaller bite.

"Chew a little slower," Dex said with a smile. Tomorrow he'd bring two sandwiches. He always ended up giving Red the lion's share and then he was hungry by mid-afternoon. On the other hand, his apartment was just over the garage and he relished the freedom of walking up the stairs and grabbing something to eat whenever he wanted. Right now, he didn't think he'd ever get enough beer and peanut butter.

"You watch over Dani." He scratched the base of the dog's ear. "She has a lot on her plate."

He glanced wistfully over his shoulder. Red had come from the south so that meant Dani was riding. If he walked to the other side of the ridge, he'd probably spot her. She used to ride from six to noon, then they'd both quit for lunch. However, he had no idea of her schedule now.

He'd always been in charge of the broncs, the rank horses who needed to be cowboyed out. Hopefully Jeffrey could handle the buckers. Dani had too much skill to be wasting her time on rough stock. Besides, those types of horses were dangerous. He dragged a hand over his jaw, wondering what kind of rider Jeffrey was. The man didn't even drive a truck. That fact alone made his abilities suspect.

Red trotted toward the ridge, then stopped and gave an inviting whine, as if aware Dex was torn.

"I can't," Dex said. He was no stalker and besides, he really didn't want to see Dani and Jeffrey riding together.

Red tilted his head, his eyes stark with appeal. He gave another pleading whine.

"You're killing me, dog," Dex muttered. But he rechecked the time. The boys purposely left his schedule light. He had a brake job at two and a couple oil changes after that. It wouldn't hurt to climb the ridge and make sure Red returned safely. At least it wouldn't hurt anyone but him.

Red was literally dancing now, racing back and forth between Dex and the tree line, sensing victory. Dex slowly rose.

Dani stopped the mare at the far end of the ring. She waited several minutes, determined to teach the eager horse patience, then finally lifted her hand to the right and moved the horse into a smooth spin. She counted every time they passed the fencepost, one, two, three—a blur of movement—until she hit seven rotations.

"Whoa," she said, dropping her seat and hand. The mare stopped, her nose perfectly aligned with the post. She only needed one-eighth of a rotation to stop after a wicked spin. Some of the bigger striding spinners needed a quarter of the circle, so it was important to say 'whoa' at the proper time.

When Dani had first started training, she'd always spun four times, the number specified in a reining pattern. But horses quickly learned to anticipate and it affected the quality of their spins when they slowed on their own. Now she always changed the number.

She also avoided lead changes and spinning in the middle of the ring, the usual spot for those maneuvers. Reining horses had enough reason to anticipate commands, so she generally schooled in other locations.

But now the mare's spins were excellent. Tomorrow they'd work on sliding stops. The ring would have to be harrowed first though, and she didn't have time to do that until the end of the week. She needed to squeeze in some painting today too and Cracker needed more groundwork, lots of it. He'd been a brute this morning, almost trampling her in the pen. If she did another session this afternoon, it might be possible to toss a saddle on him by Friday.

At least this mare was a joy to work with. However, the reining-bred horses were always special. She loved their athleticism and work ethic. She let the mare relax on a loose rein, rewarding the horse for her efforts. The sun was warm on Dani's face, the birds trilled and she sat on a lovely horse. There really was nowhere else she'd rather be. She closed her eyes, letting her mind drift, relishing the serenity.

When she opened her eyes, Dex was leaning on the fence. Or someone who looked exactly like him. She blinked. Sometimes the spins made her a little dizzy, especially with horses that spun as fast as this mare.

But no, it was Dex. She could tell by the way her dog acted. Red pressed against Dex's leg, tongue lolling and looking proud, as if he'd conjured up her ex-husband all on his own.

"You plussed those spins," Dex said.

She nodded. The spins had felt good, but sometimes it was hard to tell. It had been a while since anyone watched her ride. But it was reassuring that a reining judge might have scored them high. The mare's owner would be happy.

She gulped, still staring. Dex's face appeared carved in concrete and it was definitely more angled. But he hadn't lost weight, at least not in his upper body. On the contrary, his shirt couldn't conceal the ridges. He looked tough and hardened and unaffected by her presence—so far removed from the biker cowboy she'd fallen in love with that he seemed like a stranger.

She jerked her head away and smoothed the mare's mane. She couldn't believe they were talking about reining and spins and scoring maneuvers when all she really wanted to know was that he was fine and that prison hadn't been such a horrible experience. But her throat closed over and the back of her eyes pricked and she could only mourn all that they had lost.

"She might score another half point if the ground was better," Dex said.

"I didn't have time to drag the ring yet," Dani managed.

"Want me to come by tomorrow and harrow?"

No! She did not want that. Jeffrey would not want that. But she didn't say anything. Her head gave a brief nod, seemingly disconnected from her brain.

"All right. See you tomorrow. Stay, Red," he added, as her traitor dog turned to follow.

Red whined in protest but obediently dropped to the ground, his ears pricked. Even the mare's ears shot forward. All three of them watched as Dex strode across the field and climbed the hill. He definitely was bigger. Even at this distance he cut an imposing figure.

She waited until he disappeared. Then she frowned at Red. "I wondered why you kept sneaking off. How did you find him? Is that why you're so happy?"

Red didn't even act ashamed. He merely wagged his tail and looked proud.

CHAPTER TWENTY-EIGHT

Dani pointed her arm, extending the lunge whip and asking Cracker to circle to the left. But the buckskin still faced her, ears flat, small eyes resentful. He even had the audacity to shake his head.

She made a clucking noise and tapped him on the hip. He finally turned and trotted to the left. A little progress. Yesterday, he'd charged forward, almost trampling her, and she'd been forced to crack him on the chest. He was a challenging horse, rebellious the first five minutes, seeming to forget everything he'd learned the previous session.

This morning she'd saddled him in the hope she'd be able to mount, but he definitely needed more groundwork. She couldn't afford any broken bones.

"Hey, Dani," Jeffrey called, stepping up on the rails and peering into the round pen. "I've been looking for you. I'm going to the hardware store. Don't use the new toilet. There's a leak somewhere. I'll stop at the grocery store too and pick up some food for tonight."

"Great," she said, glancing sideways and giving him a grateful smile.

Cracker noticed her inattention. He ducked his head and abruptly changed direction, kicking out first toward her and then aiming high at Jeffrey.

"Wow, he's happy," Jeffrey said, misinterpreting the horse's lethal kicks.

"He's grossly disobedient," Dani said, giving the horse a punishing crack of the whip. "And I don't trust him."

"He sure is a pretty color though," Jeffrey said. "And remember, a few more months and you'll have a receptionist's job. Weekends off and no more barns to clean. Speaking of that, why is the dog locked in a stall?"

"If he sees a horse kicking at me," Dani said, "he'll bite their heels. And I don't want him running around the pen trying to help."

"He sure loves you. He never leaves your side, even when you're riding."

"Not always." Dani gripped the whip tighter. Jeffrey had worked a late shift and was still sleeping when she rose to feed the horses. There'd been no chance to tell him about Dex's visit, about how Dex was coming back today to drag the ring. But there was time now.

She squared her shoulders. "Yesterday Red disappeared while I was riding," she said, "and when he came back—"

"Gotta go," Jeffrey said, checking his phone. "Lorna wants some house measurements finalized and I have a couple other meetings. Have fun playing with the pretty horse."

Dani blinked and dropped her hand, the tip of the whip dragging in the dirt. Playing? Sometimes she played, but most certainly not with this horse. Besides, training was her job, and Jeffrey's tone had been utterly dismissive. Not that it mattered anymore.

Soon she'd have a nine-to-five job. She wouldn't have to worry about problem horses or about how she couldn't afford new fencing. Dex was probably disappointed at the ranch's condition. He hadn't said much though, just stared at her with those inky dark eyes. Jeffrey teased that she didn't talk much, but she was a chatterbox compared to Dex.

She automatically touched her mouth. He'd be here soon. Maybe she should slip into the house and add some lipstick.

Not for Dex, of course, but the sun was overhead and she should have sunscreen. Besides, it was only natural that she wanted to look good, although probably any female would look appealing to Dex after being locked up.

She sighed, hating her ambivalence, her skipping thoughts. She'd heard too many prison shower stories and she didn't want to agonize about Dex anymore, didn't want to worry if he'd been okay surrounded by all those aggressive men.

Heck, if the prison employed female guards, he probably hadn't lacked for companionship. Women always swarmed around him. That was another good thing about Jeffrey. He was good looking but he lacked Dex's blatant sex appeal. There'd be no need to fight off single women or lonely wives or the random ranch visitor. Jeffrey wouldn't leave her bed to sneak off with a sex worker... At least she hoped he wouldn't.

But who knew what a man would do? Dex had certainly been full of surprises. And not the good kind.

Something brushed her shoulder. She turned, uncertain how long she'd been daydreaming. Cracker sniffed at her shirt, evidently puzzled by her stillness. She always wished she had more time to relax and hang out with the horses, more time to figure out their personalities. However, owners paid the bills and they preferred quick and tangible results. And she had to be riding this horse soon.

She stroked his shoulder but Cracker ignored her overture. Instead, he stepped away, his suspicious ears pricked toward the road. Moments later, a truck engine roared in the distance. Her heart pounded and she smoothed her shirt, guessing it was Dex. This road didn't get much traffic, and the tow truck had a distinctively powerful engine.

Moments later, the truck rumbled up the driveway. Jeffrey's police car sat in front of the house, but Dex clearly wasn't intimidated or even curious. He parked mere feet from the marked car.

He stepped from the truck, not looking at the house they had renovated, or at the barn where he had labored building stalls, or at his irrigation contraption that had garnered statewide accolades. He simply walked toward the round pen, moving with his peculiar lazy grace, glancing neither to the right or left.

She wasn't sure how he knew her location. She intended to call out a greeting but her throat constricted and all she could do was stare. It was clear he was so over this ranch. She was the one clinging to the past, the foolish spouse who had stayed, trying to keep it afloat. She'd thought he loved the horses, the dog, the land, every bit as much as her. And she'd wanted to keep it intact. She was an idiot.

"Hi," he said.

"Hi." She fumbled with the whip, switching it to her other hand—anything to keep busy.

"Keys in the tractor?"

"Yes," she said. "The starter's a little wonky, but it should go."

"All right." But he didn't move. She could feel his proximity, her racing heart, and wished now he hadn't come. It would be helpful to have the ring dragged. It had been a couple weeks and the ground was hard and uneven. But seeing Dex churned up too many painful emotions. She'd never even had the chance to yell.

He wasn't looking at her. His dark eyes were narrowed on the buckskin. "You ridden that horse yet?" he asked.

"No. Hopefully later this week."

"Be careful. He has the look."

She nodded. She still had great respect for Dex's horse sense, and after four days of working with Cracker, it was apparent the gelding had an ornery streak. "He's been tough," she admitted, "even on the ground. The owner wants to get rid of him. Thought a couple weeks' riding would help."

"Not many people need a horse like that," Dex said. "Too bad he's a pretty color. Someone will think they scored a deal and end up getting hurt."

"That tends to happen with the good-looking boys." Dani snapped a lead line onto the horse's halter. "They should come branded with a warning. It would save a lot of pain."

Her eyes caught Dex's and for an instant she glimpsed a flash of such anguish, it left her unbalanced. "I was talking about horses not husbands," she added quickly. Then she clamped her mouth, annoyed for even worrying about his feelings. Dex certainly hadn't worried about hers.

"I'll get the tractor," he said, his jaw stiff. "Want the track dragged as well?"

It was clear he didn't intend to talk about the night of his arrest, his time in prison, or even the shambles of their marriage. But it did seem as if he genuinely wanted to help. And there was no better man than Dex around a ranch.

"That would be great," she said. "I haven't dragged it since Tizzy's gallop last month. He's at Santa Anita by the way… Just in case you're wondering. That's why I needed his papers signed."

"How's he doing?"

"Good. Eve—she's a jockey I met when my truck broke down—thought he might make a racehorse. So her boss has Tizzy now."

"What was wrong with your truck? The boys couldn't keep it going?"

Dani stopped Cracker, surprised Dex was more interested in her vehicle than Tizzy. "Well, it's an old truck," she said defensively. "And Dad's mechanic said it wasn't worth wasting any more money."

"The garage would have fixed it for free."

"I couldn't go there," she said. And even though she tried to bury the hurt, her voice quavered. There were too many memories: Dex's apartment with the big soft bed, Red's pen with the three-story doghouse, the special chair Dex had carved so she could watch while he tinkered—she'd thought they shared a relationship that would last a lifetime. Yet it had collapsed in one night.

"I understand," Dex said. But his face was so stony, it was clear he didn't. He certainly wasn't softened by old memories. In fact, his head had already turned to the tractor. He seemed to hesitate a beat, then turned and walked away.

CHAPTER TWENTY-NINE

The ring was perfect, two inches of loose dirt over a firm base. Dex must have dragged it twice. Even Gunner was enjoying it.

Dani deepened her seat in the saddle. "Whoa," she said. The gelding instantly tucked his hind end and slid to a smooth stop. She glanced back, gleefully checking the tracks. It looked like fifteen feet, possibly more.

"What do you think, Red?" she asked. "Fifteen, maybe twenty?" It was always nice to share a spectacular slide, even with a dog. But Red wasn't sitting in his usual spot by the gate. He wasn't anywhere to be seen. She sighed and glanced to where Dex and the tractor chugged around the oval.

Yes, there was her errant dog, trotting happily behind the harrow. She wasn't sure when he'd snuck off. He'd been sniffing by the gate at the beginning of her ride. Now his tongue was lolling and he looked deliriously happy. She hoped Dex knew Red was there. The harrow and tractor wheels were dangerous.

She shifted uneasily, debating about riding over. Dex wouldn't even know Red was loose; the dog had still been locked up when he left on the tractor.

But Dex abruptly stopped and Red charged forward and scrambled into the cab. She blew out a sigh of relief. Dex leaned out, raised his hand and she automatically waved back. No need to worry.

Sometimes Jeffrey wasn't very observant but Dex was different. It was rather nice to ride when someone else was around, when someone would notice if she were bucked off. She and Dex had always worked together, not talking much but aware of each other's presence. Like now.

She jerked her head away, walked the horse forward a few steps then moved him into an easy lope. One more stop. If he slid as good as the first time, she'd end the ride. She could squeeze in one more horse before lunch, or wait and ride in the evening. Probably best to ride the mare now. She wouldn't feel like moving after a big supper. Besides, Jeffrey would want her company.

She circled at the far end, lifted her rein hand and collected Gunner for the rundown. His speed increased until he was galloping down the long end of the ring. She sat back and said, "Whoa."

He tucked his hind end nicely, keeping his head and neck relaxed but this stop wasn't nearly so fluid. His hindquarters twisted to the right and she popped slightly in the saddle. She liked to end her ride on a good maneuver but this was disappointing. The horse felt like he'd been trying, and he'd certainly been set up properly, but the slide had been ragged.

She glanced back, analyzing their tracks, already calculating the best correction. And then she understood. Sometime during their last circle, Gunner had thrown a shoe. She stepped down from the saddle and checked his hind feet. There was still a wide sliding shoe on his left foot but the right hind was bare.

"Guess we'll call it a day, fellow," she said, patting his neck. The farrier wasn't due for another week. She'd have to give him a call. Usually she tried to stretch the time between visits in order to save money. However, when animals were in for training, it was important they receive full value. And she couldn't do much training without sliders. Hopefully she could find the shoe and save some money.

She walked around the ring, leading the horse and following her tracks. The reining plates were wider than normal shoes, giving a better base for the horse to slide, but they were still difficult to spot. She kicked at the dirt as she walked, hoping to feel the metal against her boot.

The tractor rumbled closer and she looked up. Dex cut the engine and stepped down, followed by an eager Red. "Lose a shoe?" he asked.

Red charged up, wagging his tail and acting as if he hadn't known she was in the ring. "Yes," she said, dropping the reins and patting her dog. "But we got some good slides in."

"Looked like he was getting about fifteen feet," Dex said.

"More like twenty," she said quickly.

His low chuckle surprised her. She glanced back then wished she hadn't. Dex was devastatingly attractive but when he smiled his whole face changed, reminding her of the younger, happier man she'd married. And those memories hurt.

Her heart gave a helpless kick and she couldn't help but smile back. "Maybe the slides weren't quite twenty," she admitted, "but I bet they're more than fifteen."

"You're on," Dex said. He opened the gate, walked in and began pacing off Gunner's tracks. Red trotted after him, as if serving as a partisan referee.

"Wait," she said. "Our longest slide was on the other side. And what do I get if I win?"

He looked past her, his eyes glinting with amusement. "A drive back to the barn," he said.

She wheeled. Gunner was already sidling through the gate Dex had left open, grabbing at stalks of grass as he walked, being careful not to step on the dangling reins.

"Hey," she called, rushing after him. But he flattened his ears and broke into a trot, and it was clearly a futile chase. She just prayed he wouldn't step on the reins and snap the leather, or worse, yank the bit and hurt his mouth.

"Sorry about that," Dex said.

"It's all right," she muttered. The old Dex never made mistakes around horses; he was freaky observant. But in prison, guards probably looked after shutting doors, and she didn't want him to feel bad. No doubt, it was a tough transition, from prison to freedom. "That horse is smart about the reins," she added, hiding her worry. "I've let him loose before to eat grass. It's no big deal."

Dex just stared at her, so closely she fidgeted. He always said she was a lousy liar. "You don't have to worry about him stepping on the reins," he said quietly. "The horse just slipped his bridle."

She pivoted in disbelief. She wasn't surprised Gunner had pulled off his bridle. The old headstall didn't have a throatlatch, but Dex had been watching her the whole time. How had he seen? There was no question though. Gunner's head was bare now and he was happily grazing, keen to take full advantage of his freedom.

"We can pick up the headstall on the way back," Dex said. He turned and seconds later scooped up the missing shoe.

"It's not twisted," he said, inspecting the metal. "I can nail this back on, if you want."

"That would be great," she said. More than great. It would save her forty dollars. And Gunner wouldn't miss any training days. Naturally Dex had found the shoe in seconds while she'd searched for five minutes without success. He was so damn capable it was almost irritating. Except she wasn't irritated; she was relieved. And that was annoying in itself.

She crossed her arms and edged away. "I'm going to go catch Gunner. He shouldn't be wandering around loose. And Jeffrey will be back soon."

"Don't you want to see how far you slid?" Dex continued pacing off the slide, totally unfazed by her reference to Jeffrey. "Surprising," he said, staring at the ground.

"What?" she asked. And just like Red, she followed Dex. "Is it twenty feet?"

"Only eighteen. Let's check the one on the other side."

She nodded, positive the stop on the left side of the ring had been her best. And if this slide measured eighteen, the other had to be twenty. Maybe even more. This was an element she'd sorely missed, the camaraderie of another rider, someone who could stoke her competitive nature.

"Are you sure you're measuring correctly?" she asked. "Do you remember your stride length?" Her eyes dropped to his stiff new boots. Of course, he would have needed to buy everything. He'd probably walked out of prison with only the shirt on his back.

"Your clothes are boxed up in the spare bedroom," she added. "There's no need to buy new stuff. Your tack is still here too."

His stride shortened. If she hadn't been watching his feet, she would have missed it.

"I expected you to sell my tack," he said. "The ranch as well." His eyes flickered over the sagging posts. "Clearly it's too much for you."

She lifted her chin, hiding her hurt. He'd left her high and dry, without a thought as to how she'd manage. And yes, it had been a struggle. Too many nights she'd cried herself to sleep. But the ranch was still here and that was a triumph in itself, even if he didn't realize, or care.

"We managed... Jeffrey and I," she said. "But I've decided to sell now. The real estate agent was out last week. We'll need to work out how to split any assets."

She drew in a fortifying breath, preparing to discuss numbers, but he just glanced around the land.

"Is selling what you want?" he asked.

She nodded. "Jeffrey thinks he can find me a job at the town office. And his place is only a ten-minute commute."

"I can't imagine you living without horses," Dex said.

"And I couldn't imagine you living in prison," she snapped. "Or picking up a hooker." The words rushed out, unbidden but truthful. It was impossible to pretend his betrayal didn't still ache. And it was bewildering he didn't have any regrets, that he could walk away from the ranch, from her, with no worries about anything except giving money to the family of a dead woman.

But he just looked at her, his face stony. "I told you I didn't have sex with her."

"You rented a room, she had no cl-clothes—" Dani shook her head, horrified to feel the sting of tears. She twisted, trying to conceal the wetness staining her cheeks. But Dex's hands wrapped around her shoulders, preventing her from leaving. And her tight control finally snapped.

She wheeled, pummeling his chest with her fists, her emotions erupting in a mixture of frustration, rage and sorrow.

She cried until she was empty, until her face was pressed against his soaked shirt and her breath came in shuddering gasps.

"I'm sorry, Dani." His hands were entwined in her hair, his voice so raspy it was unrecognizable.

She glanced up, shocked to see the unmistakable sheen of tears in his eyes.

"Why," she whispered brokenly. "So many nights I wondered what I did wrong. If I had dressed different, acted different—"

"No." He cupped her face in his big callused hands. "It wasn't you. Never you."

"Then why?" She hiccupped, unable to control her quaking voice. "I thought you were happy. That we were happy."

"I was. We were." He stared down, his eyes dark with intensity. "We could be again."

She almost choked with disbelief. "No." She flattened her palms over his chest and pushed him away. "Do you think I'm an idiot? After what you did. How could anyone trust you?"

He didn't speak for a moment. "At least let me help you get the place ready for sale," he finally said, stooping and patting Red.

She scrubbed at her cheeks while he wasn't looking, glad she had a chance to harness her emotions. To match his composure. And his offer, while tempting was problematic. Dex would be a tremendous help but Jeffrey would resent his presence. On the other hand, it would be a good way to prove to herself that she no longer loved Dex.

"I can pick up some fence posts tomorrow," Dex went on, as if sensing her indecision. "How many do we need? About twenty?"

"More like forty." She tugged at her lower lip. "But what about your work at the garage?"

"I'll juggle my time. The job was mainly to satisfy the Parole Board. Let me help. It's the least I can do."

True. And it would help them both. She pressed her lips together then nodded, her stomach giving an uneasy flip. However, there was nobody handier than Dex and she'd be a fool to turn down free help. Even Jeffrey couldn't argue with that.

CHAPTER THIRTY

Dex slowed the tractor and leaned across the cab, pretending to examine the string of fence posts. Dani twisted in the seat, following his gaze.

"That section of fence is okay," she said.

"I'm not so sure," he said. Her head was only inches away and he drew in her familiar scent, reveling in her closeness. "We should check them all," he went on, feigning rapt attention in a post. "Is that rot on the bottom?"

She peered to her right. So did Red, who was crammed in the space between them. She'd wanted to walk back and catch her horse, but the dog's presence seemed to reassure her, and Dex had been able to coax her into the tractor under the guise of checking the fencing. Of course, he had no intention of driving back to the barn anytime soon. Being with her was a slice of heaven, and he intended to grasp every minute. Helping her horse escape earlier had been well worth it.

"Yes," he said firmly. "That looks like rot. We better check the other side." He swung the wheel and turned the tractor.

"Wait. I'm sure it's only dirt. Besides," she checked over her shoulder, "I have to go back. Gunner is loose."

"He's happily grazing," Dex said.

"But it's lunchtime and I need to feed hay. Besides, I'm hungry too. Just stop and I'll walk back."

"Here." He kept the tractor rumbling forward but reached below his seat and pulled out a brown bag. "You can share my lunch."

"That's okay." She paused. "What do you have?" She peeked in the bag, then glanced up, her smile so beautiful, so open, his breath stalled. "Is that peanut butter and jam?"

He nodded, not speaking, simply absorbing her expression. This was the first time she'd looked like that, unguarded, without the hurt confusion that ripped at his chest. They'd always enjoyed these simple moments, had never needed much of anything except each other.

"I haven't had one of those in a while," she said, giving an appreciative sniff. But she reluctantly closed the bag. "I'm not going to eat your lunch though. I can get something back at the house."

He pulled out a sandwich and placed it in her hand, grabbing any excuse to touch her. "I brought two," he said. Red whined and placed his paw over their joined hands, urging them to hurry and eat. They both smiled. Unfortunately her expression reverted to its familiar wariness.

He replaced his hand on the steering wheel knowing that if he pushed, she'd bolt. On the positive side, she hadn't said she loved Jeffrey... Only that she didn't trust him. And while he'd convinced himself that he only wanted the best for her, Jeffrey definitely lacked substance. "There's bottled water," Dex said. "And coffee in the thermos."

He increased the tractor's speed, gunning toward the far end of the pasture. It was obvious she didn't want to linger and have lunch with him. But the sandwich was in her hand and he guessed she hadn't eaten since breakfast.

He glanced sideways, relieved when she finally took a bite. Of course, she'd be too generous to eat alone. In another second, she'd stop chewing and worry about his appetite. He increased the speed of the tractor, putting even more distance between them and the house. If Jeffrey returned within the next half hour, it would be a long hot walk.

She swallowed her first bite then paused, as he knew she would. "You must be hungry too. Do you want to eat while you're driving?" Her voice turned hopeful. "Or wait until you're back at the barn?"

"No, I'll eat with you." He stopped and shut off the engine, ignoring her dismay. "So it looks like we need forty posts," he added, "and twenty-five gallons of paint. Do you have someone lined up for the painting?"

"I've been painting a few hours every afternoon," she said, passing over the lunch bag.

"That's a lot of work." He pulled out the remaining sandwich, trying not to be distracted when she licked some jam off her top lip. He jerked his head away and cleared his throat. "Are you sanding the holes and priming?"

"I thought it would be fine with just one coat," she said. "The fence by the ring looks okay."

"But savvy buyers are going to check. I can prepare the fence for you. Won't take long…with the two of us."

"Okay, thanks." She pulled off a piece of crust and fed it to a grateful Red, not appearing to notice the way he'd linked them. "Jeffrey is updating the bathroom so he doesn't have time to paint. He works a lot of shifts."

Okay, so she had noticed. But at least Jeffrey was busy. Dex opened the cooler and passed her a bottle of water. "I'll come over early tomorrow," he said. "Do some shoeing while you're riding. How many reiners are here?"

"Three." She tilted her head. "But you don't usually trim reiners. You always said they were complicated."

"I did a lot of farrier work in prison." He almost winced, hating the 'p' word. Being around Dani reminded him of how sweet and untarnished some people were. "We had a good library," he added. "Now I can do more than nail on a shoe."

"You always were good. And I'm glad you were able to get outside. I didn't realize there were horses there." She gave Red another piece of crust, her voice empathetic. "Being around the animals must have helped."

He nodded, his throat tight. "There was one mare in particular, a big pinto named Gypsy. She saved me." He was surprised to be talking about his time inside but Dani had always been able to slip beneath his surface. "You would have liked her," he said. "She was brave, strong and loyal. A good horse."

"So you rode a lot?"

"No. Horses were trained for resale, but I mainly did farrier work."

He went on to talk about Quentin and the setup of the work farm, then couldn't believe the way he rambled. But she listened with big expressive eyes, even nodding in understanding when he spoke of Sandy's greenness and Tinker's irritating tendency to talk.

"Will you ever see them again?" she asked. "Maybe when they get out?" Her phone chimed and she twisted, tugging it from the pocket of her jeans. "Excuse me," she murmured, pressing the phone to her ear.

"Hi, Jeffrey," she said. "I'm in the tractor with Dex. We're checking the fencing."

She paused. Dex couldn't hear Jeffrey's words but his tone was authoritative and Dani's smile quickly turned to a frown. Her chin even lifted in a stubborn tilt. *Good. Very good.* She never liked to be pushed around.

"No, I think it's a good idea," she said. "It's his place too."

And then Jeffrey said something else, his voice softening. She smiled again and Dex's heart sank.

"Great," she said. "See you in a few minutes."

She cut the connection and shoved the phone back into her pocket. "I really need to go back." She paused, folding and refolding the empty sandwich wrap. "Sometime we need to talk about the asset split," she said. "A lawyer is looking at the agreement you left, but Eve's brother-in-law said it seemed straightforward."

"You hired someone?" He'd wanted to make things easy, hadn't wanted her to go through the expense and hassle of finding a lawyer.

"No, the service is free," she said. "Eve arranged it. Her brother-in-law, Scott, is a private investigator. He took it to his lawyer."

"So you haven't filed yet?" He bent down and pulled out his thermos, trying to pretend her answer was unimportant.

She shook her head. "Scott's coming out with it soon. But we... I thought someone should look it over before signing."

"So legally we're still married?"

"Yes," she said.

"The important thing now," he said, almost giddy with relief, "is to fix this place up. I'll start with the fencing and anything else after that."

She automatically took the coffee he passed her, apparently forgetting her rush to return to the house. "That would be great," she said. "I'd like to have the ranch on the market soon. But I don't know...Will you be okay with Jeffrey?"

She studied him over the coffee, her eyes blue and wide and troubled. His hand twitched with longing, remembering the curve of her neck, the smoothness of her skin, and how her eyes darkened when he tilted her head and kissed her. And she was sitting right here beside him. Such a well of contentment filled him, he thought he might burst.

"Dex?"

He gulped. "Pardon?"

"Jeffrey? And you being around. Don't you think it might be awkward?"

Dex forced a negligent shrug. "No reason to be," he said.

CHAPTER THIRTY-ONE

Dani peered into the bathroom. Jeffrey was still on his knees, tools scattered around the base of the toilet. "Is it still leaking?" she asked.

"Yes." Jeffrey sighed and tossed a wrench on the floor, clearly frustrated. "I can't figure out what's wrong," he said. "When Eve and that PI come, have them use the other bathroom, just in case."

Dani nodded. It was tempting to ask Dex to fix the leak. He could probably do it in five minutes. But that would only hurt Jeffrey's feelings. For the last couple of days, the two men had skirted each other like dogs circling before a fight. She needed to keep them apart. And while Jeffrey had good intentions, few men were as capable as Dex. Of course, once the ranch was sold, Jeffrey's handiness, or lack of it, wouldn't matter. Not in the least.

Jeffrey rose and wiped his hands, then followed her into the kitchen. "It'll be good to get that agreement in front of a judge," he said. "Dex is a good worker but I don't trust his motives. He's probably angling to claim more of the ranch."

"He made the down payment," Dani said.

"And you made more than two years of mortgage payments while he was locked up." Jeffrey's voice rose. "And now he's walking around like the risen Christ."

"I just want to be fair. Let's see what Scott Taylor says."

"Scott Taylor?" Jeffrey's voice changed, his eyes widening. "*He's* Eve's brother-in-law?"

"Yes, do you know him?"

"The man's a legend," Jeffrey said. "He was part of that group who stormed the Sanchez cartel a few years ago. When's he coming? I want to meet him."

"They'll be here around three." She glanced out the window. Dex was making good headway with the poles, despite the noon heat. He stopped to pat Red then abruptly lifted his arms, his muscles bunching.

Oh no, now he was pulling off his shirt. The skin glistened over his back. He didn't seem to have any new tattoos and there was definitely no prison pallor. But he certainly had new muscles. Everything was hard and smooth and defined, the color of bourbon but twice as potent. She wet her lips, then yanked her gaze away.

"Think I'll tell him to check the septic." Jeffrey moved closer to the window, his eyes narrowing. "We should make good use of him while he's here. Those ex-cons are accustomed to grunt work."

She turned from the window. Dex had slipped so easily back into her day, it was easy to forget where he'd been. And why.

"We'll have to keep him away from Scott Taylor too," Jeffrey went on. "Scott has zero tolerance for drugs, and for cowards like Dex who protect their dealers."

Dani scooped the lunch dishes from the table, rattling the plates in disapproval. Eve had mentioned a similar thing about Scott, and everything Jeffrey said was true. However, Dani didn't like people bashing. Ever. "It must be very hard to move on after prison," she said, "if people refuse to forgive."

"I'm just upset at how he treated you." Jeffrey turned and splayed his hands around her hips. "It's not something that should be forgiven. He put you through hell."

She gripped the plates, determined not to obsess. But it had been hell. And Dex might be working hard but it was based on self-interest. She hadn't heard a word from him when he was in prison. Even her frantic letters after the wind destroyed the barn roof had been returned, unopened. He'd cut her from his life and that was fine. However, his helpful act now was too late. Naturally he wanted to raise the value of the ranch. But she'd moved on. With Jeffrey.

Red barked, leaving Dex's side and trotting down the driveway to greet the approaching sports car.

"Looks like the real estate agent," Dani said, placing the plates in the sink. "She'll be happy to see all the new fencing."

She and Jeffrey walked outside, waiting on the verandah as Lorna Thompson opened her car door and walked toward them.

"I have a release here," she said, patting her leather case. "Dani, if you could have your husband sign, that would be perfect. Will obtaining his signature be a problem?"

Dani's gaze drifted to the field. "No, he's eager for the sale too. He's the one who fixed all the fences."

Lorna glanced over her shoulder. She stiffened then adjusted her sunglasses, studying the long string of posts. "Oh, my," she said. "If *he* came with the property, I could charge an extra twenty percent."

"He's an ex-con," Jeffrey said. "They're good at hard labor."

"I'm not talking about his labor," Lorna said, her voice husky. "Would you mind," she said, her eyes still on Dex, "if I witnessed the signing of this paper myself?"

"Not at all," Dani said. "He probably needs a break."

Lorna pivoted and hurried across the rough ground. Dani watched, amused, wondering how she could possibly slip between the rails in her tight skirt. And Dex wasn't making it easy. He'd turned his back, effortlessly positioning the earth auger and ignoring the approaching woman.

"I don't get it." Jeffrey blew out a frustrated sigh. "Why are women always attracted to cons?"

Dani indulged in a last peek of her shirtless ex, but prudently refrained from explaining. If Jeffrey didn't understand Dex's attraction, he never would. "Don't worry," she said, giving his arm a reassuring pat. "Most women prefer a gun and a uniform."

"But what about you?" He captured her hand. "What do you like? Cop or con?"

"That's obvious," she said, trying to deflect the question.

"But sometimes it's not," Jeffrey said. His hand tightened and it was clear he needed her answer.

She swallowed, trying to choose her words carefully yet still be honest. "I was madly in love with Dex once," she said. "But that was back when I was young and naïve. It might not be possible for me to love like that again, but I'm ready to try. And it's more important to be with someone I trust, someone who has my back and who knows I have theirs."

"Good." Jeffrey gave her hand a relieved squeeze. "That certainly rules out Dex."

"Yes," Dani said, proud her voice was devoid of even a hint of wistfulness. "That certainly does."

Jeffrey glanced at the two figures by the post. Lorna was gesturing now, her hands flying around her face, standing so close to Dex there was barely any space between them.

"I've always considered Lorna an ice princess but she looks ready to do him right in the field." Jeffrey shook his head in reluctant admiration. "Let's give them some privacy. Dex won't need a motel room for her."

Dani pulled her hand away. "Please don't do that anymore," she said.

"What?" Jeffrey asked, his voice innocent.

"Those constant pokes about Dex. It's not necessary. Bad enough I have to listen to Dad. I don't need that from you."

"I'm sorry," Jeffrey said. "But I can't help worrying. I don't know what he's up to but the way he looks at you is scary."

Dani shook her head. Beneath his rugged exterior, Dex was the kindest person she knew. Maybe he didn't smile a lot and he often looked rather fierce, but that was just his way. "He'd never hurt me," she said.

"I know he wouldn't hurt you," Jeffrey said. "That's not what I'm afraid of."

CHAPTER THIRTY-TWO

Dani tightened the cinch, watching as Cracker's ears flattened.

"Stop it," she said, tugging downward on the bit. It was time to climb onto his back and this was the ideal day. The sun was high and hot, and he might be a little less feisty. Besides, she was in the mood for a tough ride. And it was *not* because Lorna had returned to the house with flushed cheeks and a dreamy look in her mascara-caked eyes.

Besides, Lorna had only been with Dex for fifteen minutes and that certainly wasn't enough time for sex. Dex preferred to make love slow. Or usually he did.

She swallowed, remembering a few occasions when it had been hard and fast, and that had been fabulous too. Maybe, as Jeffrey said, the long prison stay had left Dex sex starved. But surely he would have been with plenty of women by now. There was no need to hook up with the real estate agent in their back yard. It was impolite and improper. Definitely not good use of his work time.

She shook her head with growing indignation. He could have fixed three fence posts in the time he'd spent with Lorna.

"You riding that horse today?" Dex's low voice sounded from the side of the round pen.

"Yes," she said, not turning around.

"Probably someone should be watching." His voice moved closer as he climbed onto the rail. "That buckskin appears a tad unpredictable."

"Jeffrey's in the house," she said.

"That won't help if you fall off and hit your head."

Her teeth clenched. "I've ridden alone for the last twenty-nine months," she snapped, "so forgive me if your concern doesn't feel genuine."

Boots thudded as Dex dropped to the ground behind her. "What's wrong?" he asked.

He stood way too close, and her skin danced with a familiar awareness. It was much easier to be close to Dex when he was driving the tractor or pounding posts. She didn't like being the subject of his laser focus. Was too afraid of what he might see. And she certainly didn't want to stare at a bare, sweaty chest...probably still marked with Lorna's lipstick.

She pushed Cracker's head to the right and led the horse several steps away, creating some distance. Only then did she glance over her shoulder. "Nothing's wrong," she said, relieved to see he'd replaced his shirt. Not that it did much to hide his body; it merely emphasized the strong arms, that rippled chest, his broad shoulders. She gulped. Little wonder Lorna had been crawling all over him.

"If you've finished socializing," she said, "perhaps you could check the septic. I have no idea when it was last emptied or who to call."

"Socializing?" Dex arched an eyebrow. "I'm not sure if that's what you and I are doing. But I believe this horse could be dangerous. So I'm going to hang around here until you've finished riding."

He sounded both amused and implacable, and she knew from experience there was little sense in arguing. Besides, he clearly wasn't thinking of Lorna. It really wasn't his fault the agent had been hitting on him. He had that effect on women.

"Fine," she said, her voice not quite as crisp. "But you'll have to stand outside the pen. And watch your head. He's a kicker."

"Yes, ma'am." Dex's exaggerated salute almost made her smile, but he turned and climbed over the rails. She grabbed the chance to admire his lean hips tucked into those long faded jeans, quite certain only the horse heard her admiring sigh.

Actually she was rather relieved by his capable presence. It was always wise to have someone around when riding tough horses.

She collected the reins and stepped onto Cracker's back. He stood quietly, his ears and body relaxed. Any unsuspecting rider would never imagine he was capable of throwing a fit. She squeezed her legs, asking him to walk. Cracker flattened his ears but stepped forward, turning obediently to the left when she picked up the rein. She had a snaffle in his mouth and she kept two hands on the reins, determined to keep her body relaxed, to give him no reason to be concerned.

She picked up the left rein again, asking him to turn in small circles. He remained supple and relaxed so she switched to the right rein and repeated the exercise. So far, so good.

She moved back to the left rein and pushed him into a trot. He jogged easily, turning every time she lifted her hand. She changed directions, switching to a jog on the right rein. He pinned his ears, his body stiffening. She tightened her legs and clucked, insisting on a jog. His head abruptly shot down and he tried to buck, but she yanked his nose to the left. He crow hopped around the round pen, but she kept him circling and after several attempts, he settled and jogged smoothly, turning to the right every time she picked up the rein.

She stopped in the middle of the pen and loosened the reins, rewarding him for his efforts. "Maybe he's not so bad," she said, turning toward Dex. "I'll take him to the ring tomorrow and try some loping. He's not real strong and it's easy to keep his head up."

"Yeah," Dex said, his eyes narrowed on the horse. "But I don't like the look in his eyes. I've only seen that a couple times, like he's scheming—"

Cracker's head abruptly lowered. He lashed out with a jarring buck and Dani's chest smashed into the saddle horn. She dropped one of the reins but was able to grab the horn and regain her seat before he bucked again. She leaned back, desperately yanking on the rein, trying to pull him off balance. Soon his bucks softened to ineffectual crow hops. She gave him a punishing kick and pushed him around the pen, furious at his sneakiness.

Five minutes later, she let him stop in the center of the pen. She relaxed the reins but kept a careful feel, prepared for his tricks now. He stood obediently, his neck relaxed. He even rested a hind leg.

"I wonder if it's when you talk," Dex said. "Maybe he's learned it's easier to dump riders when they're not paying attention."

Dani grinned, rather exhilarated from the ride. "So he'll be a good horse for a quiet person—"

Cracker immediately bucked again but this time she was ready and easily kept his head up. He swelled up, humping his back, but he wasn't super athletic and it was easy to keep him between her hands and legs. He squealed in frustration, sounding so much like a pig that she laughed.

Her laugh seemed to infuriate him. He shot forward, twisting at the last minute and trying to ram her leg into the wooden rails of the pen. She kicked his ribs and he squealed again, leaping high into the air.

Dani kept his nose up but something wasn't right. He was all crooked, his head to the side. She stiffened, abruptly realizing his intent and jammed her leg back, lifting the stirrup toward his hip just before his side hit the ground.

She heard Dex's curse but stayed on the horse's back, refusing to jump off and reward Cracker for another nasty trick. She kicked him until he rose to his feet, then loped him in circles. Ten minutes later, she stopped in the middle of the pen and cautiously lowered the reins.

Dex popped up beside her and grabbed the reins. "Get off," he said, his voice low and urgent. "Don't speak. Just get off. He's not worth it."

She wavered, breathless with exertion. Her legs felt like jelly. The buckskin's neck was lathered too, his left side caked with dust from his suicide drop to the ground. If he rebelled again, she'd have to keep riding, and that wouldn't be healthy for either her or Cracker. Probably best to quit while they were ahead.

She nodded and stepped off.

Dex wordlessly removed the bridle, replacing it with a rope halter. His movements were oddly jerky. "I'll cool him out," he muttered.

"That's okay. I can do it." She pulled off her helmet and wiped her brow. Dex's face appeared carved in granite, and he didn't look at her. Clearly he wasn't impressed with her riding, but Cracker had surprised her. And unlike Dex, she wasn't used to nasty outlaws.

"Would you have done anything differently?" she asked. "Should I wear spurs next time? I'd really appreciate any tips."

Dex dropped the bridle and whirled. Seconds later, his arms squeezed her so tightly she could barely breathe.

"Goddammit, Dani," he muttered. "You shouldn't be doing this alone."

His heart pounded so loudly she could barely hear his words, and for a moment she simply stood there, absorbing his concern and just wishing they could wipe away the past…

Then she pushed him away.

He immediately dropped his hands, but he didn't step back, and their ragged breathing mingled in the hot air. He stared down, the concern in his eyes unmistakable. Traitorous warmth flooded her chest. He might not love her but at least he still cared about her safety.

"I'll work with the horse the rest of the week," he said, his voice almost angry. "But he shouldn't be run through any auction. It's criminal."

Her chest turned cold. Clearly she'd misunderstood his concern, and it stung that he believed she'd want to dupe the public. "I'm not the one selling him," she said, crossing her arms. "But I guess you know all about criminal."

"That's right," he said. "I do." His face shuttered and the quiet lengthened into a brittle silence.

She fiddled with the buckle of her helmet, aware she'd hurt him, and just wishing the words could be pulled back. "I'm sorry about that criminal crack," she finally said. "I'm not being very Christian. You're working hard and I appreciate that. Jeffrey and I both do. But it's hard to forgive. I'm sorry but I'll always resent what happened. I do appreciate your help with Cracker though. It made me braver that you were here. So...thank you."

"Did you have many broncs come in for training?" he asked, his jaw still tight.

"A few. Sometimes I pretended you were here," she admitted, "so the customers would have more confidence. I wrote a lot of letters, telling you about the horses and asking advice. But they came back unopened." She kept her voice carefully level. "It was then I realized you no longer cared about the ranch...or anything on it."

"I couldn't see you." His voice lowered, so soft his words were barely audible. "I couldn't even think about you. You have to understand. I wouldn't have made it."

She shrugged. "It doesn't matter now."

She grabbed Cracker's lead line and led him toward the gate. The fact that Dex hadn't thought about her was a revelation in itself. He was a strong-minded man but how could someone just shut off thoughts and feelings? She certainly couldn't.

"Do you want to see Red?" she asked, her voice cool. "I locked him in a stall so he wouldn't get kicked, but he'd probably like to hang out with you. Just be careful of him around the septic."

Dex didn't answer and she glanced back, her hand on the latch. He stood unmoving. His powerful fists were clenched, but his dark eyes were oddly helpless. For a moment she waffled. A part of her would always love him—she'd admit that. But he didn't deserve any more of her tears. The only thing they could do was finish this.

"Scott's coming by with the divorce papers this afternoon," she said. "Sorry I took so long. I just wasn't ready to sign... Not until you were released." She took a big breath, hating this messy part, but it couldn't be ignored any longer. "You had them drawn up over two years ago? Is there anything you want changed?"

He just looked blank so she kept talking.

"I know you made the down payment," she said, "but I was still hoping for thirty percent of the proceeds. I don't want to squabble though. And of course Tizzy is all yours. I had to have my name on the papers so he could go to Santa Anita. But I'll sign him back. I hope he races well and gives you a lot of fun."

She blew out a liberating breath. She hadn't been able to talk about the division of assets before, had been afraid she'd start crying. But she was on a roll now and if she spoke quickly, it was easy to ignore the growing tightness behind her eyes.

"I guess the big issue is Red," she went on. "I'll always love him, but I think he'd rather be with you." Her lower lip quivered and it felt like her throat was jamming. Perhaps she wasn't quite as strong as she hoped.

"Anyway, I can't talk about this right now," she muttered.

She pushed open the gate and rushed Cracker from the round pen, retreating toward the dark barn where she could wipe her eyes in private.

CHAPTER THIRTY-THREE

"Scott Taylor's here," Jeffrey called, not even mentioning Eve. He pushed open the door and hurried out to greet the gray sedan.

Dani followed more slowly, amused Jeffrey was so impressed with the private investigator. Usually he didn't say anything complimentary about investigators, relegating them to a spot somewhere between lawyers and criminals.

She glanced toward the pasture, instinctively scanning for Dex. He appeared to be finished with the septic and was back sweating over the posts. She brushed aside her stab of guilt. His hard work increased the value of the property and that would mean more money in his pocket.

"Hi, Dani," Eve called, stepping out of the car and giving Red a quick pat. Her gaze swept the property. "Wow, this place looks great. You've done a lot of work."

"It's mainly Dex," Dani admitted. "He accomplishes a lot in a short time."

"He's definitely building up his man points." Eve shielded her eyes with her hand and glanced across the field. "Good God. Is that him?" Her voice lowered. "The pictures don't do him justice. How do you deal with that?" she whispered. "How does Jeffrey?"

Dani jammed her hands in her pockets, faking nonchalance. "We're just happy he's getting the work done. Jeffrey ignores him. He knows Dex and I are through."

"Yes," Eve said, "but men get jealous, just like women. And forgive the observation," she paused to theatrically fan her face, "but Dex makes me think of break-the-bed sex."

Dani sighed. It would help if Dex kept his shirt on. Women circled him like mares in heat. She'd never worried about his faithfulness before, but the hooker incident had rocked everything. Of course, it didn't matter anymore. "Go talk to him." She waved an airy hand. "He probably needs a break."

"I have a boyfriend." Eve's dark eyes flashed with mischief. "But that's no reason I can't admire the scenery. So yes, thanks. Think I'll wander out and give Dex an update on Tizzy."

"Oh, wait," Dani said. "He's probably thirsty. Do you mind taking him a bottle of water? There's a cooler by the barn."

She ignored Eve's knowing smile and turned to Scott who was already deep in conversation with Jeffrey. She hesitated, wishing she could meet with Scott alone. Jeffrey would only complicate things. Besides, it wasn't his business how she and Dex split the property.

Scott nodded at something Jeffrey was saying. But when his eyes settled on Dani he immediately walked around the car. "Good afternoon," he said, reaching out and shaking Dani's hand. "This won't take long. Do you have a room where we can talk privately?"

"Yes, of course." She gestured at the house, thankful he'd sensed her desire for privacy.

He walked beside her to the house, his interested gaze sweeping the paddocks. "You have some different horses this month," he said.

"Yes. A couple new ones are in for training. And Tizzy is at Santa Anita now. We own about half of the twenty here. But by next month, most of our private horses should be sold."

"It's tough leaving a ranch," Scott said, following her inside. "It's not just a home, but a way of life. Hopefully you can find a way to keep riding."

"I'd like to keep Peppy, my retired barrel racer," she said, settling into a kitchen chair. "I've had him since I was fourteen. I don't think Dex would insist I sell him?" But her voice rose in a question because she'd been making lists for weeks. And no matter how they split things, the division always gave her a headache, especially since she and Dex valued the same things.

"No," Scott said. "I think you can bank on keeping Peppy." He didn't explain his comment though, just clicked open his briefcase and flipped through a collection of papers. She spotted the butt of a gun, a set of handcuffs and a velvet display of silver-feathered earrings.

"Those earrings aren't mine." Scott smiled, following her gaze. "My wife makes jewelry."

"They're beautiful," Dani said politely, folding her hands and trying to ignore her jitters. One signature—then all that remained was to drive the papers to the courthouse. No big deal.

"Did your lawyer find any reason why I shouldn't sign?" she asked. "I was hoping for thirty percent but if Dex thinks it should be a little less, that's okay. I just want it over."

"Actually," Scott pushed over a single legal-sized page, "Saul said this was the easiest divorce agreement he's ever vetted. He recommended you sign quickly, before your husband changes his mind."

Dani stared at the typed summary with a lawyer's impressive credentials adorned in black at the top. Scott's lawyer had helpfully itemized everything, with notations on the side. The division of assets was extremely short.

Dex wanted nothing.

Her throat tightened in disbelief. "But that's not fair," she said.

Scott gave a wry smile. "Most people would be ecstatic. But sell or keep the ranch, he wants you to have everything. Even the dog."

Dani gripped the paper so tightly her fingers hurt. "But he made the down payment. He built up this ranch and he's still working hard, even now." She shook her head. "It doesn't make sense."

"Sometimes people feel guilty. They go to prison, never expecting to get out." Scott leaned back in the chair, his voice thoughtful. "Your husband was offered a deal in exchange for information. Unfortunately he wouldn't bite. Although if he had, the cartel most certainly would have been displeased."

Her neck prickled. "Displeased?"

"No need to worry now," Scott said. "That particular cartel is much weakened. Several of their main dealers have disappeared. Either fled back to Mexico or…" He shrugged, his mouth tightening in an ominous line. "They're still rounding them up. Either way, the channel that supplied the tainted heroin is plugged."

She crossed her legs, struggling to absorb his words. *Big dealers and Mexican cartels.* They sounded foreign in her insular world. Luckily her father would never know. He constantly preached that the Tattrie club was responsible for all the town's vice. This would only give more ammunition.

Scott pushed over a yellow sheet of paper. "This contact information was also in the envelope your husband prepared."

She glanced down at the page filled with Dex's distinctive print, then leaned forward, blinking.

The list was filled with names, numbers and notations of people who owed Dex favors: vet, hay supplier, farrier, leather repair, chiro, electrician, plumber, mechanic, carpenter, roofer, fertilizer, real estate broker, water, septic, painter, accountant, lawyer. Even through her blurring eyesight, she found it moving that he'd listed the animal suppliers first, knowing they would be her primary concern.

"This was in the envelope?" She gripped the page, her voice cracking.

"Yes, it was with the agreement," Scott said.

"I didn't see it." She stared at the sheet. This list would have made life much easier, but more important was the fact that he hadn't completely turned his back. He had cared, enough to prepare a detailed list. He'd even provided the names of two cowboys who would be happy to come over if she had any troublesome horses.

"It looks like a very helpful list," she managed, over the growing lump in her throat.

"What it looks like," Scott said, "is directions from a man who didn't expect to get out for a very long time. Maybe never. And that he desperately wanted to take care of you."

"But it doesn't make sense. He wouldn't let me visit or write. He never called. It didn't seem like he cared."

"That might have been the impression he wanted to create," Scott said. "Do you think he'd talk to me? I don't want to abuse my position here, but he might appreciate an update on the cartel."

Dani hesitated. According to Eve, Scott had no tolerance for drug dealers. His goal in this was most assuredly not in Dex's best interest. On the other hand, Dex was no fool. Obviously he'd been interrogated before, and rather aggressively. He either had no information or he didn't intend to give it. And when Dex didn't feel like talking, a horse was more vocal.

"Eight people died, including Tawny." Scott leaned over the table, his eyes compelling. "Dex has done his time. But he could still help. We're aware he wasn't selling the heroin. But he must know who came to the motel room that night."

Dani fingered a corner of the yellow sheet, creasing it back and forth. "He's out in the field," she said after a moment.

"But if he asks you to leave, I want your promise that you'll go."

Scott gave a grim nod.

"Say it," Dani said, her voice turning fierce.

"I promise," Scott said.

CHAPTER THIRTY-FOUR

"I like your ex," Eve said, moving to the kitchen window. "He asked some good questions about Tizzy. Wanted to know the farrier's name." She pressed closer to the window, making no effort to hide her curiosity. "He and Scott are still talking. And they haven't come to blows yet."

Dani set down her water bottle and joined Eve by the window. She didn't want to spy. However, Scott had promised not to hassle Dex and she intended to make sure he kept his word. She still couldn't fathom that Dex had taken the time to make such a helpful list so soon after he was arrested. The fact that he'd signed over ownership of the Double D was secondary to the knowledge that he'd worried about her alone on the ranch. And that left a happy glow in her chest.

Which was ridiculous. She might feel more kindly toward Dex but it didn't erase the hooker. She crossed her arms. "Scott seems intent on finding the person who sold the drugs."

Eve nodded. "He's like a bulldog. He doesn't talk much about his work, but I know there were already several arrests. Those cartels destroy a lot of families." Her voice turned wistful. "I can't help wondering what life would be like if Joey were alive. He never saw our baby. I was only nineteen when we met. But I doubt I'll ever love anyone as much."

"Just because you fall in love when you're young," Dani said, her attention shooting back to Dex, "doesn't mean it's any less."

"That's right," Eve said, following Dani's gaze. "Think you could ever forgive him?"

"Enough to be cordial," Dani said. "But I care too much to be friends. And I could never trust him again. Women like him. It didn't bother me before, not when I thought he loved me. Now…" She gave a helpless shrug. "The trust is gone."

Eve nodded. "Men are no good without trust. It's like riding a horse that behaves ninety-five percent of the time. But you know a big buck is coming. And when it does, it's going to hurt."

"We have a horse like that," Dani said. "He just came in for training."

"We? You and Jeffrey?"

Dani fumbled for her water bottle. She hadn't been talking about Jeffrey at all. She was letting Dex ease back into her life, already linking them together. And that was a mistake. "Yes, Jeffrey," she said, pausing to take a cooling sip of water. "He doesn't ride but he helps out. Not with the horses but other things—like the toilet. And he's been staying here lately because we're getting the place ready to sell."

"He probably doesn't want to leave you alone with Dex."

"I don't think Jeffrey worries too much," Dani said.

"Really? Does he always clean his gun on the verandah?" Eve glanced outside to where Jeffrey was bent over his disassembled service gun. His police vest hung prominently on the back of a chair.

"He was trying to give Scott and me some privacy earlier so he stayed outside," Dani said. "It's no big deal."

"Maybe not to you. But Dex probably doesn't appreciate having a cop around. Not after being in prison." Eve gave an exaggerated shiver. "It would give me the willies."

Dani rubbed her forehead. Eve disliked cops and was always very honest. However, perhaps she had a valid point. In addition to the gun, Jeffrey's police car was often parked in the driveway. After being herded around by guards in uniform, that might rankle.

"I guess Dex wouldn't come here if it bothered him," Dani said slowly. "But tomorrow I'm taking the papers to the courthouse. We'll finally get this finished."

"Did Scott's lawyer help?" Eve asked. "Did he say it was okay to sign?"

"Dex was crazy generous." Dani fought her guilt. "He signed the Double D over to me. But I'm going to give him seventy percent once it's sold, more if he keeps doing all the work."

"But who gets Tizzy?"

"He will," Dani said. "Tizzy was always his horse."

"What about your dog?"

Dani's mouth tightened. Red was a more difficult decision. He'd been her buddy, confidant and protector. Many nights he'd licked the tears from her cheeks, his faithfulness her sole comfort. But she had Jeffrey now; Dex had nobody. He needed Red more than she did. And Red adored Dex.

She glanced out the window to where Dex and Scott leaned against the fence. Red sat by Dex's knee, his head tilted upward, following the men's voices as if participating in the conversation.

"Red will go with Dex," Dani said slowly. "He'll be happy at the garage. He's lived there before."

"Dex is taking the dog?" Jeffrey stepped inside, carrying a rag stained with pungent gun oil. "Hallelujah. But what about the papers? Did Scott say they were okay to sign?"

Dani nodded. "I'm going to the courthouse tomorrow."

Jeffrey grinned and tossed the rag on the table. "Scott's a good man," he said. "So is his lawyer." He looked out the window, his smile fading. "Wonder what they're talking about for so long?"

"Not sure," Eve said, checking the kitchen clock. "But Megan is babysitting so Scott and I need to go soon. You two should come to the track some morning and watch Tizzy gallop." She shot Dani a mischievous smile. "You might want to think twice before giving Tizzy away. That horse looks awesome."

Jeffrey frowned and turned to Dani. "You're giving away an expensive racehorse?"

"Tizzy was always Dex's horse," Dani said. "But we should watch him gallop while we can."

"But isn't that boring? Running around in practice circles." Jeffrey's nose wrinkled. "Wouldn't it be more fun to wait for a race?"

Dani's eyes met Eve's in tacit understanding. Jeffrey wasn't a horse person or he'd understand the appeal of watching Thoroughbreds train. But it didn't matter. She wasn't dating him for his love of animals. However, she was definitely going to drive to Santa Anita. Alone. There was nothing worse than being with an impatient man who wished he was somewhere else.

"I'd love to see Tizzy," Dani said to Eve. "What morning would be best?"

"Tuesday," Eve said. "I'll ask Jack to put him in the last set so that'll give you more time. Did you mail your application for credentials?"

"Sure did." Dani smiled. "I've never had owner credentials before. Does that mean I can wander around the backside and get in free on race days?"

"Absolutely." Eve grinned. "It's better than Disney."

Dani bounced on her toes. She'd only been to the track once, and she'd never been backside where the animals were stabled. She and Dex had talked about the fun of

Thoroughbred ownership, but they'd never had the chance to actually race.

"Think I'll walk down and get Scott," Jeffrey said, clearly bored with the horse talk. "He probably doesn't realize I'm waiting. Maybe he'd like to try my new pistol." He glanced at Dani. "Would gunfire scare the horses?"

"They might be a little startled but they're far enough away," she said, rather reluctant Jeffrey was joining the men in the pasture. And she didn't like to admit her concern wasn't totally about the horses, but more for Dex, surrounded by two armed and hostile law officials.

"I remember that horse." Scott chuckled. "If you drew Widow Maker, you were in for a tough ride. You did better than me. I never made eight seconds."

"A bit of luck," Dex said, genuinely liking the investigator. And it had been enjoyable comparing their rodeo experiences. Hell, the man had even ridden a Harley.

They both turned as Jeffrey marched toward them. His shoulders swung with purpose and a gleaming leather gun belt was strapped over his hips.

"Looks like he's on patrol," Scott said.

Now it was Dex's turn to chuckle.

Jeffrey stepped closer, his mouth flattening at their laughter. "Is everything all right here, Scott? As you're aware, this man is a convicted felon. There's no need to tolerate any insolence."

"That's not something I generally do," Scott said. He reached out and shook Dex's hand. "Good luck," he said. "I'll be in touch."

He nodded at Jeffrey and strode toward the house.

"What did you say to make him leave?" Jeffrey asked, scowling at Dex.

"He's meeting his wife," Dex said. He pulled his work gloves back on and picked up a post.

"But what were you talking about all that time?"

Dex wrapped his hands around the post and angled it into the next hole. It wasn't quite deep enough. He'd have to use the iron bar and do a little more digging.

"Listen to me when I speak," Jeffrey snapped. "Or you might find you're only out of prison on a sabbatical. I just need to make one call to your parole officer."

Dex tossed the post aside and picked up the bar.

Jeffrey jerked backwards then realized Dex was only digging in the dirt. "Dammit, Tattrie. How can you keep ignoring me?" The man's breath thickened with frustration. "Come on. Hit me. Just imagine how good it'll feel."

Jeffrey edged closer, turning braver now. Dex caught the familiar smells of a kitchen, *his* kitchen—coffee, apples and the potpourri Dani loved—mingled with the more acrid smell of gun oil on the man's hands.

Red growled.

"Just think," Jeffrey said, shooting a frustrated scowl at the dog. "After tomorrow, I'll be sleeping with her. I'm going to love that. *She's* going to love that."

Dex jammed the bar to the left, widening the hole. He refused to be goaded into a fight and end up back behind bars. But he couldn't control his curiosity. "What happens tomorrow?"

"Why do you think Scott Taylor came today?" Jeffrey sneered. "Not to waste time with scum like you. No, the divorce papers were approved for Dani's signature."

She hadn't slept with Jeffrey yet! Dex squeezed his eyes shut, swept with relief. This was a game changer. And Jeffrey was unbelievably stupid to announce that he hadn't been invited into her bed.

"If you're going to stand there and jaw," Dex said, concealing his elation, "could you at least pass me that post?"

Jeffrey's face reddened. His fingers twitched over his holster but he absorbed the iron bar in Dex's hand, as well as the protective dog. "I'm busy," he hissed. "Decent folk are going to church tonight."

He kicked the post with his boot, sending it rolling further out of Dex's reach, turned and stomped toward the house.

"Now this is a positive development," Dex said, grinning at Red.

He pounded in two more posts in record time, totally re-energized, but all the while watching the driveway. Twenty minutes later, Jeffrey's car sped away, leaving Dani alone.

He pulled off his gloves and headed for the house. Red trotted beside him, his tail wagging gaily, his mood exactly mirroring Dex's.

He climbed the verandah steps, deliberately making lots of noise. He didn't want to surprise Dani but neither did he intend to knock. It was his house too. And as of now, his strategy had changed.

He pushed open the screen door. "Dani," he called. Red rushed past him and down the hall.

Heels clicked on the wooden floor. Seconds later, she appeared. She'd added lipstick, just enough to make her lips a little more glossy, a little more kissable. Her eyes looked darker too and her honey-blond hair was swept up. He'd always liked it pinned up like that, but only because he looked forward to releasing it when they returned home. He loved the silky feel beneath his fingers, liked to slip his hand around the side of her neck and watch her eyes when he touched her.

He swallowed. It was important to keep his head clear, but that was difficult when he always had such a physical reaction to his wife. "Going out?" he managed.

She nodded, her eyes wary. "Church service. Jeffrey is picking me up."

"He doesn't stay here?"

"Sometimes," she said, not meeting his eyes. "Are you thirsty? There are drinks in the cooler at the barn."

"No, I'm through for the day." He kept his voice mild. "Jeffrey said the divorce papers were ready so I'm just checking on them."

"Of course." She turned toward the kitchen table, and he grabbed the chance to admire her toned legs and the flattering curve of her dress. She waved a sheet of paper, and he yanked his gaze up, his expression innocent.

"Since you drew this up more than two years ago," she said, "there's another affidavit required, confirming that it's current. You just have to sign again." She tilted her head, her eyes troubled. "And I appreciate your generosity in trying to give me the ranch but we'll definitely share the proceeds. I didn't read the agreement before today. I think you deserve seventy percent but right now, it's more important to get this in front of a judge."

"Where's the main agreement?" he asked.

She pointed at the coffee table.

He walked past and scooped up the envelope. "As you already mentioned," he said, "it's been a long time since this was prepared. And obviously there's a need for reassessment."

"Reassessment?"

He nodded gravely. "I have to evaluate all the assets. It won't take long, a couple weeks maybe."

"But why?" Dismay filled her face. "I'll give you seventy…eighty percent. Whatever you want. Please, let's just get this filed." She stepped forward and tried to tug the envelope from his hand.

He almost grinned, jubilant with relief and the pure pleasure of her hand on his wrist—something he'd scarcely dared to imagine. But he kept his face impassive and raised the envelope higher.

"Don't you trust me?" she asked, blinking with hurt.

"I don't trust anyone," he said. But of course, that was a lie. She was the one person he did trust. He'd always been moved by her loyalty which was why he hadn't wanted her waiting around for his release, didn't want her burdened with a shell of a man shuffling out from prison. But she was still here. And he didn't feel empty.

This was an unbelievable, undeserved gift. Even now, he couldn't quite get his head around it. She hadn't had sex with Jeffrey…which meant she must have some reservations.

Her hand was still on his arm. They both looked down and she pulled it away. "Fine," she said, edging around the table. "Take it to your lawyer. It's just a formality anyway."

"My lawyer also advises that I shouldn't give up possession of the ranch," he said, watching her reaction. "That I should…sleep here."

Her mouth opened but nothing escaped except a feeble choke.

"Is that back bedroom still empty?" he asked.

"Yes, but you can have any room you want." Her eyes changed, blazing now with a familiar stubbornness. "I'll move in with Jeffrey tonight."

"No," he said. *Hell, no.* "You deserve the house. I'll continue to sleep at the garage. As long as I can use the kitchen and bathroom during the day, that's fine."

Her hands gripped the chair, her mouth turning mutinous.

"I'm going to lengthen my work day here," he added quickly. "Get this place shaped up so the sign can go up faster. That's what you want, right?"

She gave a curt nod.

"So you want to sell the place and live in town? You really want to work in an office?" His voice softened. "Is that what you want, Dani?"

She didn't speak. She just looked at him, and the hopelessness in her eyes twisted at his chest. Red rose from the mat and crossed the kitchen, the click of his nails loud in the room. He pressed his nose against Dani's hand, as if concerned by her stillness.

"I just want a normal life," she finally said, her voice ragged. "No ugly surprises. What happened with you almost broke me. Jeffrey follows conventions. And that's what I want."

Conventions. Dex swallowed. "I'll take these papers," he said. "Do some evaluations. We'll figure it out."

He kept a tight hold on the divorce agreement and headed toward the door. He'd never been a conventional man but if that's what she wanted, he would certainly give it his best shot.

And if memory served him correctly, the evening church service started at seven.

CHAPTER THIRTY-FIVE

The church parking lot was jammed full. Jeffrey parked on the side street, angling his car between a rusty minivan and a compact sedan. Dani stepped out. She gave him an apologetic smile when he rushed around, trying to open her door, but it seemed silly to wait, especially since they were already late.

Her father held an evening service every fourth Sunday. She preferred them at night, since morning chores weren't so rushed. The sermons were rather random though. She suspected her dad intended to prepare them on the weekends but if his time was required elsewhere, he simply spoke about whatever issue was foremost on the congregation's mind. Or his.

"Dad might be preaching about parking today," she joked as she and Jeffrey slipped into the cool building.

"Shush," he said.

She squeezed her purse. Jeffrey always worried about other people's opinions. Besides, they were barely through the door. It was doubtful anyone could hear. But no, almost every head whipped around, staring with varying degrees of disapproval.

She instinctively raised her chin. She'd been the object of their fascinated sympathy for over two years and her skin had necessarily hardened.

It took a moment to realize they weren't staring at her. Or Jeffrey. They eyed the lone man in the back pew, the man surrounded by empty seats, despite that it was standing room only and at least ten people lingered by the wall.

"Breaking one's marriage vows goes against the word of God," her father went on.

She studied Dex's broad shoulders. He seemed relaxed, apparently unconcerned that worshipers preferred to stand rather than be tainted by his proximity. It had been a similar situation at the rodeos. The cowboys had excluded him, maybe not intentionally but because he was different. And now he was the estranged husband of the minister's daughter, and the congregation was simply following her father's lead. Yet Dex needed the church more than ever.

She clasped her purse in front of her. Her father should have made this easier. He could have spoken about forgiveness, rather than intolerance. If she'd forgiven Dex, why couldn't everyone else? Tightening her mouth, she stepped forward and slid into the pew beside him.

"Rebel," Dex whispered, giving her an irreverent wink. He'd always lightened this place up. Back when they were a couple, she'd suspected his attendance was only to make her happy. However, he never once complained and she'd certainly appreciated his presence.

Jeffrey followed, settling in the seat beside her. It was as if the floodgates opened. The lurkers in the back immediately rushed forward and snagged the remaining space.

Dani couldn't help but notice that the woman who pressed into the pew on Dex's left was single and wore a transparent silver blouse quite inappropriate for the occasion. Dani pulled her attention to the front of the church, trying to ignore Dex's presence and instead concentrate on her father's words.

She thought she did a fine job. She went through all the motions, singing when everyone sang, standing when everybody stood. She even gave Jeffrey several forced smiles. But Dex's presence was totally distracting. And he sat way too close. They weren't touching—only when he brushed her elbow as he reached for a hymnbook—but her entire body was on high alert. Her skin turned hot and itchy, and she had no idea what her father was saying.

She eased toward Jeffrey but it didn't help. There was no escaping Dex's primal heat or her own irritating reaction.

By the time her father completed the hour-long service, she was exhausted. She squeezed her hands together and eyed the exit. Only a few more minutes...including the predictable closing which always contained a lengthy update about Matt's volunteer work in Zimbabwe.

"So," her father went on, "we can't all travel to Africa and help the needy. Some of us grapple with finding worthy work, a worthy spouse and to live within a law-abiding community."

Her breath escaped in a tormented sigh. Dex stared straight ahead, but she caught the amused twitch of his lip and when he pressed his toe against her ankle, the show of solidarity made her feel better. Dex had always been able to shrug off her father's comments, and heck, if they didn't bother him, why should she care?

'He's your father,' Dex had said, back when they were first married. 'And he loves you. If it means being polite and respectful twice a week, I can do that. He and I both want the same thing.'

'Which is?' she'd asked, skimming her hands over his bare chest.

'To keep you safe. And happy.' Then he'd flipped her over on the bed and proceeded to make her very happy.

She wiggled on the hard pew, annoyed by the vivid memories, then realized the service was over and everyone was standing. She scrambled to her feet, keeping her back to Dex.

"Are you okay?" Jeffrey asked. "You look flushed."

"I'm fine," she said.

"Don't forget your purse," Dex said, touching her elbow.

She turned, praying he wouldn't guess the nature of her thoughts. "Thanks," she murmured, accepting her purse. "I didn't expect to see you here."

"Services provide comfort," Dex said. "I appreciated them even more in prison. And I intend to come back...every week, the rest of my life." He stared at her for a long moment as if his words were important.

"So glad to see you again, Dex," a feminine voice behind them trilled. "You should join us downstairs for the social."

Dani caught a flash of impatience on his face before he turned toward the woman. Judging by the rush of people, they were accepting him back with open arms. And she couldn't help but notice that the majority of those arms were female.

Jeffrey noticed too. He stared at the swarm of women, shaking his head. "Everyone loves an outlaw," he said glumly.

"Yes," she said, fighting her own despair. "Let's skip the social. Say hello to Dad and go home."

"An excellent idea," Jeffrey said, cupping her elbow and guiding her toward the church office.

Minutes later, Dani's father joined them. He closed the door behind him, his eyes bright with excitement. "Matt called unexpectedly last night," he said, "so I was able to include more details in tonight's service. Everyone appreciates updates on how their donations are being spent. It was interesting, wasn't it?"

He pulled off his ministerial robe, not waiting for their answer, and hung it on a steel hanger. "Matt wants you to have his car, Dani. This is the third time he mentioned it."

"That's generous. And selling it will help with expenses," Jeffrey said, glancing at Dani. "But don't include it in the ranch sale. Keep the proceeds separate since it's a gift after your marriage broke down."

Dani perched on a hardback chair, distracted by the muted murmurs rising from the vestibule. She could no longer pick

up Dex's deep voice but there was an undercurrent of
excitement, so no doubt he was there. Single, attractive men
were scarce in the congregation.

"Dani?" Jeffrey touched her arm.

She straightened. "Yes, of course," she said. "That's very
kind of Matt. But are you sure he wants me to have it?"

"Absolutely." Her father beamed with pride. "He's giving
it to the Double D. To sell or keep, whatever you want. Very
generous. I must say he's grown up down there."

Dani blinked. This was the first time her father had ever
alluded that Matt was self-centered. It couldn't have been
easy for her dad, raising two kids alone. He'd indulged Matt
with cars and supported Dani's love for horses, never
understanding either passion. But as Dex always said, if the
man's perceptions of his offspring were a little colored, it was
only because he loved them.

"Thanks, Dad." She rose and kissed her father's cheek.
"Yes, Matt is generous. I'm not sure if the Camaro will start,
but I'll check it out."

"Are you doing all right?" He squeezed her hand. "I saw
where you were sitting. I know it's not easy." He gave Jeffrey
an approving nod. "At least this time your partner is on the
right side of the law."

"Did Matt intend to give the car to the Double D or
Dani?" Jeffrey asked, rising from his chair.

Her father shrugged. "He said the Double D. Does it
matter?"

"No, not a bit," Dani said, rather resenting Jeffrey's
interference. "We're going now. See you Thursday. I'll bring a
salmon to grill."

"Excellent," her father said, escorting them to the door.

"It does matter though, Dani," Jeffrey said, once they
stepped into the empty hallway. "You shouldn't have to share
the money from Matt's car." He looped an arm around her
waist. "We could use the proceeds to buy a bigger bed."

"I already have a king-sized bed," she said.

"Yes, but we should buy a new one. Make new memories."

She fingered her purse. It couldn't be easy for Jeffrey, following after a man like Dex. But everything would be better once they sold the ranch and were able to make a fresh start.

"And tomorrow," Jeffrey went on, "we'll drive to the courthouse. I know everyone there. We'll get it filed."

"But I don't have the papers anymore," she said. "Dex wants to review them."

Jeffrey jerked to a stop. "I thought it was a simple fifty-fifty split? I was trying to negotiate a little more, but half would be enough. What happened?"

"The original agreement gave everything to me," she said. "Which wasn't fair. But I didn't read it. There was also a contact list of suppliers. He went to a lot of work—"

"So if you had signed two years ago, you would have owned everything?" Jeffrey groaned and flattened his palm over his forehead. "So this could drag on?"

"It won't," she said. "Dex wants it settled too. But when he prepared the agreement he was going to prison for five years. I'm sure things look differently now. And he'll need money to start a new life."

"He's the same man who didn't care enough to put you on his visitors' list," Jeffrey snapped.

"He explained that," Dani said, crossing her arms, annoyed at Jeffrey's tone. "It was too difficult. That's why he didn't want any visitors."

"And you believe him?"

"Of course," she said. "He doesn't lie. It's how he handles things. He just closes up."

"Not to all women," Jeffrey sneered.

"I asked you not to keep reminding me of that." Her head was pounding now and she edged away. "Maybe I'll stay and get a drive home with Dad. I need to use the bathroom anyway."

"I'm sorry," Jeffrey said stiffly, without sounding sorry at all. "I'll bring the car around. Take your time."

He stalked outside, slamming the door behind him. Dani rubbed her forehead. They never fought, except about Dex. And there was nothing she could do about that. History couldn't be erased.

"Trouble with loverboy?"

She turned toward Dex's quiet voice.

"No," she said, wondering how much he'd heard. "But please do me a favor. Have your lawyer look at those papers and then sign them quickly. I'll be happy with twenty percent."

"It's not that easy," he said, moving closer. "My lawyer is away for a bit. But he wants you to write everything down. Go through the house, the barn, the animals, the equipment. Make a detailed list of everything you want. Shouldn't take you more than a couple weeks."

The throb behind her left temple intensified. More lists, more decisions, more good- byes. Things she'd never thought about before were suddenly precious. She'd been trying to keep the ranch and everything on it intact, had struggled to keep creditors at bay. Thought she'd accepted the reality of selling. But both Dex and Jeffrey spoke so casually, as if the ranch consisted of assets now, not cherished possessions.

"I like my bed," she said, backing up and gripping the doorknob. "I don't want a new one. And the potato peeler with the white handle. I'd like to keep that."

Dex's eyes narrowed, his face appearing almost stricken. He stared for a moment then reached out and wrapped her in his arms. "Don't worry," he said, his voice muffled against her hair. "Don't even think about it. You keep anything. Everything. Whatever you want."

His fingers tunneled through her hair then skimmed over her neck and shoulders, his touch gentle but with a hint of urgency. "You feel thin," he murmured. "Why don't you sleep in tomorrow? I'll come by and look after the horses. You won't even know I'm there."

She almost choked, her face still pressed against his soft shirt. Of course she'd know he was there. She'd sense it with every fiber of her being.

"Bet it's a long time since you had a morning off," he went on, his voice persuasive. "I can feed, clean stalls, even ride that sneaky buckskin."

She drew in a shuddery breath, definitely tempted. "You can't use as much bedding as we did before," she warned, stepping back. "There's no shavings left and the straw has to last until the end of the month. And the gelding on stall rest will need his legs rewrapped. But Jeffrey is on call this week, so I don't know—"

"Good," Dex said. "It's settled then." His hands lingered on her arms, his eyes compelling. "I'll come by at five-thirty tomorrow. Right?"

She stared up and when he nodded, she automatically nodded back. Five-thirty was breakfast time and clearly he remembered the routine. It would be nice to have a morning off. Besides, she'd barely see him and even if she did, it certainly wouldn't change anything.

CHAPTER THIRTY-SIX

Dani woke to bright sunlight filtering through the curtains. She gave a luxurious stretch and checked the bedside clock. Eleven thirty. She hadn't slept this late since her honeymoon.

Despite Dex's generous offer to feed the horses, she hadn't expected to sleep so long. He must have let Red out too. Probably found the spare key beneath the planter or else he'd picked the lock. Didn't matter; he was immensely capable and just knowing he was looking after things made her feel much lighter.

Humming, she wandered into the shower then changed her mind and indulged in a sudsy bath. She dressed carefully, even adding coral lipstick, convincing herself it was for ultraviolet protection. And her best jeans and pretty V-necked shirt were most assuredly in case Jeffrey dropped by.

She glanced out the window. Dex's truck was parked close to the barn. The horses were all in their paddocks. She couldn't see Dex or Red, but everything looked orderly. And she hadn't lifted a finger. What a lovely day.

Smiling, she made herself a cup of coffee, then poured another for Dex. She pushed open the door, carefully balancing the cups, and headed toward the barn.

Dust rose from the round pen and she veered toward the sound of hoofbeats. Dex must be riding Cracker. Red ran to meet her, his pink tongue lolling, his eyes bright. He turned and trotted toward the pen, keen to show her current developments.

"Good morning," she called, trying not to surprise either the horse or the rider. But especially the horse. Cracker was the type to grab any excuse to buck. "How's it going with him?" she asked.

Dex grinned from the saddle, his eyes shaded by his cowboy hat. "We had a couple arguments. But now I think we reached an understanding." He reached down and stroked Cracker's neck, still looking at Dani. "You look...rested."

"I just woke up," she said. "Thanks for this day. I feel a lot better. Sorry for my meltdown yesterday."

"Hardly a meltdown."

"But I was a little needy." She took a sip of coffee, searching for the right words. "I can make a list, if that's what you want," she said. "But I was thinking, we've been through enough that we're always going to be friends, right? I mean, we can get along?"

He nodded. His hand rested on the saddle horn but he turned so still he seemed like part of the horse.

"Then," she said, pulling in a deep breath, "I know your lawyer wants a complete list and everything fairly split, but do you think we'd be able to share Red?"

He abruptly sat back, the saddle squeaking beneath his weight. Disapproval radiated from his body and even Cracker flattened his ears.

"It would have to be convenient of course," she said hurriedly. "Jeffrey and I would be flexible. I know Red likes you more, but I love him."

Dex didn't speak for a moment, just stared down at her from beneath his big hat. "Love can be a kicker," he finally said, his voice flat. "Did you bring that coffee for me?"

"Yes. Can you drink it on him?"

"I can now," Dex said. He moved Cracker closer to the rail and reached for the cup. "But he's going to challenge every rider that climbs on his back. I don't like him."

Dani climbed higher on the rails now that she had her second hand free. Dex sounded testy. In fact, she'd never heard him say he didn't like a horse. "He's not bucking now," she said. "And he looks very respectful."

"Looks are deceiving. That's what makes him dangerous."

Dani stared at Cracker, her good mood withering. There wasn't much future for a gelding who was dangerous, not only to ride but to handle. He wouldn't even make a good companion horse. "Maybe a cowboy would want him?" she asked hopefully. "Someone who can ride like you?"

Dex shook his head. "He's not athletic enough to do much. And he's not even a reliable bucker. He's just sneaky."

"I promised the owner I'd give him a month of riding. I can't just give up."

"You do sometimes," Dex said.

"There was one gray mare that was unrideable," Dani said. "But I didn't quit. I found her a home."

"Then why are you quitting now?" he asked.

She stared, stunned by his unfairness. "Are we talking about something else here?" she finally asked. "Because I wasn't the jerk who cheated."

She jumped from the rail, spilling her coffee which only fanned her rising anger. She didn't hear Dex until the ground thudded behind her.

"Dani, wait," he said. His hand slipped over her shoulder and he turned her around. "I didn't cheat. I haven't been with anyone but you."

"So you only watch naked hookers?" she snapped. "Is that supposed to make me feel better? And you certainly cared enough to send money to Tawny's family."

"I felt responsible," he said. "And Luther looked after that, not me."

"But why were you at that motel? I don't understand. Please tell me." She stared up. But his expression only turned stony, the way it did when he wasn't going to change his mind.

"It doesn't matter." She pushed away his hands. "Dammit. This started out as such a nice day."

He raised his palms and stepped back. "Don't worry about the horse," he said. "I know a place that will take him. But I need to see how he acts with other animals. It would help if you rode with me."

She was already edging away but she paused. "Ride where?"

"In the ring. And around the pasture."

"All right," she said slowly. "I'll saddle Peppy." She didn't really want to be in Dex's company. He churned up too many emotions. However, she couldn't refuse, not if it would help find Cracker a home. And though she certainly didn't intend to talk more than necessary, she couldn't hide her curiosity. "Who could use a horse like that?" she asked. "A rancher? A cowboy friend?"

"No," Dex said. "A prison friend."

"Tell me more about the riding lessons?" Dani moved her horse closer to Dex's. She'd been determined not to talk, but his tales of hardened convicts learning to deal with sensitive horses were fascinating. "Do they fall off much?"

Dex chuckled and slowed Cracker's walk. "Yes, but the falls keep them humble. Most of the cons come with too much attitude. The horses straighten them out. And when required, Quentin puts them on a tough horse. Gypsy was great for that."

His voice softened whenever he spoke of Gypsy. If the mare had been a woman, she might have been jealous. *But he hasn't slept with anyone.* The whole time they'd been riding, his statement had played over and over in her head. He'd been out of prison for a month. He would have had more than his fair share of offers.

She glanced sideways, studying his handsome face. And a sigh of relief leaked out.

"Tired?" Dex asked. "Want to go back?"

"Maybe we better," she said, straightening her thoughts. "Jeffrey's on call. He usually swings by for supper if he's not busy." She paused, hating her defensiveness. "I know you never really liked him but he's been a huge help while you were gone."

"I'm sure your father approves," Dex said.

"Yes, but it has nothing to do with Dad. I like Jeffrey. A lot. I'm not saying we're going to get married or anything, but he's good company." She pressed her mouth shut because up to this moment, she'd thought they probably would get married someday.

Dex's smile was a little too complacent. "Want to ride down to the creek before we go back?" he asked.

"It's too far." She shook her head, annoyed at how he seemed to pull out her private thoughts, even before she knew them herself.

"But I need to see what this guy is like with water." His voice turned teasing. "Don't want my fellow felons getting wet."

She couldn't help but smile back. Dex had talked more about prison today than he had in weeks. He'd even laughed a few times. "You seem all right after being locked up," she said. "No worse for wear. I'm glad."

"It was questionable how it would go though." His words turned halting. "You need to understand. I didn't want you waiting…for someone not worth waiting for. That's why I thought a divorce was best."

"Don't." Her hands tightened around the reins. "It's too late. We should have talked like this before you pleaded guilty. You wouldn't even let me visit."

"I didn't let anyone visit."

She shook her head and pushed Peppy into a trot. Dex refused to speak for over two years and now he was almost garrulous. The turnaround left her unbalanced and utterly fragile. She wasn't prepared for this. And he still wouldn't talk about what had hurt the most.

Peppy's trot turned into a canter and then he was galloping, as if understanding her need for speed. Wind cut her face even as tears wet her cheeks. She'd probably always love Dex but their relationship was ruined. Jeffrey might not make her heart race but he was safe. Just like good old horses—they didn't provide much exhilaration but they didn't leave you bruised and broken either.

She glanced back and almost choked. Case in point. Cracker had stopped to pitch a fit. His head was between his knees, his tail pointed to the sky. Trail dust rose in an angry swirl. She quickly circled Peppy, rubbing the telltale tears from her cheeks before stopping to watch the commotion.

If it were any other rider, she would have felt guilty for galloping ahead and possibly causing the horse behind to throw a tantrum. But Dex was built to ride broncos and bikes…and women. She hardened her heart, rested her hands on the horn and simply enjoyed the show.

Cracker was frustrated, either because he couldn't throw his rider or because Dex remained impervious to anything he did. The horse sun fished, twisting his body in a crescent and looking much more athletic than he had in the round pen.

Dani winced as Dex hit the front of the saddle. "That couldn't have felt good," she murmured to Peppy who watched with pricked ears, equally entertained by the rodeo in the middle of the field. Even Red sat back, tongue lolling, completely unconcerned. If it had been Dani riding, he would have been nipping at the horse's heels, determined to help.

As abruptly as it started, Cracker stopped. Dex pushed him forward and joined Dani. "Don't think this horse will be good for trail rides," he said, calmly adjusting his hat.

"No." Her mouth twitched. "But he's fun to watch. Glad you were on him, not me. Would the prison farm really want a horse like that?"

"They'd be a perfect match," Dex said, his eyes lingering on her face. "Be a shame to keep anything apart, when they're so well suited."

She looked away, determined to ignore his innuendo. "If I ride off," she asked, "will he start bucking again?"

"Probably."

"Good," she said. "Then I'm in control."

"You most definitely are," Dex said.

"I need a break," Dani said, stepping back and surveying the freshly painted fence. "Want a drink or something?"

She swiped her face with the back of her wrist. Her paintbrush waved, adding another dot of white to her cheek and splattering a streak on Dex's bare chest.

"Hell, woman," he said, "you are the messiest painter." But he couldn't stop smiling. They'd been working side by side for the last two hours, ever since their ride in the field. She'd wanted him to pound more posts in the far pasture but he knew she hated painting and guessed that with a little push, she'd accept his help. And other than a few glitches while riding, he figured he had made considerable progress. In fact, it was almost as if he'd never been away.

"You turned all prissy in prison," she said. "It's just a little paint. At least you're not wrecking clothes." She smiled and reached out to rub the paint off his chest, then jerked her hand back.

Damn. For a hopeful moment he'd stopped breathing. She wasn't totally immune to him, insisting he keep his shirt on while he'd been equally insistent that he couldn't stain the few clothes he owned. It was a hot day and she was too kind to protest. He hoped he wasn't misinterpreting her sideways glances. But now she'd turned away, eagerly scanning the road for Jeffrey's car.

And that cop didn't deserve her. He hadn't stepped back from their marriage so she could end up with a weasel like Jeffrey Nicholson.

He blew out a frustrated sigh. "Is loverboy late?"

"He's on call," she said. "The police are surprisingly busy for a Monday."

Not so surprising, Dex thought. He'd asked Luther to arrange a series of calls, decoys and distractions. "Probably nothing more important than a cat up a tree," he said, keeping his expression solemn.

"And please don't call him loverboy again," Dani said, dropping her brush beside the paint can. "It sounds derogatory. Now do you want a drink or what?"

"A drink," he said, putting down his brush. "I'll walk up with you."

"No, stay—"

"Then you won't have to walk all the way back," he said. "You can shower, feed the horses, be ready when *Jeffrey* arrives."

"All right, thanks." She nodded but her eyes remained wary. "I did buy some peanut butter, the crunchy kind, if you want to make a sandwich."

"My favorite," he said pulling on his shirt and scooping up her brush. "I'll rinse this out so you can paint again tomorrow."

"No painting for me," she said. "I'm going to Santa Anita tomorrow."

"To see Tizzy?"

She nodded, her eyes suddenly stricken. Even her face flushed, like it always did when she felt guilty. She was so honorable, could always be counted on for fair play. He loved that in her, loved everything about her. But this was an opportunity he couldn't ignore. And he didn't always play fair.

"You're going to Santa Anita?" He hardened his voice. "To see *my* horse? That's hardly fair. How do I know his value if I can't watch him gallop too?"

"You can go up whenever you want."

"But how would I get past security?" he asked. "It wouldn't be easy."

"I think anyone can walk into Clockers' Corner. But if it's restricted, you could just call Eve and set up a day and time. Then she checks it with the trainer. Or maybe you should call the trainer directly." Dani shuffled her feet, her voice trailing off. "I'm not really sure if you need credentials for the stable area though."

"I can't believe you'd make this so hard," he said, using his coldest tone which was rather difficult when all he wanted to do was wrap her against his chest and take away her stricken look. "I haven't seen Tizzy in years." He crossed his arms, really laying it on.

"You haven't asked about him in years either," she snapped, and her gumption almost made him smile. Even hardened cons backed away when he frowned and folded his arms.

But he didn't smile. In fact, he roughened his voice. "You sent Jeffrey to prison in his cop uniform, deliberately intimidating me into signing away Tizzy. And now you don't even let me see him. Frankly, I'm disappointed."

Her eyes widened. "Jeffrey wore his uniform? To prison? I'm sorry." She reached out and touched his arm. "I needed to send Tizzy to the track. It was never about ownership."

"So I still own him too?" Dex asked, pushing his advantage despite the fact that her touch left him breathless. "You agree it's only fair that we both see him?"

"Well, yes, of course," she said, so flustered her hand still pressed against his forearm. "But you can go up by yourself another time. I'll even arrange it. Just pick a day that's convenient."

"But tomorrow is convenient." He tilted his head, as if considering a very busy schedule. "Actually," he said, "tomorrow is the only day that will work."

CHAPTER THIRTY-SEVEN

Morning sun slanted through the truck window, making it tricky to weave through traffic. Dani munched one of the doughnuts, rather glad now of Dex's company. She was a little intimidated about driving to the track alone as well as nervous about Tizzy's progress. And, in addition to being an excellent driver, Dex had brought a thermos of coffee and some very delicious doughnuts.

She licked strawberry filling off her lower lip, then paused to study the doughnut. Dex didn't like strawberries so either he was a good guesser or he remembered her favorites. But she doubted he'd remember something so obscure.

"I remembered your favorites," he said. "And the coffee's black."

"Great, thanks," she murmured, turning to look through the passenger window. There was no denying he'd always sensed her thoughts from the very first day they'd met, when he'd cooled out Peppy after her fall. And it was both irritating and reassuring that his company was so easy.

"Think Tizzy will recognize you?" she asked, scrambling for a safer topic.

"We'll know soon enough," Dex said, turning into Santa Anita's huge parking lot. He veered to the left, joining a scattering of vehicles parked in front of an expansive and confusing grandstand.

"How do you know which door to use?" she asked.

"Any one that isn't padlocked," Dex said. He gave a wry smile. "And it helped that Scott told me to use the furthest entrance on the left."

"Scott questioned you again? That's not right." She jerked her seatbelt off, so annoyed the buckle bounced off the side of the door. "He promised not to hound you. I'm so sorry."

"It's okay, tiger." Dex reached over and grazed her cheek with the pad of his thumb. "He's doing me a favor. Come on. Let's go watch our horse."

He took her hand and tugged her across the bench seat toward the driver's side. And though she'd resolved to keep a careful distance, it was only natural to let him help her to the ground. Besides, the affectionate way he'd touched her cheek was totally disarming.

He used to do that a lot—just a little touch as they worked side by side—along with that patented smoldering look that always left her eager for the night. And often they hadn't waited.

But it was unhealthy to wallow in memories. She'd already resolved to set boundaries, to shut him down if he moved too close. Like now. She stiffened, preparing to pull away, but it wasn't even necessary. He released her hand as soon as her feet hit the ground.

"Let's follow that guy to Clockers' Corner," he said, pointing at a gray-haired man with a program tucked under his arm. "Unless you want to go to the backside first?"

Dani shook her head, rather disappointed he'd released her before she even had time to ask. "Eve said it was hectic in the morning. Her boss won't have time to talk until they finish training. Tizzy will be coming out in the last set. That's still an hour away. Guess we should just sit and wait."

She adjusted her sunglasses. "I'm a little nervous," she admitted. "What if his lack of training shows? Our little field is nothing like this. Worse, what if he looks unhappy?"

"Then we'll take him home," Dex said.

She blinked. He spoke so matter-of-factly, not at all concerned about increasing Tizzy's value or gathering numbers for his lawyer's list. "I'm glad you feel that way," she said slowly. "Jeffrey thinks Tizzy's going to be a big money maker just because he's a Thoroughbred."

"If the horse isn't happy," Dex said, "he's not going to win many races."

"So what would we do with him?" She tugged at her lower lip. It would simplify things if Tizzy could be sold as a racehorse.

"We'll find something he likes to do and train him for that," Dex said, putting his hand on her hip and guiding her toward the entrance.

He spoke so firmly, his goals so aligned with hers, that she breathed a little lighter. It seemed she'd harbored so much uncertainty, for so long, a tightness had permanently lodged in her chest. But now Dex was back, and everything was easy again.

She paused at the bottom of the grandstand, not even bothered by his hand on her back. "I'm glad you're here," she said sincerely. "At first I didn't want you to come today, but I know we can work this out. And stay friends."

Movement flashed and she glanced past him. Less than twenty feet away horses walked and jogged and galloped, moving in perfect symmetry against a backdrop of mountains and palm trees. "Wow," she said. "It's gorgeous. Let's sit a little higher where we can see everything."

She bounded up the steps. "I'd like to be close to the rail when Tizzy's on the track," she called over her shoulder, "but we can move back down later."

She chose two seats where they could see across the infield and view the entire oval. It was amazing how the riders controlled a thousand pounds of horsepower despite their tiny saddles. "I don't think I could ever ride in a little saddle like that," she said, staring raptly. "But maybe I can get Eve to teach me."

Dex still hadn't spoken, hadn't even commented on the total awesomeness of the track. She tore her gaze off a spectacular gray horse with the biggest stride imaginable. "What do you think of that gray?" she asked. But he wasn't looking at the horses. Instead, he stared at her with an oddly wistful expression.

"Dex?"

His eyes immediately shuttered. "Nice horse," he said. "Wings a bit on the left front."

She leaned forward, surprised he'd noticed. He hadn't even appeared to be watching the gray although she'd learned from experience never to question his powers of observation.

"I didn't catch that," she said. "Wait, there's Eve."

She scrambled from her seat and rushed to the rail.

Eve instantly stopped her horse. "Glad you both made it." Her welcoming smile moved past Dani to include Dex. "I'll be riding Tizzy after this one. He'll be working four furlongs in company." She leaned forward, her voice lowering. "Did you see the gray? The owner is Bert Howard. That guy has thirty horses in training."

Eve's horse pawed, clearly impatient to get to work, and Eve turned him along the rail. "Gotta go," she said. "Walk back to the shedrow with Tizzy afterwards. We can all talk then."

Dani nodded happily. "This is so much fun," she said to Dex. "But it's weird not to be riding, don't you think?"

He didn't answer. In fact, he'd barely spoken the last fifteen minutes, not so unusual for Dex, but somehow this silence felt strained. She glanced around. Over fifty people were scattered around the seats. And there were mesh fences and a security booth and two uniformed guards. She was ecstatic to be here, but maybe it was a little overwhelming for him, after being locked up in prison for so long.

Her voice softened and she turned away from the beautiful horses. "Do you need more space? We could sit higher in the stands. Or even go back to the truck for a while. Or if you just want to be alone—"

"Don't, Dani," he said, so curtly she flinched. She'd heard him use that tone before, but not on her. Never on her.

She gripped the rail, pretending sudden absorption with a bay colt trotting past. He wore a white bridle and matching shadow roll and all the equipment looked new and clean and well oiled, and she was so happy to be at the track. But she couldn't stop her blink of tears.

Dex's fingers abruptly covered her hands. "Sorry," he whispered, his voice ragged.

"I just thought this might be too much," she said miserably. "That you might want a break."

"Your sympathy isn't what I want."

"It's not sympathy," she said, staring across the track, struggling to talk around the big lump in her throat. And hating that he could still so easily put it there. "It's just …caring. How I'd care about anyone," she added.

His fingers stroked her hands and even though they were hard and callused, his touch was velvet soft. "I snapped and I apologize," he said. "Your thoughtfulness is one of the things I loved about you."

He spoke in the past tense and somehow that hurt more than it should. "What were the other things you loved about me?" She shrugged as if it didn't really matter. "Just for the record."

His fingers stilled as if he might lower his arms. But she felt him take a big breath. "I love your sense of fair play," he said slowly. "How you always support the underdog. How you sit a horse."

How I sit a horse. No wonder they hadn't made it. No wonder he'd run to a hooker. Her breath leaked out in a humorless laugh.

"I'm not finished," he said. "I love how you look in your jeans. And the way you look out of them. I love your rumpled hair in the morning and how you always smiled and let me have the toothpaste first. I love how you sit up all night with a sick horse, that you make dinner for your dad every Thursday night, and how sweet you are with the girl in the wheelchair who comes for free riding lessons."

"She moved away last year," Dani managed.

Dex's arms tightened, his fingers squeezing her hands. "Seeing you in prison would have gutted me, Dani. You have to believe that." And his voice was so urgent, so sincere, she did believe him.

The right side of her sunglasses was crooked, but she didn't want to move her hand from his to adjust them. Her heart still thumped from his bittersweet words. It seemed like they were in a time warp and she was wrapped in his caring arms just as he'd held her so many times before. The sun shone, the horses beckoned and their problems seemed a world away.

Dex seemed to feel the same way. "That big paint ponying the chestnut reminds me of Gypsy," he said, resting his chin on the top of Dani's hair. "Same regal look in the eye. Gypsy's hooves were dark though. She had great feet."

Dani smiled. She tended to look at a horse's head first while Dex always checked their legs and feet. Some things never changed.

The paint was big boned and tall, almost seventeen hands high. She disciplined the rambunctious colt at her side merely by flattening her ears, and it was obvious her presence made the rider's job much easier.

"Was Gypsy bossy like that?" Dani asked.

"Probably bossier," Dex said. "They sent her to Skyview Buckers, a breeding farm for rodeo stock."

Dani didn't intend to move, not yet, but the wistfulness in his voice made her turn around and study his face. "Sounds like Gypsy meant a lot to you," she said.

"Every once in a while I fall hard." He lowered his arms and looked to the left. "Tizzy's coming on the track now."

She leaned over the rail, studying the familiar bay walking through the gap and onto the track. Tizzy's eyes were bright, his neck arched and he had a new strut to his walk. "Oh," she breathed. "He looks fabulous."

Tizzy looked even better as he moved closer. The whiskers around his muzzle were trimmed and his head and neck were sleek and refined.

"They shortened his mane," she said, the same time as Dex said, "His feet look a little long."

They both laughed and Dex wrapped his hand over hers again, but it was okay because today they were just two proud parents. Eve nodded from her perch on his back but she didn't frustrate Tizzy by trying to stop when he was clearly ready to run.

"You did a good job with him," Dex said, his gaze following the horse.

"It was the people here," Dani said. "Tizzy didn't look like that when he left."

"But you taught him the basics. He's more businesslike than some of the other horses."

"I'm glad he looks happy," Dani said. "I don't know if he can run fast, but he seems to think he can."

"That he does," Dex said, and when he squeezed her hand, she squeezed back.

They watched in delight as Tizzy warmed up, cantering without an escort, moving big and bold and beautiful.

"Eve has a good feel for him," Dani said. "If Tizzy makes it to a race, he'll already know his jockey. And the trainer is good at picking races. One horse was so good Eve said they sent him to a big turf race in Ontario."

She glanced sideways. Dex wasn't even looking at Tizzy. He just stared at her, his expression enigmatic.

"I'm just dreaming," she added quickly. "I know most Thoroughbreds don't make it to the starting gate, let alone into a big race. But it's fun to imagine. I'd like to visit Canada."

"It would be ten years before a country like that would let me in," Dex said.

Dani frowned. "But your probation is up way before then."

"I'll still have a record."

He spoke matter-of-factly but she couldn't help but feel a well of sympathy. The repercussions of his conviction were endless, affecting everything from job prospects to travel. Of course, he should have considered all that before he broke the law.

"Well, if Tizzy becomes famous," she said, forcing a smile, "we'll just have to make sure we run him locally. No Dubai World Cup."

"We're keeping him then?"

She flushed. Of course, they couldn't keep Tizzy. The last thing she needed was to co-own a racehorse with her ex. She'd been living too much in the moment, too seduced by the sight of galloping horses, the sound of pounding hooves...and the feel of Dex's hand.

She freed her fingers and inched further along the rail. "Looks like he'll be working with the chestnut horse in the blinkers," she said. "They're moving up to the half-mile pole."

"Tizzy's on the inside. Good," Dex said, following her cue and edging several inches in the opposite direction.

"Why is that good?" she asked. And of course she was relieved he'd backed off. But deep down, a part of her wished he'd drop to his knees and beg her forgiveness. A grand gesture—something, anything—that would prove he really cared. She'd always suspected she loved him more than he loved her. And that hadn't mattered so much, until *that night.*

"Two young horses," Dex said. "If the blinkered horse blows the turn, he won't take out Tizzy."

She nodded, struggling to remember her question. They'd come to watch this workout, but his presence jumbled her senses and now all she could think about was the possibility of owning a racehorse together. Yet Dex was so cool, he was already analyzing the horse's position.

She stared across the track. The two horses moved together to the red half-mile pole, their strides lengthening as they hugged the rail, moving in tandem around the turn. The blinkered horse had a nose in front while Eve kept Tizzy under a tight hold, content to remain a neck back. But when they straightened down the stretch, Tizzy surged forward, his stride quickening. And by the eighth pole, Tizzy had already moved a length in front, seemingly galloping for the fun of it.

Dani craned forward, following the blur of horse, but all she could see was Tizzy's gloriously streaming tail. She didn't speak for a moment, didn't want to harbor false hope. Probably all owners thought their horses looked fabulous in the morning. And racing in the afternoon was much different. But heck, Tizzy looked awesome, like an unbeatable, unstoppable race machine. "He looked good, didn't he?" she asked.

Dex grinned, a smile cutting the corners of his strong jaw, and he looked so shockingly handsome she could only grin back. He rarely gave away smiles like that. And of course, he'd handpicked Tizzy as a colt. Naturally he was pleased.

But he just looked at her, his eyes smiling. "It's been awhile since I've seen you look so happy," he said.

Because you're happy, she thought. But she just shrugged. "I smile a lot."

"Not like that," he said. "You should keep Tizzy. It would be a lot of fun watching. Let another trainer worry for a change."

Dani nibbled at the inside of her cheek. It would be fun, but racing was expensive. And most horses didn't pay their way. Jeffrey would certainly consider it an extravagance. It would be different if she were with someone who shared the same interests... Someone like Dex.

"Tizzy's on his way back now," Dex said, his perceptive eyes still on her face.

She turned and leaned over the rail, watching Eve and Tizzy as they walked back along the outer rail. This time, Eve stopped to talk.

"He did great," Eve said, her breath slightly labored. "Jack will be pleased. I bet he'll want to keep Tizzy in training." She pointed to the gap where the horses entered the track. "Follow me to the backside, barn fourteen. We can talk more there."

Tizzy's ears locked on Dex before Eve turned him away.

"He seemed to recognize you," Dani said. "Think he wonders where you've been?"

"Probably not," Dex said. "Horses have excellent memories but they live in the moment. Humans, unfortunately, tend to brood." There was no doubt he was referring to her.

"I'm not brooding," she muttered. "But it's impossible to forget, even if I wanted to. What would you have done? If it had been me in that motel room?"

"I don't know," he said. "It's not the same thing."

"Not the same thing?" Her voice rose. "Well of course it is. Why should men do what they want while wives are just supposed to accept this stuff? And that poor woman might still be alive if you'd stayed home—"

A couple people turned, studying them with avid curiosity, so she pressed her mouth shut. However, she was charged with too much emotion to stand still. She turned and stalked toward the gap, her hands clenched in frustration.

She didn't even notice the man in the guardhouse.

"Stop, miss," he called. "You need to show your credentials."

She flushed and turned back to the window. "I applied for an owner's license, but it didn't arrive yet."

The guard glanced over her shoulder, waving several people through the restricted gate. "What's your trainer's name?" he asked, looking back at her.

She rubbed her forehead. She remembered the man's first name was Jack. Eve had said his last name too, and Dani had written it on her application. But it was an unusual name and now her mind blanked.

The guard's eyes narrowed. "When did you apply? Licenses don't usually take long to process." He gave a condescending smile. "Not unless you have a criminal record."

Dani clutched her hands, fighting a growing panic. Maybe that's why her owner's license hadn't arrived; maybe they knew her husband was a felon. More people milled behind her, filling the walkway, impatient to reach the backside.

She felt Dex's reassuring hand on her shoulder. "I'm sure we're on your visitors' list," he said to the guard. "It's Dani and Dex Tattrie."

The guard frowned. "But what's the trainer's name?"

Dex glanced at Dani, his eyes amused. If he was at all annoyed about her memory loss, he didn't show it. But this was awful. If the guard asked pointblank if Dex had a record, what would she say? And Dex might be embarrassed. Heat rose to her cheeks.

"Tattrie? Dex Tattrie?" The authoritative voice came from behind them. A silver-haired man pushed through the jam of people, his eyes fixed on Dex. "Are you Dex Tattrie, the farrier?"

Dex paused, then gave a brief nod.

The man's hand shot out. His Rolex flashed as he pumped Dex's hand. "Well, this is an honor," he said. "I'm Bert Howard. You taught my son, Sandy, to shoe." He turned to the guard. "They're with me," he said, imperiously ushering them through the checkpoint.

"Please join me for a coffee," he went on. "Or I could meet you for lunch, any day you want. Maybe tomorrow? Sandy told us what you did," he said, still staring at Dex as if fearful he might disappear. "And my wife and I are exceedingly grateful. Please meet with me. I have so many questions, so many concerns."

"We're going to barn fourteen," Dex said, "but after perhaps." He looked at Dani. "Unless you need to get back to ride?"

"It's okay," Dani said, moved by the man's obvious desperation. "I'm not in a hurry."

Bert Howard shot her a grateful smile and she nodded back. It wouldn't hurt to give the horses a day off. If this man's son was in jail, naturally he was eager to talk to Dex. And she certainly hoped they'd let her listen.

Bert's shoulders sagged with relief. "Barn fourteen. That's Jack Zeggelaar's barn," he said. "My horses are just opposite, over there."

He pointed to a shedrow with hanging flowerpots where two grooms bathed a well-muscled gray, the same horse Eve had pointed out earlier. The barn was clearly prosperous. It was more flamboyant than the adjoining buildings, a little better maintained. Even the hot walkers were fancier.

"All right," Dex said. "I'll find you." He slipped a hand around Dani's hip and guided her toward Zeggelaar's barn, completely dismissing Bert Howard.

And that was one of the reasons she loved him, Dani thought. He was completely unaffected by wealth, power and privilege.

She still loved him.

She stumbled, would have fallen except for his quick arm. Flustered, she stared down at her boots, pretending the ground was uncommonly rough.

"Hey," Eve called, stepping out from the shedrow. "Your horse earned a lot of attention today." She hurried closer, lowering her voice but still visibly excited. "Jack thinks he can sell Tizzy for fifty thousand. And I have to tell you, there was a whole lot left in the tank. I think you should keep him."

Dani glanced at Dex. "What do you want to do?" she asked.

"Keep him," he said. "Let's race him...together."

She pushed a strand of hair back, warring with indecision. It was apparent this wasn't just about the horse, but also about renewing their relationship. However, Dex had hurt her badly. And there was no guarantee he wouldn't do it again.

A man with brown hair and astute eyes stepped up and shook their hands, giving her a reprieve. He introduced himself as Jack Zeggelaar and it was clear he held Eve in high esteem. No wonder Eve had been able to talk him into taking Tizzy on trial.

"I like to give them lots of time," Jack was saying to Dex. "Make sure they're ready, mentally and physically. If your horse stays with me, we're probably looking at his first race in three or four months. He definitely has potential."

"If you want help with the training bill," Jack went on, "we do have ownership consortiums. With this horse, I'd even be interested in purchasing a share myself."

"We'll continue as is, for now," Dex said, his eyes sweeping over Dani, as if aware of her ambivalence. "Is Tizzy in his stall?"

"On the hot walker," Jack said. "Come this way."

Dani started to follow but Eve grabbed her arm. "Keep him," she whispered, "if it's at all possible. Tizzy's just starting to put it all together. The fact that Jack's interested is huge."

Dani tugged at her lip. Yes, it was significant the trainer was high on their horse. However, the first month's training bill had totaled more than thirteen hundred dollars. The second bill was due in a week. And Tizzy's first race was at least ninety days away.

"I understand things are tight," Eve said, her voice sympathetic. "I can gallop him for free, maybe work out something with Jack. But training is labor intensive and expensive. As you and Dex both know."

Dani gave a wry nod. Training was also cyclic and it was difficult to estimate cash flow. Once they sold the ranch, she'd have a regular paycheck. Jeffrey said the receptionist's job at the town hall was hers if she wanted. Maybe then she could manage Tizzy's training costs. However, it would still be tough. "Does Jack need more riders to gallop in the morning?" she asked, only half-joking.

"There's already too many people knocking on his door," Eve said, "and you don't want that life. If it weren't for Megan and Scott, I'd be in the poor house." She pointed at a familiar gray Mercedes. "There they are now. I met Megan at jockey school. She's one of the best things that ever happened to me."

Car doors clicked. Megan stepped out, looking more like a model than a jockey. She wore buttery soft leather boots, a stunning necklace, and had an oversized diaper bag looped over her shoulder. Even Scott looked intimidating, dressed in a gray suit and crisp white shirt.

"We're late," Megan said, including Dani in her warm smile. "Joey's asleep in his car seat."

"Thanks for looking after him." Eve gestured. "This is Dani. She has a horse in training."

"Oh, nice," Megan said, still smiling. "We've sent three horses to Jack. He sent them all back after a couple months. Said they weren't good enough. But it was still fun."

Dani instantly relaxed. Megan was totally unpretentious despite her elegant beauty. The conversation moved to upcoming races and it was clear that, in addition to helping with childcare, Megan was a staunch supporter of Eve's riding career.

Scott stepped closer, seizing a lull in the conversation. "Is Dex here?" he asked.

Dani nodded. "He's probably still with Jack by the hot walker."

"Looks like he's over there now," Scott said, staring at the adjacent barn. "Getting into the white limo."

Eve gave a wistful sigh. "That's Bert Howard. He's the most influential owner at Santa Anita, but he's difficult to approach. How does Dex know him?"

Dani jammed her hands in her pockets, not sure if it was public knowledge that Howard's son was incarcerated. She did know that Dex was intensely private, and she had no intention of revealing anything about his affairs.

"Howard has a lot of business interests," Scott said smoothly, seeming to pick up on Dani's reluctance. "And he doesn't just own race horses. He's also into fox hunting and steeplechase."

Dani studied the stretch limo, sharing Eve's wistfulness but for a different reason. She wanted to hear more about prison and Dex's time there. Clearly though, Dex didn't want her included. He'd slipped into the car when she wasn't looking. He'd always been an island, doing what he wanted, when he wanted, with little explanation.

And it was difficult to love someone like that. Difficult, if not impossible. She blew out a tormented sigh, not sure if she dared do it again.

CHAPTER THIRTY-EIGHT

Dex glanced sideways at Dani, his hands tightening around the steering wheel. She'd been quiet since leaving the track. Unusually quiet. Almost resigned. And all he wanted to do was make her smile, like she did before he went to prison…like she had when dancing with Jeffrey at the lounge. It rankled that *he* couldn't take her out, at least not anywhere with liquor.

So much frustration bubbled inside, he wanted to stop and pound the dashboard of his truck. Instead he concentrated on loosening his grip on the wheel. He understood the consequences of jail time, and in fact, thanks to her kindness, being together like this was more then he'd ever expected. But it was bittersweet.

"The trainer seems competent," he said, trying once again to engage her in conversation, which was rather bizarre because generally he prized silence. Except from Dani.

She could talk about her newest pair of shoes and he would hang on every word. Except now she wasn't talking about anything. Not how good Tizzy looked, or how the bedding at the track was so deep, or how sweet the alfalfa smelled. He'd exhausted every subject of importance. Even his statement that Quentin had agreed to take Cracker had drawn few questions.

She pushed a strand of silky hair behind her ear.

"Those are pretty earrings," he said, almost desperately.

"Did you notice Megan's," Dani asked, her head turning slightly.

He barely remembered Scott's wife and he certainly hadn't noticed her earrings. However, he nodded. "Yes, they were real nice," he said.

"She made them. And that necklace too. I couldn't stop staring."

Dex nodded again, keeping his eyes on the road.

"They're a nice couple," Dani went on. "I wonder if they talk about Scott's cases, you know, share things that are important."

"I don't know," Dex said cautiously. "Some things are probably best kept confidential."

"Like your two-hour discussion in Bert Howard's limo?"

"I didn't realize it was two hours," he said. "But you looked like you were having fun, hanging out in the shedrow with Eve."

"Eve and Megan stayed to keep me company," Dani said sharply. "They didn't want to be there. When Joey started crying, Scott took him home. *He's* the type who puts himself out for his wife."

Sweat beaded on Dex's forehead. He reached forward and adjusted the air conditioning. She'd said it was okay to talk to Howard, but it probably wasn't prudent to bring up that detail. On the positive side, she'd referred to husbands and wives, linking him in the same category. That had to be a good thing.

"We talked about Howard's son," he said slowly. "The man wanted to thank me. And find out what he could do to keep Sandy safe."

"Safe? Don't the guards do that?"

"Not so well," he said.

He caught her tiny gasp of dismay. "Were you raped?" she asked, after a taut moment.

"No." He glanced sideways. "But Sandy is smaller. More vulnerable."

"Oh, Dex." Tears brimmed in her eyes and she wrung her hands, staring at him with a mixture of helplessness and pity.

His jaw clenched so tightly it hurt.

"I'm sorry it was like that," she went on. "So very sorry."

He wished she wouldn't look at him like that. His ribs squeezed and his heart pounded in a painful staccato. He veered onto the dirt shoulder and bounced the truck to an abrupt stop.

"I don't want your sympathy," he muttered, gripping the wheel. "It's over now. It is what it is."

They sat in silence. She was probably trying to control her revulsion, probably picturing the things he'd seen. Then her seatbelt clicked. She slid across the seat and wrapped her arms around his neck. She didn't speak, just hugged him, and he couldn't remember a hug ever feeling so good.

Cars whizzed by and a truck honked, but he only gripped her tighter. Simply being close to her made him feel better. Her hair was soft and silky and fresh. She'd changed her shampoo to one with a hint of apples. But her breasts felt the same, pressed against his heart, and such longing filled him he could barely breathe.

But he didn't let his hands roam. Didn't want to push his luck. Experiencing the pleasure of her touch after such a long absence was a treat in itself.

"Sorry I was snappy earlier," she said, her face still pressed against his skin. "Guess I didn't want you to shut me out. And I'm glad you were able to talk to that man. I hope it helps you, and his son. I realize it's none of my business."

His fingers tightened around the back of her neck. He had shut her out. Had always done that, trying to protect her. But he wanted it to be her business.

"Howard asked me to visit the work farm," he said slowly. "To make sure Sandy stays safe. And at the same time teach inmates about shoeing."

Her head jerked up, her eyes widening. "But isn't that asking a lot? How do you feel about going back?"

"It'd be okay. And it would only be once a week."

"But is it safe? You said the guards weren't great."

He loved the concern heating her eyes, the way she gripped his shirt as if she'd never let go. "It's safe for me," he said.

"I see." She swallowed. "I guess it's generous to volunteer like that."

"It's not exactly volunteering," he admitted. Howard was a very astute businessman. Dex had been sold on teaching the inmates a valuable trade, but there had been other incentives. Huge ones.

Not only had Howard offered a shoeing contract but he'd also proposed to send some two-year-olds to the Double D for basic training. His horse ownership was vast so Dani could choose the animals she wanted. That is, if she wasn't working in a stuffy office somewhere in town. "Do you really want to sell the Double D?" he asked.

"I think sharing a day like this makes us both think differently." She slipped from his arms and back to the passenger's side. "And that's a mistake."

She took out her phone and checked her messages. "Red will be glad to see us," she said. "Jeffrey was planning to drop by so I hope he let him out."

Dex started up the truck. "Is Jeffrey there?" he asked, already knowing the man was on his way to a Dodgers game with two ball tickets, courtesy of Luther.

She shook her head and put away her phone. "He's busy. But I'm starving, aren't you?" She reached into the crumbled bag on the floor and pulled out the last remaining doughnut. Carefully broke it in two and offered him the biggest half.

"No, thanks," he said, wondering how he could convince her to let him stick around tonight and paint. "I ate in Howard's car."

"You ate? Without me?" Her voice was small and shocked and hurt.

His chest squeezed. He hadn't been thinking. Of course, she would have missed lunch. He certainly didn't want to admit that he'd enjoyed sushi, sandwiches, and even a beer.

"What did you have?" she asked.

His palms were suddenly sweaty and stuck to the wheel. "Does it matter?" he asked.

"You're so selfish," she said, but she didn't sound angry, just resigned. And that scared him even more. She took a half-hearted nibble of the stale doughnut then thrust it back into the bag. Even her hands looked reproachful.

"I had sushi," he said. "Salmon and tuna, I think. And there were little cucumber sandwiches. The fridge was stocked with cheeses too, and a man came to the limo every once in a while to clear our plates. It didn't seem like a car, more like an office. But mainly I stared out the window and wished I was with Tizzy...and you."

She gave a tight smile, but the hurt in her eyes remained. "Probably a long time since you had sushi," was all she said.

"Do you want to stop?" he asked desperately. "Get something to eat? There's that nice Mexican restaurant just ahead."

"It's too expensive," she said.

"But you need to eat."

"It's okay. We're almost home anyway. And the horses will be hungry."

"There are a few good hours before dark," he said. "Guess I'll paint a little before I go."

"No, don't bother—"

"The agent wants to take some pictures this week," he said. "The front fences are the most important. Best I stay and work for a bit." He shot her an apologetic smile. "Since I've eaten and all."

Her mouth twitched.

She'd always been too big-hearted to sulk for long, but despite her reluctant smile it was obvious he'd backslid. And it was equally obvious he needed to step it up before Jeffrey arrived on the scene.

CHAPTER THIRTY-NINE

Dani straightened the overturned bucket, then inserted the hose and filled it with bubbling water. Day trips were great but they also resulted in extra work. And impatient horses were harder to handle, seeming to need more time whenever she tried to rush.

Her stomach rumbled with hunger. And she was hot, thirsty and rather drained. She splashed her face and hands, determined not to check on Dex. She half hoped he'd help with the chores, but he'd driven off for more paint and then just wandered around, not seeming to accomplish anything except steal her dog and wreck her concentration.

She grabbed a hammer and replaced a paddock board that Peppy had splintered. "Bad horse," she muttered. But he just complacently munched his hay, as if saying 'that's what happens when you leave us alone too long.'

She reluctantly checked the driveway. Dex's truck was gone again. She hoped he had the good sense to keep Red from following his vehicle. It was strange he hadn't bothered to say good-bye. Not that it mattered if he simply drove off. It was just that they had shared a fun day. Unfortunately, he did what he wanted, how he wanted, without any explanation.

She trudged toward the outbuildings, her heart giving a little leap when she spotted his truck. So he hadn't left after all. He'd just parked closer to the barn. Red trotted from the doorway and licked her hand in greeting.

"You faithless dog," she said, only half teasing. But his eyes were bright and his tail thumped, and she couldn't begrudge his happiness. He turned and led her inside, checking over his shoulder to make sure she followed.

She stepped into the cooler shadows of the barn, walking slowly, her eyes adjusting to the light. "Do you want a peanut butter sandwich, Dex?" she called. "I'm going to the house now."

She jerked to a standstill. Hay bales were carefully arranged in the center of the aisle. A red horse blanket covered the middle bale and on top of that sat a huge pitcher. Frosty and brimmed with salt.

Dex walked around the corner, carrying a large glass. "Have some supper," he said, pouring her a margarita.

She couldn't stop her smile or the way her mouth watered. "A liquid supper?"

"Fajitas are in the bag," he said. "And nachos. They're still warm."

She blinked then dipped her nose in the glass, glad he couldn't see her expression. Dex wasn't a big talker, but when he was sweet, there was nobody sweeter.

She sank down on a bale, cupping the glass like it was treasure. Dex sat down beside her while Red flopped at their feet.

"This is really nice," she said after a long moment. "I love these."

He reached over and wiped the top of her lip, then licked his finger. "I know," he said softly.

Her heart hammered at his touch. "You don't want one?" she asked.

"My PO wouldn't like me driving with alcohol on my breath."

She tilted her head. "What's a PO?"

"Probation officer."

She nodded, then squeezed her eyes shut and took another appreciative sip. Dex had always been able to mix the perfect margarita. Now she understood why he had roared off in his truck. He had gone to a lot of trouble to serve this delightful supper. It seemed a waste if he couldn't enjoy it too.

"Maybe Jeffrey could drive you home," she said, surprised to see her glass was almost empty, "if you wanted to have a drink. I'm sure he wouldn't mind."

Dex arched a skeptical eyebrow but said nothing. He simply refilled her glass.

"He's not a bad guy," she went on. She swirled the glass, studying the crushed ice, then drew a wavy line in the condensation. Dex didn't speak. He seemed absorbed with manning the bar and food.

The barn was peaceful. Red's eyes were shut, his breathing deep and contented. She sipped her drink and crunched nachos with Dex but otherwise it was companionably silent.

"I do wish Jeffrey liked horses a little more," she finally admitted.

"Seems important for you," Dex said.

"A lot of people get along fine without them." She wrinkled her nose in thought. One of her friends didn't even like animals, and she seemed happy enough.

"I like horses," Dex said.

"You like women too," Dani said, keeping her voice light. She didn't want to wreck this impromptu dinner when he'd tried so hard to serve her favorite things.

He picked up her hand, tracing her bare finger where her wedding ring used to be. "I've never slept with anyone but you," he said, "not since the day you climbed onto my bike."

"Wish I could believe that."

"Then that's the real issue." He leaned closer, his eyes intent. "Do you trust me?"

She gave a hard swallow. Of course she did, for the little things. But there were varying levels of trust. She could trust him to be on time, to sit up with her when she was sick and to take good care of the animals. But while she'd take a bullet for him, she suspected he'd stop and grab a bulletproof vest first.

"I've never lied to you, Dani," he said urgently. "And I never will."

She knew that. It was probably why she'd never dared to ask many questions. Dex was painfully honest—or else he just closed up. She drew in an achy breath. "Were you with that woman...Tawny...that night?"

"I was in the motel room," Dex said. "But it wasn't a sexual thing."

"Were you selling drugs? While we were married?"

"No."

His answer was so quick and curt, she sensed there was something else, something buried. "Did your uncle, Luther, ask you to do something illegal?"

"No."

But his body tightened and she knew she was close. Maybe Luther hadn't asked Dex to do something illegal but clearly it had been borderline. "I hate the Tattrie club," she said, her voice rising in frustration. "There's so much bad stuff. Even though you left, you can't get away. Did family drag you in?"

He stared at her for a long moment, his eyes dark and bottomless. "Yes," he admitted.

"Dex," she said, her voice breaking. "Over two years in jail. Was it worth it?" She crossed her arms, feeling small and cold and helpless. Because essentially he'd chosen the Tattries over her. He'd been willing to throw away their marriage for the club.

He pulled her close, stroking her hair and murmuring soothingly and despite her anguish, she felt a bittersweet relief. Because he hadn't been unfaithful. True, she wasn't top on his priority list, not like he was on hers. But maybe she could live with that. If he were half as content as her, maybe it would be enough.

"Were you happy?" she whispered. "Living here with me?"

"It's all I ever wanted," he said, his voice husky. "But I'd be happy living with you on a desert island."

She blinked. "An island...with horses?"

"No horses," he said. "Just you."

"Oh." Warmth flooded her chest. "That's probably the nicest thing you ever said to me."

"Then I've been negligent." He lifted her hand, pressing his mouth against each of her fingers.

"What else would you like?" she asked, rather flustered by the feel of his warm mouth and how it made every inch of her tingle. "On our island? You can pick two more things."

"Red and Gypsy," he said, still holding her hand. "What would you like?"

She swallowed, hesitating for a long moment. It felt like she was jumping off a cliff, and she wasn't certain if he'd be there to catch her. But it wasn't fair to ask for honesty and not give it back. "You," she finally said.

His head swooped then, his mouth covering hers, his tongue and touch and taste achingly familiar.

"Please give me another chance, sweetheart," he said after a minute...or ten or twenty. Time was hard to measure after his kissing. Her mind might have reservations but her body certainly didn't. She arched against him, clutching his shoulders, knowing she never wanted to let go.

He trailed his lips over her neck, talking about Tizzy and Red and how they should keep the ranch. His words were warm and seductive and she accepted she'd always love him, and really, she didn't need to hear anymore. She just wanted to go back to their bedroom.

"I can get the bank off our back," he was saying. "Work longer hours at the garage. There's no need to sell."

"Stop talking," she whispered, pressing a finger over his lips. "Husband."

He stilled, scanned her face, then scooped her up, so quickly he knocked over the margarita pitcher. He compensated for his unusual clumsiness by kissing her the entire way to the house, yet somehow managed to remove her bra before they reached the kitchen.

He pushed the front door shut with his foot. "Stay, Red," he muttered.

He carried her into their bedroom and laid her on the bed, then yanked at his belt buckle.

She reached up and helped him pull off his shirt, her breath stalling at his sheer magnificence. He was ridged and rutted and ready, hard everywhere, and she didn't know where to touch first.

He already had her clothes off, showing no such indecision. One hand was on her breast, the other between her legs, touching and teasing and making her quiver with wanting.

"I didn't wait for two years to have this over quick," she said, breathless, but needing to let him know she hadn't slept with Jeffrey.

"It won't be over quick," he said.

CHAPTER FORTY

Dex stared at the sleeping woman curled against his chest. His arms tightened convulsively. Their marriage wasn't repaired yet, and he accepted that. But she was letting him back into her life, and his gratitude was limitless.

He didn't want to wake her. On the other hand, he couldn't resist sliding a hand over the curve of her hip. He'd never been able to get enough of her, from the moment he'd seen her whipping around the barrels, riding Peppy like the horse was her trusted friend and partner. It was clearly all or nothing with her. And he'd wanted it all.

The first couple weekends she'd been the only one brave enough to talk to him, the fearless competitor who looked like a rodeo queen but ran barrels like a hellion. She never worried what people thought—rather remarkable since her father was the most judgmental man in town.

She opened her eyes. "You're frowning," she said, blinking with sleep. "Did I take advantage of you?"

Her words were flippant and certainly didn't do justice to the passionate night they'd shared, and frustration now mingled with his gratitude. He tilted her head with his thumb. "I thought of you while I was away," he said. "Your mouth, your hair. This." He cupped her breast. "I tried not to. But you're in my heart, Dani."

"Wow," she said. "You turned rather eloquent in prison." But despite her smile her eyes remained shadowed.

He traced her jaw with his finger, fighting his panic. They'd made love most of the night, but it hadn't banished that wary look in her eyes. And that was unlike her. She was usually open and honest, incapable of telling a lie. Maybe sleeping with an ex-con wasn't so easy for a minister's daughter. Perhaps it was too big a cross to bear.

He drew in a deep breath. "What's wrong?" he asked.

"Do you love me?"

He jerked back, so incredulous his breath stalled.

"It's just that you don't say it," she went on. "And women really like you. It's difficult sometimes…especially with what happened."

He still couldn't speak. His throat balled so tightly, he could barely breathe, let alone talk.

She was staring at him, waiting. But after a long moment her eyes filled with disappointment.

"It's okay," she said, generous as always. "I love you. When you're around, it's like I'm walking on air. But I don't want to be in this alone. I can't." She gave a trembling smile. "The ground hurts too much when it hits."

She slid from his frozen arms, all dignity and grace. Bent to scoop up her clothes and his inertia disappeared. He leaped across the bed, hooked his arm around her waist and flattened her across the tangle of sheets.

"I love you, you fool," he said.

And probably that wasn't the most romantic way to say it, but it was certainly forceful. Because even Red trotted into the room. He jumped up on the bed and stuck his head between them, whining with concern.

"It's okay, Red," Dex said, pushing the dog away. "I'm not going to hurt her."

He cupped Dani's face, desperate for her to believe. "I said I loved you when I asked you to marry me. Remember?"

She gave a little nod.

"And again that time when you had your hair cut short and thought it was ugly. And also when you had the lump removed." He paused to kiss the scar on her left breast. "And we were afraid it was cancer. And a bunch of other times, like when that crazy woman delivered the barrel horse and took off her shirt. Why would you possibly think I had changed?"

A fat tear brimmed in the corner of her eye.

He tried to blot it away, but his hand was too big, too shaky. "Because of Tawny, I guess," he said heavily. "Fair enough."

He slumped on his back. He'd always thought talk was trite, that actions meant much more than words. Certainly they were more difficult. At least, for him.

A well of frustration filled his throat. *Over two years in prison.* He shook his head, fighting the bitter taste of injustice.

"So, what now?" he asked, studying the ceiling, afraid to look at her.

"I need to explain to Jeffrey," she said, "before I see you again. Keep your apartment at the garage. We'll take it slow. See how it goes."

"Okay," he said quickly. They weren't out of the woods yet, but at least there'd only be the two of them. "I'll feed the horses," he said. "You can stay in bed." His hopeful gaze drifted over her breasts, but she shook her head and swung her legs over the mattress.

She pulled on her clothes with an odd urgency, and it was then he understood.

"You want me out of here?" he said. "In case Jeffrey comes?"

She paused, her hands over the zipper of her jeans. "I just don't want to hurt him this way. He deserves more."

Dex stared, rather distracted by the expanse of beautiful smooth skin being covered much too quickly.

"You understand, don't you?" she asked, pulling her hair back in a ponytail.

He nodded but didn't move. Her thoughtfulness was sometimes damn inconvenient. Besides, he wanted to relax and appreciate the privilege of watching her dress, of sharing their morning ritual, familiar but new. Never again would he take such intimacy for granted.

"Dex?"

"Yes. I'm going." He reached for his clothes, his eyes still locked on her. Sneaking off because of Jeffrey rankled, and he had the overpowering urge to mark his spot, like a dog pissing on a tree. "If I can get Matt's car going," he said casually, "I'll take it to the garage for a tune-up...and leave my truck here."

"Great, thanks," she said, already heading toward the door. "I'll put Matt's keys on the table."

And then she and Red disappeared. No hug, no kiss, no coffee. Not even the slightest chance of enticing her back into bed. And he was left with an achy sense of longing and an even deeper sense of unease.

Dani dragged a brush over Peppy's gleaming coat and glanced nervously toward the driveway. She dreaded seeing Jeffrey. While she didn't regret one minute of the last twenty-four hours, she sincerely wished she could have ended their relationship first.

And she wished Dex would leave. She was jumpy as a cat, aware that if he looked at her as he had in the bedroom, full of such heated promise, her insides would turn all mushy and she'd race him back to the bed and melt in his arms.

He was still in the shed though. The Camaro's engine had turned over a couple times but it hadn't moved yet. She had no doubt he'd be able to start the car, despite that it had been parked for over two years. The man had magical fingers.

Yes, indeed. She gave a little shiver of delight followed by another nervous glance toward the road. If Jeffrey didn't come soon she'd drive to his house, before her guilt magnified.

Dex sauntered from the shed, walking as if he had all the time in the world. He didn't move fast...except when he did. Like when he'd pulled her back onto the bed. He moved like a panther then. One minute she was on the other side of the room, the next she was flattened beneath him.

And he'd said he loved her.

She clasped the brush tighter. He might not say those words again for another three years, but that was okay. At least there had been no other women, or more correctly, he hadn't had sex with any other women. Dex didn't talk much but he didn't lie either. He just omitted.

She brushed Peppy's shoulder even harder, the brush smacking against his muscles. *Tawny.* It was still there...an insidious betrayal that would probably never leave.

"You beating that old horse up?" Dex asked.

She whirled, her eyes meeting his through the bars of the paddock. "Just thinking," she said.

He studied her in silence. "I think Matt's car will make it to the garage," he finally said. "Found a few mouse nests beneath the hood, but I'll drive it over and get it up on the hoist."

"Okay."

"I'll leave my truck by the house," he added. "And wait for you to call."

"It might be a couple days," she said. "I need to sort out some things."

"Take as long as you want." He shrugged as if it didn't really matter. She scanned his face, searching for a glimmer of eagerness but his face was granite hard, as if their lovemaking had already been forgotten.

She lifted her shoulders, copying his shrug, and turned back to Peppy.

The latch clicked. Dex swung open the gate and pressed his hand over her shoulder. "Don't let Jeffrey give you a hard time. I'll be at the garage." He grazed his mouth over her forehead. "I love you."

The brush fell from her stiff fingers and ricocheted off her foot. There were other things to work out besides Jeffrey, and a few horse arrangements to make, but for now she was too shocked to speak.

Dex stooped and picked up the brush. He placed it in her hand then stepped outside the paddock. "I cleaned the stalls," he said, "and mixed the grain for tonight. I'll leave now."

She merely gaped as he walked away. *I love you.* Twice in one day he'd said it. Not during sex either and not after she'd said it first. She gave her head a shake. And if she hadn't been holding the brush so tightly that it pinched her fingers, she would have suspected she was dreaming.

CHAPTER FORTY-ONE

"I have to work in an hour," Jeffrey said, pulling out a kitchen chair, "so I didn't have time to come by this morning. But I'm glad you dropped in. The last two days have been crazy. I even won a couple tickets to the Dodgers' game last night. Some biker fundraiser. Don't remember entering the draw, but I'm not complaining."

He shot Dani an apologetic look. "Sorry. There wasn't time to call. My partner and I went. Besides, do you even like baseball? I wasn't really thinking about you."

She shook her head, struggling with her guilt. She hadn't been thinking of Jeffrey either, not when she and Dex were driving to Santa Anita, not when they'd been watching Tizzy, and certainly not when Dex's tongue had been halfway down her throat.

"I've been busy too," she said, heat rising in her cheeks. "Dex and I have had some time to talk, and, well, we think, since we're still married—"

"You're taking him back?" Jeffrey shot to his feet, his eyes widening. "You're kidding? Hell, you aren't?" His voice rose with incredulity.

Dani gulped. "I'm truly sorry, Jeffrey. I do care for you but—"

"Dammit!" Jeffrey slammed his fist on the table, the sound cracking through the kitchen. "I can't believe you picked a con over me. Can you imagine how embarrassing that is?"

Dani leaned so far away from the shaking table that the chair cut into her back. But Jeffrey looked quite different when he was angry, the uniform and gun not as benign. And just like her dad, he placed an inflated value on appearances.

"I'm sorry," she said stiffly. "I hadn't considered the embarrassing aspect."

"It's not just that, of course," Jeffrey said quickly. "I care about you. Very much. And I'm worried. Where will you work? That job with the town was offered because of your relationship with me. They can't hire someone who's linked to a man with a record."

He paced around the table, his throat moving convulsively. "Have you even thought about this? Have you considered how your father will feel?"

"This has nothing to do with Dad."

"But you're his daughter. He's always been embarrassed about your connection with the Tattries. Can you imagine how difficult this will be? For him to stand in front of the congregation, knowing his daughter was married to a convict?"

"Is," Dani said. "We're still married."

"I hardly need a reminder," Jeffrey snapped.

He kneeled and grabbed her hand, his voice softening. "Look, I see the way you two stare at each other. And I know you don't love me like that. But we might, in time. And you wouldn't have to worry about me being arrested and I certainly wouldn't pick up hookers."

Dani felt her face freeze.

Jeffrey's voice turned more insistent. "I saw what you went through when he was in prison. Dex is an outlaw. He's not the man for you. He's ruthless, tough and selfish."

"He's also kind and compassionate."

"He's a lot of things," Jeffrey said. "But kind and compassionate aren't what come to mind."

He rose and circled the table, his movements jerky. "What are you going to do," he asked, his lip curling with distaste, "when he comes home reeking of cheap perfume? You know it's going to happen. People don't change."

"He doesn't have to change." Dani crossed her arms. "He wasn't with that hooker. Not like that."

"Come on. It's obvious he has women everywhere. He was probably doing most of the female guards." Jeffrey gave a spiteful smile. "And I can't blame him. If a woman wants to spread her legs for him, why not?"

Dani recoiled, surprised by his crudity. On the positive side, it made their split much easier. She rose from the chair. Jeffrey was hurt and people said cruel things when they were hurting. Maybe later, they could have a more civil conversation.

"You've known me for eighteen years," Jeffrey said, his frustration escaping in a low hiss. "Yet you still don't believe me? You accept a con's promises?" He pulled a file from the top of his fridge and slapped it on the table. "You want proof. Look at this. He had his women, lots of them. *That's* why he didn't want you to visit. He was already getting plenty."

She stared down at the scatter of pictures, her throat drying. Some of the photos were just grainy images of women in uniform but others were unquestionably Dex. Dex smiling with a pretty lady by a long low barn, Dex hugging a tall brunette in a sterile visiting room...the room where he said he never had any visitors.

"I didn't want to hurt you," Jeffrey said. "So I didn't show you these."

"And now you want to hurt me?" she whispered, her voice cracking.

Jeffrey shook his head "No. I just don't want you to make the same stupid mistake twice."

She jammed her hands in her pockets and stumbled for the door.

"Dani, stop. Don't drive yet." He grabbed her arm. "Wait a minute."

He guided her back into the chair and to his credit, even moved the pictures. "Have some coffee before you drive anywhere," he said. "Or maybe you'd like water?"

"I'm fine," she muttered. But her face felt stiff, her legs boneless. And her gaze kept shooting to the file.

"You really love him, don't you?" Jeffrey said, his voice grudging.

She said nothing, just crossed her arms, her throat still convulsing with pain.

"I was always afraid of him getting released," Jeffrey said. "You two were always so tight." He blew out a heavy sigh. "I'm here, you know, if you can't work it out. Dex probably told you that I caused him some trouble?"

"No," she said. "He didn't."

Jeffrey sank into the chair beside her and rubbed his face. "Guess it's true then, what the chief said. That Tattries don't tattle. I had some guards prod him a bit," he admitted.

"Is that why you have those pictures?"

Jeffrey gave a sheepish nod. "But no one really hurt him. And it didn't make any difference. He handled...everything, even that horse owner who didn't want to pay."

"I have to get out of here." Anger now mixed with her pain. She jerked from the chair. A file on Dex, pictures of him with women, Jeffrey trying to hurt Dex...it was all too much. She needed to be alone, to think.

She'd been elated earlier when Dex said he loved her. And maybe she was a fool to trust him. But without trust, they wouldn't have much of a marriage. Because the reality was he'd always have women hitting on him. So she could either believe that he loved her...or she couldn't.

And that required a lot of soul searching, as well as considerable faith in her own instincts.

CHAPTER FORTY-TWO

Dex poked his head out from beneath the bottom of Matt's car, every one of his senses on high alert. He didn't need to hear the loud muffler or the tick of the engine to know that Dani's truck had driven into the parking lot of the Tattrie garage. He just knew she was here.

The side door opened. Seconds later, her boots clicked on the concrete. She walked unerringly past three vehicles and toward Matt's car, seemingly drawn by a shared radar.

"Good afternoon," she said, bending over and peering down at him. "Do you want to come by for supper tonight?"

"Yes," he said.

It had been days since he'd seen her, ninety-six excruciating hours when he'd agonized over what she'd been thinking, what Jeffrey might have said, and how long he'd have to wait. She'd only called once. A frustratingly short call when she'd asked if he ever had any visitors at prison.

'Only Cindy,' he'd said, 'to help with my parole hearing.'

And now Dani was sitting on the old wooden chair, looking fresh and pretty in a scooped white T-shirt and shapely jeans, watching the way she'd first watched him seven years ago.

"I brought coffee but wasn't sure if you could take a break." She gestured at the paper tray with two large cups.

He hadn't even noticed the coffee. Couldn't pull his gaze from her face. "I can take a break," he said, pushing out from beneath the car. "I'm finished with Matt's car."

He pulled the rag from his back pocket and wiped his hands, still looking at her. "Want to take it for a test drive?" he asked.

"Sure." She rose and opened the driver's door, still not revealing any of her thoughts. Or her decisions.

"I better come with you." He hesitated, hating to ask but unable not to. "Did you finish it with Jeffrey?"

"Yes." Her voice muffled as she bent down and struggled to adjust the driver's seat. "This seat is stuck," she added.

He tossed the rag aside, grinning with relief. "It's manual. Reach below the seat and lift the handle."

He strode to the wall and pressed the red button on the control panel. The wide bay door slowly rose. "Just back it out," he called, over the noise of the rising door, "so I can lock up. We're not open on Sunday anyway."

He walked around and closed the office door then returned to the panel, eager to leave. But she still hadn't backed the car out. She remained motionless, one hand clutching the driver's door, the other gripping a gold card.

"Dani?"

"Your name is on this," she said, staring down at a credit card. "It was under the front seat."

His mouth dried. Oh, hell. But he forced a negligent shrug. "I must have dropped it when I was driving the car over." He reached for the credit card.

She pulled her hand back, squeezing the card. "But it expired last year. And you had it the night you paid for that motel. The room and drinks were on it." She tilted her head, her voice thoughtful. "You had your truck that night," she added. "So Matt must have been there. With his car. Why didn't he say that?"

"It was a long time ago," Dex said, feeling his stomach cave. "Let's go."

"But he left for Africa three days later. And he never said he was there that night." She straightened by the door, the card clutched in her fist. "Why didn't I know that?"

Sweat tickled Dex's neck. "It's probably in the police report," he said. "Come on. We need to leave before a customer shows up."

Her mouth set in a stubborn line. "Did Matt steal your card?" she asked.

"Of course not." Dex shook his head and bent down, making a show of fiddling with the car seat.

"Please tell me." And even though her voice wavered, it had a steely core. "Don't shut me out. I won't have it. Not again."

He straightened, staring at her over the door of the Camaro. "Matt didn't steal my card," he said. "I gave it to him."

"So he bought those drinks. He paid for the motel room…was *he* with Tawny?" Her voice quavered. "Was this M-Matt's fault?"

"No, it was my fault," Dex said. "I gave him the card, told him to have some fun before he went to Africa. The Tattrie name took him a little too far."

"I don't understand." Her visible anguish yanked at Dex's chest. "Matt was with you? He bought the heroin. That means he saw the dealer. But he never said a word." She sagged, clutching at the door with both hands.

"And why didn't he talk to the police?" She shook her head in bewilderment. "All they really wanted was the dealer. You would have received a lighter sentence. And why wasn't he charged too?"

Dex swallowed, desperately trying to wet his throat. "The cartel sold the heroin because they thought they were dealing with a Tattrie." He paused, his throat oddly rusty. "They wouldn't have trusted Matt not to talk. And if he didn't cooperate with the police, he would have gone to prison."

"But he would have cooperated," Dani said. "He would have been scared shitless. And a description would have helped the police track down the dealer." She stared at Dex in growing horror. "You think the cartel would have hurt him? So you took the blame? To help Matt?"

"It wasn't just to help Matt," Dex said. "You're his sister. Luther didn't think we could keep you safe."

"But that's not fair." Her head whipped back and forth in growing horror. "We have to tell the police. Matt has to come home and deal with this."

Dex moved around the door and placed his hands on her shoulders. "Matt wouldn't last six months in prison. And if he talked to the cops, the cartel would have been very annoyed."

"But we have to make this right. It wasn't only you involved." Her eyes widened with dawning comprehension. "You weren't even there? That's why you swore you didn't see the dealer?"

"Matt called me in a panic that night," Dex admitted. "Said Tawny was in trouble."

"But why didn't you tell me?"

He cupped her face. "Because you wouldn't have let me do it."

"Of course not." She jerked away, her voice breaking. "And I'm going to call my cowardly brother right now and tell him to come home. He has to tell the truth. I can't believe he ran away."

"I told him to, Dani. I wanted him out of here. It was the only way to keep him safe. And more importantly, you."

She shook her head, her face so bloodless her skin appeared translucent. "It doesn't matter. This isn't right. People have to know. Maybe your record can be overturned."

"Dani, it's done. This is exactly why I didn't tell you."

"But you went to prison. For something you didn't do." Her voice turned fierce. "And he's getting accolades while everyone thinks you're a criminal. I called you selfish, and you rotted in a cell for my cowardly brother—" She clamped her hand over her mouth, backed up a step then bolted for the bathroom.

He wet a paper towel, giving her some time before following the sounds of her retching.

"You can't say anything," he said, kneeling beside her in the cramped bathroom. "The cartel is still watching. But Scott says authorities are closing in and Matt did give him an off-the-record description."

She groaned and clutched the toilet bowl, her entire body shaking. "You should have t-told me. Why make me think you wanted to end our marriage?"

"Prison changes people," he said, trying to wipe her mouth. "I didn't want you waiting five years for a bitter shell of a man. And you would have waited, if you had known. I don't want you that way."

He couldn't keep the regret from his voice. She'd never leave him now. She'd probably invite him back to the Double D tonight. But now he'd never be certain if it was based on gratitude.

Sighing, he adjusted his hip against the wall. The bathroom was tiny and his legs barely fit. But she still clutched the toilet, pulling in big quivery breaths, clearly not ready to leave.

"I thought you were selfish." She gave another pitiful groan. "But you did so much for Matt. And Dad. Yet he always attacks you, your family. He'd be mortified if he'd known. How can we ever thank you?"

"This wasn't for your father, or Matt," Dex said roughly. "And it was my fault for giving him my credit card. So don't thank me."

She looked at him then. "More than two years, Dex… That's not right." Her face crumbled and the sobs burst out. But this time she let go of the toilet and pressed into his chest, and even though they were crammed into an airless bathroom, now he had no desire to leave.

Eventually her sobs changed to heartrending hiccups. "I'm going to wring his neck," she said. "Matt never should have let you do that."

"He didn't have much choice," Dex said, gently wiping her face.

"You really think he wouldn't have survived in prison?"

"I know he wouldn't," Dex said.

She was silent a moment, as if absorbing a place where people weren't safe. "We need to tell Dad."

"No." He gripped her shoulders. "There's no reason. It will only hurt him. And he'd feel compelled to go to the police."

"But we can't let this go." Her mouth tightened in a stubborn line. "You've sacrificed so much. It's not fair."

"Don't make my time in prison a waste," Dex said. "Eight people died, including Tawny. Investigators aren't giving up. Scott says they've located several witnesses."

"Witnesses braver than my brother," she said bitterly.

"Witnesses who are now hiding in a protection program," Dex said, "with their families. But *we* don't have to do that."

"Why did the cartel trust you?"

"Luther assured them I was solid. And reminded them I was accessible in prison. If their belief changed, they could...fix me."

She sagged against him, motionless except for her ragged breath feathering his throat. "You must have been on edge every single day." She clutched at his shirt. "So Jeffrey coming to visit in uniform couldn't have been good?"

"No," he said. "But it was reassuring everyone believed we were divorced. And that I didn't care about you." He tilted her head, scanning her face. "Please understand. It was the only way."

"No." Her jaw clenched. "Matt shouldn't have called you that night. He should have pressed nine-one-one and then called a lawyer."

"And you would have resented me for giving him my credit card," Dex said. "For introducing him to the Tattrie crowd. He was drinking with them that night. And when he was hurt in prison, you would have blamed me."

She shook her head. "No, I wouldn't," she said.

"And if he had made a deal with the prosecution," Dex went on, "Matt would be looking over his shoulder the rest of his life. And you never would have been safe."

"It wouldn't have been like that," she muttered. But her eyes shadowed and it was clear she was at least picturing the scenario.

He pressed a hard kiss over her forehead. "This is over now. And we're not leaving until you promise not to speak of it."

"I can't promise that. Matt is a selfish spoiled brat, and I'm going to tell him." She tilted her head, her face mutinous. "Besides, you can't keep me in here forever."

"Can't I?" He wrapped his hand around her neck, lowering his voice to its most threatening. "Luther has a room made for people like you."

"Really?" She raised her head, giving him more access to her neck, not at all intimidated.

"I mean it, Dani." He stroked her fluttering pulse with his thumb. "If not for your family, do it for me. Don't make my prison time a waste. Please."

She tugged at her lower lip then blew out a breath. Then a short nod.

"Say it," he said.

"Okay," she said, her eyes stricken. "After all you did, yes, I promise. We owe you."

We owe you. And so it began. But the words cut more deeply than even he had imagined. He lowered his arms, hating to use the favor card, but knowing it would always be out there.

"You should move back to the ranch tonight," she went on, rising to her feet. "We've never really celebrated your release."

He rose more slowly. "Cindy had a party for me last month. My family was all there."

Her face whitened and he immediately felt like a jerk. Of course, she hadn't welcomed him back with open arms. And he wasn't an easy man; he'd certainly never been overly demonstrative. He was working on that though.

He followed her out of the bathroom then turned her around and kissed her on the cheek. "I love you, Dani."

"I love you too," she said quickly, almost mechanically, and he felt another little shot of despair. But it was clear she was thinking of something else. Even now, she was glancing at Matt's Camaro as if keen to leave. Of course, she had just experienced a major shock.

"I better drive," he said, guiding her to the passenger door. "You'll be able to feel how well the car is working."

She just nodded, not speaking again until Dex had backed out of the garage and closed the bay door. "Did Jeffrey know...what you did?"

Dex shook his head. "He's just a small town cop." His tone was deliberately disparaging. However, her concern for Jeffrey bothered him. And she had taken four long days to deal with the man, while Dex had been twiddling his thumbs—waiting, wondering.

She obviously had developed strong feelings for the cop. Only natural. Jeffrey had helped her through a rough patch. But Dex remembered how happy she looked dancing. He couldn't remember the last time he and Dani had gone out. They tended to ride hard and hit the bed early. And he'd been delighted with that. However, he'd sown his wild oats. Dani was younger. And he'd been her first love. She probably would enjoy some nightlife.

"Guess we should go slow," he said, turning the car onto the highway. "Like you planned. Make sure ranch life is really what you want." He glanced sideways, gauging her reaction.

She didn't seem to be listening. She sat silently in the seat, staring at the passing road signs.

"We could still sell the ranch and get a place in town though." He waited a beat. Still nothing.

"Or I can live at the garage and you could get an apartment," he added. "Maybe that's best? Take six months and be carefree again. You've never really had a chance to kick up your heels."

He gulped. Dani could be quieter than him when she wanted.

He wracked his brain, trying to think what else might interest her. "Or maybe you still want to try an office job?" he asked. "Maybe take some classes?"

She just stared out the window, her hands clutched on her lap.

He reached over and gave her fingers a reassuring squeeze, shocked at how cold they felt. He turned up the heat.

"I feel awful," she finally said, her voice so low he could barely hear. "Calling you selfish, wishing for…more. But you shouldn't have pleaded guilty. You shouldn't have done that. Matt and I can never repay you."

He almost groaned. He thought they were over that, ready to plan a new life. Yet they'd been driving for miles and she hadn't been listening to a word. "Let it go," he said, more curtly then he intended.

But she twisted in the seat, her eyes filling with more tears. And more gratitude. He hated the gratitude.

He pressed on the accelerator and whipped past a slow-moving transport truck. "This car still has some punch," he said, almost desperately. "I changed the oil and all the filters.

Some of the hoses were chewed through, but she's running well. I'll take a look at your truck when I go back to the garage."

"Can't you take the day off? Just move your things back home?"

He squeezed the steering wheel. "That's not what you wanted four days ago."

"I know," she said. "But I had time to think. And when you said you loved me and there had been no other women, that's all I needed, and now, after what you did—" Her voice broke, and she pressed her palms to her face. "This is so unfair. I can never make this up to you."

A vise tightened around his chest. Damn that credit card. The last thing he wanted was her gratitude. He didn't want to be like her father, someone she'd never leave simply because of her incredible loyalty.

She was smiling at him now, that beautiful mouth tilting with invitation. "Move home, Dex," she was saying and he wished he could hold out but guessed he'd have his duffle bag in their bedroom that very night.

"You sure that's what you want?" he muttered.

"It's what I want," she said, but now he'd never know... Not for certain.

He reached over, taking her hand again, then turned Matt's car up their familiar driveway.

But something had changed.

He blinked, staring first to the left then to the right, trying to absorb the yellow ribbons flapping in the wind. And tied on every fencepost.

His foot slid off the pedal and the car rolled to a stop. He jerked the door open and stepped out but dammit, it was windy and grit stuck in his eyes and he could barely see. And when she wrapped her arms around his waist he buried his head in her hair, his throat convulsing.

"That's a lot of posts, sweetheart," he finally managed.

She gave him a fierce hug. "You're a lot of man," she said.

He lifted his head, staring at the yellow dots circling their entire property. All those ribbons, it would have taken days. And such an incredible lightness filled him, it felt like he might float away. "You did this…before?"

"Before what?" she asked.

But he didn't speak again, merely cupped her sweet face and kissed her, a deep kiss full of amazement and gratitude and love. And he would have kissed her for hours, but Red darted out, whining and jumping on their legs, eager to join in the celebration.

Dani patted the dancing dog. "Okay, boy. Let's show him."

Red trotted toward the paddocks, his tail waving in a gay plume. Dani grabbed Dex's hand and tugged him along, and even though he really wanted to pick her up and carry her into the house, he could only grin and follow, because both his dog and wife looked so adorably excited and he knew a moment could never be so perfect.

But then Gypsy stuck her big head over the paddock. Her long ears tilted forward and she stared at him, as if in disbelief.

Everything stilled. Colors were brighter and the yellow ribbon shone in stark contrast to her deep black chest. But there was no sound, or movement. Even the birds seemed to stop singing.

He knew he was squeezing Dani's hand a little tighter than he should, and he figured that maybe the blur in his eyes might not really be dirt at all, but he didn't care. Because somehow she'd made an unbelievably wonderful moment even more perfect.

And then Gypsy nickered, and the sounds of their ranch started up again but richer than ever before. And he knew he was finally home. He really was home.

EPILOGUE

Dani clutched her program, unable to take her eyes off Tizzy. Though it was his first race, the horse acted like a pro. He stood stock still for saddling, completely unfazed by the noisy crowd gathered around the saddling enclosure. His white bridle gleamed in the sun and she'd never seen his coat so shiny.

A line of colorful jockeys swept from the Jockeys' Room. Eve stepped forward, looking trim and toned and tiny. She shook Dex's hand, then gave Dani an affectionate hug. "He's going to win today so bet big," she whispered, her teeth flashing in a confident smile.

She wheeled away, jaunty in her polished black boots and the Double D's brand new yellow silks. Moments later, the trainer boosted her onto Tizzy's back, and the horses headed into the tunnel and toward the track.

Dani stared in rapt enjoyment. This whole experience was an utter high, and she wanted to prolong every minute. "I never thought I could be so excited," she said, glancing at Dex. "Watching, not riding."

He smiled. "It's as good as the rodeo. And an easy way to include friends and family."

She followed his gaze across the paddock to where her dad was absorbed in animated conversation with a woman wearing a faded Lakers jersey. Her father's head bobbed, and he paid no attention to the parade of horses.

"Dad and Tinker's wife have really hit it off," she said. "I'm not sure who's doing the most talking."

"They're planning the soap fundraiser for the prison," Dex said. "Your dad needs a new cause now that Matt is coming home." He squeezed her hand. "It'll be good to see him."

She gave a rueful smile. Her husband's generosity of spirit was astounding. She'd needed a little more time to forgive her brother. "I'll be glad to see Matt too," she said, relieved she was finally able to say the words with complete sincerity.

She glanced back at her father, feeling rather sorry for Tinker's wife. "Dad can talk for hours. I hope he gives her time to place a bet." Tinker only had another seven months to serve but Dani knew from experience how tight money could be. And Tizzy's odds might never be this high again.

"Don't worry," Dex said. "I took care of her bet. She and Tinker are going to be fine."

Of course they are, she thought, drinking in his beloved face. Dex's protection was no small thing. He still saw Sandy once a week and seemed to revel in teaching the intricacies of shoeing, as well as the challenges of keeping Sandy safe. And he'd even invited Quentin back to the ranch a few times, saying he thought Dani would appreciate an update on Cracker. However, it was obvious Dex held the man in high regard.

Most certainly Sandy's father appreciated Dex. Dani had six of Bert Howard's horses in her barn now, horses that brought a steady paycheck and were a delight to train. But it was Dex's farrier skills that enjoyed the biggest demand. He was extraordinarily skilled with those hands.

Very skilled. Heat rose to her cheeks, heat that couldn't be blamed on the sun. She swallowed and adjusted her sunglasses

"Maybe we shouldn't stay here all day," Dex said, running his thumb over the sensitive spot on her wrist. "Seeing as we have important things to do back at the ranch."

"Yes," Dani said. "There's lots of…things to do back home. And of course Red will be missing us."

"Of course," Dex said. But his eyes locked on her mouth, his smoldering gaze turning her breathless, as it always did.

"Fifteen minutes to post," the announcer said.

Dani wet her lips and glanced over her shoulder. The crowd had thinned. Most of the spectators had already beelined toward the betting windows or to find a seat in the grandstand. Bert Howard had provided Dex with his luxurious owner's box so there was no need to jostle for a spot. In fact, there'd been no need to leave the private suite at all except to see Tizzy in the saddling enclosure.

Luther and his family certainly had been content to remain in the spacious box. They'd lingered with Megan and Scott, high above the crowd, enjoying the salmon and champagne and making enthusiastic toasts to fast horses and faster bikes. The suite was actually the perfect place for little Joey to watch his mom ride. There was no dust or dirt, no smell of sweat or corndogs or horses. In fact, although Dani would never admit it, the owners' boxes were boringly sterile.

"Let's wait for Tizzy at the finish line," Dex said.

She twisted in delight, smiling up at the man who knew her so well. All their guests were content. Even her father. And it would be more enjoyable by the rail, closer to the horses, closer to her husband. "I'd love that," she said.

He kissed her cheek. "And I love you," he said.

***

ABOUT THE AUTHOR

Bev Pettersen is a three-time nominee in the National Readers Choice Award as well as a two-time finalist in the Romance Writers of America's Golden Heart® Contest. She competed for five years on the Alberta Thoroughbred race circuit and is an Equine Canada certified coach. She lives in Nova Scotia with her family and when not writing novels, she's riding.

Visit her at http://www.BevPettersen.com